A PLUM

PRE

JILLIAN LAUREN is a writer and performer who grew up in suburban New Jersey. She is the author of the *New York Times* bestselling memoir *Some Girls*. She lives in Los Angeles with her husband and son.

Praise for *Pretty*

"Jillian Lauren writes with stunning, furious authenticity about self-destruction and the bitter road toward redemption. *Pretty* will knock the breath right out of you."

—Janelle Brown, author of *All We Ever Wanted Was Everything*

"Jillian Lauren's prose, at times, drives with such ferocious urgency that the words seem not so much written as *willed* onto the page. Jillian Lauren is the real deal."

—Jerry Stahl, author of *Permanent Midnight*

"A harrowing journey from darkness to light to real life. Bebe's unflinching, street-level search for salvation absolutely floored me, and Jillian Lauren's writing shimmers throughout with wit and authenticity." —Antoine Wilson, author of *The Interloper*

"Bebe Baker is an unlikely, unforgettable hero with a forever-searching soul. *Pretty*'s true beauty, however, is the author's ability to lovingly capture life's microscopic details—right down to the cuticles—and offer them back up to us as communion."

—Shawna Kenney, author of *I Was a Teenage Dominatrix* and *Imposters*

"Resignation never sounded so heartbreakingly funny. Lauren is a self-deprecating genius, leading us down fluorescent-lit institutional halls looking for reasons to live and finding them in the humblest places."

—Lynn Breedlove, author of *Godspeed* and lead singer of Tribe 8

"Lauren creates an alternate world where the struggle to remain human is given the dignity it deserves—a heartbreakingly funny and not surprisingly very addictive ride."

—Bett Williams, author of *Girl Walking Backwards* and *The Wrestling Party*

Praise for *Some Girls*

Elle Readers' Nonfiction Pick

"Lauren tells the story straight, without much moralizing, but the corruption of the aristocrats, the powerlessness of the women, and the destitution of the life outside the harem speak for itself."
—*Los Angeles Times*

"One of a kind. Lauren is a fine writer who establishes an easy intimacy with her reader. Fundamentally honest and thoughtful about her experiences." —AlterNet

"This book is so good it pains me to put it down when I have to go to sleep or work. Absolutely fascinating." —Frisky Books

"Incredibly engaging. Lauren is a gifted writer—full of ease, humor, and grace. *Some Girls* truly makes you want to befriend Jillian Lauren—to learn from her daring and adventurous choices, and from the strong and funny storyteller she's become." —*Portland Mercury*

"Lauren lifts the veil off her secret harem life, sharing vivid and explosive details." —*New York Post*

"*Some Girls* intoxicatingly lures readers along a sire's tale of heartbreak, lust, love, and redemption. A fast and fascinating read."
—*Smith* Magazine

"*Some Girls* would have been riveting even if Lauren had merely illuminated the murky world of high-class prostitution. The fact that she does so with humor, candor, and a reporter's gimlet eye is an added delight. But Lauren also reveals how and why a middle-class kid found herself in such a line of work—and how she got out."
—Jennifer Egan, author of
A Visit from the Goon Squad and *Look at Me*

"A heart-stoppingly thrilling story told by a punk-rock Scheherazade . . . Lauren writes with such lyrical ease—the book is almost musical, an enduring melody of what it is to be a woman."
—Margaret Cho

"*Some Girls* takes you into a world so dramatic, it seems almost too outrageous to be true. Lauren lifts the veil on harem life and shows us the gritty truth of life in fantasyland."
—Lily Burana, author of *Strip City*

Pretty

A Novel

Jillian Lauren

A PLUME BOOK

PLUME
Published by Penguin Group
Penguin Group (USA) Inc., 375 Hudson Street, New York, New York 10014, U.S.A.
Penguin Group (Canada), 90 Eglinton Avenue East, Suite 700, Toronto, Ontario, Canada M4P 2Y3 (a division of Pearson Penguin Canada Inc.)
Penguin Books Ltd., 80 Strand, London WC2R 0RL, England
Penguin Ireland, 25 St. Stephen's Green, Dublin 2, Ireland (a division of Penguin Books Ltd.)
Penguin Group (Australia), 250 Camberwell Road, Camberwell, Victoria 3124, Australia (a division of Pearson Australia Group Pty. Ltd.)
Penguin Books India Pvt. Ltd., 11 Community Centre, Panchsheel Park, New Delhi – 110 017, India
Penguin Books (NZ), 67 Apollo Drive, Rosedale, Auckland 0632, New Zealand (a division of Pearson New Zealand Ltd.)
Penguin Books (South Africa) (Pty.) Ltd., 24 Sturdee Avenue, Rosebank, Johannesburg 2196, South Africa

Penguin Books Ltd., Registered Offices: 80 Strand, London WC2R 0RL, England

First published by Plume, a member of Penguin Group (USA) Inc.

First Printing, September 2011
10 9 8 7 6 5 4 3 2 1

Grateful acknowledgment is made for permission to reprint an excerpt from "Hallelujah" by Leonard Cohen. © 1985 Sony/ATV Music Publishing LLC. All rights administered by Sony/ATV Music Publishing LLC, 8 Music Square West, Nashville, TN 37203. All rights reserved. Used by permission.

REGISTERED TRADEMARK—MARCA REGISTRADA

LIBRARY OF CONGRESS CATALOGING-IN-PUBLICATION DATA

Lauren, Jillian.
Pretty : a novel / Jillian Lauren.
p. cm.
ISBN 978-0-452-29734-0
1. Life change events—Fiction. 2. Self-realization in women—Fiction. 3. Self-actualization (Psychology)—Fiction. I. Title.

PS3612.A9442275P74 2011
813'.6—dc22 2011005058

Printed in the United States of America
Set in ITC Esprit Std Book

PUBLISHER'S NOTE
This is a work of fiction. Names, characters, places, and incidents either are the product of the author's imagination or are used fictitiously, and any resemblance to actual persons, living or dead, businesses, companies, events, or locales is entirely coincidental.

In memory of
Sylvia

There's a blaze of light in every word
It doesn't matter which you heard
The holy or the broken Hallelujah.

—Leonard Cohen

Acknowledgments

Deepest gratitude to Alexandra Machinist and Becky Cole.

During the writing of this book, both friends and strangers were remarkably supportive and generous. Many thanks to Signe Pike, Leonard Chang, Jim Krusoe, James Russell Packard III, Joe Gratziano, Anne Dailey, Tammy Stoner, Shawna Kenney, Bett Williams, Rachel Resnick, Ivan Sokolov, Sarah Kim, Colin Summers, Nell Scovell, Claire LaZebnik, Lynn Breedlove, the Writer's Sunget, Suzanne Luke, Whitney Lee, the Dreskin family, the Shriner family, the Samuels family, Dr. Keely Kolmes, Jerry Stahl, Pamela Ezell, Arthur Avary, Pastors El and Fran Clarke, Joy Clarke, Dr. Reef Karim, and Shannon Reese. Thanks also to Connie, Monica, Linda, and Anival from Moro Beauty Academy.

I am indebted to Mark Vonnegut for his amazing book *The Eden Express* and to Milton Rokeach for his visionary *The Three Christs of Ypsilanti.*

And, always, I am grateful beyond words for my husband, Scott Shriner, who long ago told me that I was a lousy hairdresser and urged me to consider taking this writing thing more seriously.

pretty

One

How I got here the long version is a longer story than I want to tell. How I got here the short version is the story of a night a year and a half ago. I was with Aaron, who was supposed to be the love of my life.

"Did I win, baby?" I sang out to Aaron across Raji's bar, pretending I was more stupid than I actually was. We had landed in L.A. six months before and that was when I really started laying on the dumb routine. I found it advantageous to be underestimated. You have to be careful how you fake it, though, because things like that can stick and before you know it you become what you're pretending to be.

Not that I'm some kind of genius but I'm not dull enough to think I lost even when the other guy sunk the eight ball. But I hollered at Aaron anyway because he was deep in red-bar-light, sparkle-eyed conversation with a smart, dainty blonde named Madison, for Christ's sake. Madison. Madison from USC film school no doubt.

It was a bad night already. Bad even before it got worse. I was pitched sideways with the cheap well liquor and the dope we'd smoked off foils in the bathroom and the lines we'd snorted off Madison's compact mirror. I had smoked cigarettes dusted with cocaine and was tumbling too fast. I flirted with Aaron's friends just to piss him off.

"Hey, Chaaaaaaas."

I baited my hook and let my line fly. Chas was such a ridiculous mark, with his wire-rimmed glasses and his oversized-sweater-wearing, women's-college-going girlfriend. I like to taunt people like Chas because, really, what other power do I have? I have the power to make him think of me when he's fucking his girlfriend. Chas has all the rest. Chas will graduate from law school and make lots of money and the most I can hope for is that he'll still vote liberal so that when things get too bad people like me can get a bed at a state-sponsored rehab.

My mom used to say to me, "Pretty is as pretty does."

She's like the fucking cliché almanac, my mom. But she was pretty, too. Prettier than me even because she wasn't as tall and broad in the shoulders as I am. I watched her and decided that it wasn't true. Pretty isn't what pretty does. Pretty just is. Pretty is pretty and it can get you a few things. And it doesn't last long so whatever the hell you can get with it while you have it, go ahead and get it.

So that's all I was doing. Just trying to use what I had to wring the last electrical charge out of a night that was fast slipping through my fingers while Aaron turned his face away. When I remember it now I can almost see the red lights glowing in my eyes, the flecks of foam at the corners of my mouth—some animatronic horrible girlfriend monster.

I hopped up and sat on the edge of the pool table. I swung my legs and pouted.

"Be my savior, Chas. No one else is volunteering. Tell me. Did I win?"

I let it run right off the rails; let it get all out of hand. My love for Aaron was so acid it scraped my veins raw. He twinkled his liquid chocolate eyes at some other bitch, waiting a beat before he turned to me after I called out to him. I loved him so hard right then that I wanted him dead is the truth of it.

I could always see Aaron's head over the others in the bar. He was an explosion of dreadlocks and gangly limbs. He had an enigmatic not-white-not-black thing going on that inspired strangers to constantly ask him, "What are you?" Which bugged him to no end. I mean, what kind of question is that? He would simply answer, "I'm Aaron." He was nobody's easy anything.

Thick, black-rimmed eyeglasses cemented his face in place, but otherwise he was constant motion, constant, easy, seamless motion. And me, I was a long redhead glowing next to him like some Irish peasant from an old painting. What I thought when he stood behind me with his arms clasped around my waist in front of the full-length mirror was that I was something more glorious than I ever had been before. Someone I didn't recognize.

Aaron did love me. But not, I think, like I loved him. Not so that it twisted him ugly and desperate.

"You Shook Me All Night Long" came on the jukebox and it is a universal law that all strippers must dance whenever that song comes on no matter where they are. And that's what I was by then—an exotic dancer out at Jet Strip by the airport. I had meant it to be an emergency measure, something to get us by until Aaron could score another gig.

When I met him, Aaron was playing the horn on tour with Billy Coyote, a pretty well-known jazz guitarist. One humid Thursday in July he had walked into Rusty's where I worked in Toledo. My real pop was a horn player, too. There's a lot I can't remember about him, but I remember hearing him play. I live my life now with two trumpet songs like sad angel voices in my head—Aaron's and my pop's. Sometimes I can't remember anymore whose horn was whose, except that Aaron had a flaw that Billy berated him mercilessly for. He could be tentative with how he finished a phrase. Sometimes when Aaron took the horn from his lips you had the sense of another note hovering somewhere in a parallel universe, a note he could have chosen but didn't. Not so with my pop. He always hurled himself at the finish line.

When I first started working at Rusty's, Rusty had called me into the back office and showed me old pictures she'd kept of my pop. He was tall like me, taller than the other guys on the cramped stage. In my favorite picture, my pop is blowing his heart out in the smoke haze blue spotlight. Wide-collared suit, a lock of greased hair falling in his face, forehead glistening with sweat, eyes closed. I wondered where, in the Toledo I knew, was anyone half as cool. If I met someone as cool as that, I vowed I would follow him wherever he went.

And then in walked Aaron. When Aaron's band left Toledo the next morning that was exactly what I did. I climbed into the bus with them. And when I say that pretty can get you a thing or two, that's what I mean. I mean it can get you a bus ride to the West Coast with a jazz musician who hardly knows you but might already be suspecting that he loves you. We were headed to San Francisco at the end of it all, Aaron had promised me. He told me there was even a church in San Francisco that had canonized John Coltrane. Clearly the place for us. So L.A. was never really the plan, but when we got stranded here and Billy's ex-girlfriend offered to help me get a job at the club where she worked, Aaron and I both thought it was a good idea. Here's another thing pretty can get you—it can get you a job. Me being a stripper seemed real jazz to Aaron, kind of picturesque and romantic. That's how it was in our minds before I started.

Aaron and I strolled with our fingers intertwined down Hollywood Boulevard to pick out the shoes, while I wondered where the hell San Francisco had gone. Wondered what the hell Pastor Dan would say if he could see me now. Wondered how we had wound up in this desert buying a pair of heels to go hit the airport clubs for work. Wondered how many other girls had thought the very same thing walking into the very same store. I opted for the black shiny ones with the platforms and the long, thin, tapered heels. They're remarkably durable. You can get most of the scuffs out with alcohol. Dancing was another one of those choices I made that I didn't know until way later what it really meant.

By that night at Raji's a year and some change ago, dancing had shifted from an emergency measure to just being my deal. It was what I did, and I couldn't remember anymore what I had started out wanting to do. Had I wanted to be a singer? A jazz wife? A California bohemian? I don't think I wanted to be a drunken stripper. Not that it was so bad, but it wasn't so good. I mean, what it does to how you look at your real boyfriend. How all that lying all night long and all the laps of all the men can make you kind of angry and how being angry and smiling is a bad habit to get into. You can blow up and do something cruel one night. You can do something stupid that maybe you'll regret forever and that will ruin the rest of your whole life.

So "You Shook Me All Night Long" came on the jukebox just as Chas looked at me all starry-eyed, like the dork he was, and said, "Yes. You won."

"You're saying I'm a winner?"

"You are."

"Well, we should celebrate, don't you think?"

I held his gaze, got up on the pool table, recently cleared of balls by the game I had won, and handed him my pink heels. He held them away from his body like they were either worth two billion dollars or they were on fire and he couldn't decide which.

"Now, don't get all crazy and go drinking champagne out

of those, 'cause I might need to walk home in them if Aaron keeps acting like an ass."

I gave him a wink. He was so easy. All Aaron's friends were jazzmen and phony intellectuals and chatty college girls. I would never fit in with them so I settled for the next best thing and acted the wild one. Sometimes it was true.

I danced there, my bare feet on the green felt, flipping my hair back, swaying my hips, and leaning with one hand onto the low, swinging lamp. The glowing green platform was the only gash of color floating in a brown bar full of gray smoke. Glasses of one amber liquid or another reflected people's faces all distorted on their curved surfaces. Wafts of a bad smell you just ignored blew over from the direction of the crowded bathroom.

Aaron finally walked over and stood in front of me, looking concerned or annoyed or something. Chas left my shoes on the edge of the table and melted into the crowd. Aaron's forehead creased in the uneven way that it did when he was disturbed. He held his arms out to me like you would to a kid on a high wall, in that way that means jump and I'll catch you. I kept dancing and he stood there and I see him now like that, his arms extended to me, but he is moving backward away from me, getting smaller and smaller, and I am high above him, higher than the pool table even, and he is falling down a dark well. He held his arms out to me and it stopped me in mid dance move.

I ended my little performance, put my hands on his shoulders, and jumped off the table into his arms. He lifted me gently down by the waist like I was a ballerina, toes pointed, riding gracefully through the air. When I touched down I clasped my hands behind his neck and stood on his boots with my bare feet. Then, with his edges hugging mine, we danced slow like in an old movie. I don't know when he learned to dance like that or when I did. I understood that it meant we were starting over.

But even with the missteps of the evening forgiven, even with a fresh start, I was hungry and falling apart. When I was with Aaron, my molecules vibrated so fast that they flew off their gravitational path. I split into a thousand humming pieces. I closed my eyes and swam in a black velvet galaxy with no floor beneath me while I braced for my impact with the bottom. I remember thinking: I don't know if I can live with this.

We held on to each other for a minute like that, swaying dreamlike in a bubble. The rest of the room went quiet and it was just us. And if I could rewind it, I would rewind it to there.

I broke the mood and put one leg up around him, grinding on him like he was a customer. I was laughing; I was joking around, but he didn't think it was funny and he pushed me off.

"What's the matter? You want to fuck her?" I asked, meaning Madison.

"What are you talking about? Why do you always have to ruin shit?"

We were making a scene, but it was a bar where scenes

happened pretty regular. He acted superior, pretending like he was holding it together, but I could tell he was all tilted and too high and too drunk, same as me.

Aaron was into the drugs but he wasn't starving hungry need more all the time like I was. He usually kept it a little more in control, but that night he didn't. That night he was gone.

"Don't tell me how to talk, asshole. Maybe you want to talk to your fancy friend over there instead. I'm sure there's some French fucking film she's dying to discuss with you. I'm out of here," I said, fumbling for the keys in my purse, hopping and putting on my shoes as I left. I was always testing him, wanting him to stop me.

He followed me out the door and we stood on the trash-strewn sidewalk, illuminated by the headlights whizzing by.

"Give me the keys," he said. "You can't drive."

"You know who I'm talking about. You want to fuck her, you should do it. I fuck other people. Whoever I want. You don't own me. You're not my father. So go ahead."

It was a lie. I never touched anyone else if you don't count work. And you don't count work. I don't know why I said it. Maybe to see if I could make him really lose it. Maybe to measure how much he cared by how bad it could get. I was going to tell him later that I had been kidding.

Aaron grabbed my wrist hard and twisted until I dropped the keys. He leaned down to snatch them and when he stood back up I swung my arm to try to knock them out of his hand but I cuffed him square on the side of the head instead, throwing him sideways off balance. He was so calm when he righted himself that I could have sworn I knocked him sober. He turned and walked down the street and I trotted after him, trying to keep up with his long steps. I didn't want to be left behind.

"Don't say another word," he said, flat and mean. "Just get in the car."

I already regretted what I'd said, but I was still high with self-righteous fury so I wasn't about to retract it yet. I practically believed my own lie. And why shouldn't I, anyway? Why shouldn't I fuck other people? It might even the score a little bit. It might make him feel that private humiliation of knowing that you're not quite loved enough, not quite wanted enough, not quite important enough. It might make him hurt for a heartbeat like I hurt for him all the time.

There were no more words. I pulled my cheap Melrose Ave. dress out of the way of the heavy car door on Aaron's beat-up '68 Cadillac and slammed it closed. I settled down into silence, laying the bricks of a wall of indignation between us. I was convinced he was fucking that girl Madison. And if he wasn't already, then he wanted to. And even if it wasn't Madison, it had been hundreds of others and would probably be hundreds more. That's how I saw it. That's what happens to your eyes when you spend your nights in the laps of everyone else's husbands.

He gripped the wheel with both hands and glared straight ahead, teeth clenched so tight that I saw his jaw muscles twitch. I could tell he was livid, but he was also wasted. He held on to make the world stop spinning. I stubbornly sewed my mouth closed as he peeled out and headed too fast toward Sunset. I wasn't going to be the one to show weakness and tell him to slow down.

Then there was the red light and the momentum of the car, how he didn't stop. I think he simply didn't see it. He was concentrating so intensely on not weaving that he didn't even look up to see that the light was red.

I saw it coming and tried to yell for him to stop but I'm not sure the sound ever came out. It happened fast and hard. Not slow like some people say. Not slow enough to see my life pass before my eyes, whatever that means, and anyway I'm glad I didn't have to see that slide show.

It was a red minivan that T-boned us. Aaron's side completely caved in, crumpled like it was made of paper. I've seen the pictures. The impact was so massive that the van pushed the car forty feet and into a streetlight, which was what stopped us. My window was open is how my head didn't go through the glass but just got banged around pretty hard. The crash tossed me sideways and I collided with the door, then the dash. It was one of those old cars with only a bottom seat belt.

Aaron's door crushed in so far that he was practically in my lap and when I turned to see him there wasn't enough of him. Strings of blood hung off his face and off the ends of his hair and my first thought was his glasses—he lost his glasses. I grasped around for them but they were nowhere and anyway everything was turned inside out and I couldn't tell where I was reaching, what I was touching. He breathed gurgly sounds and I couldn't see his eyes through the wet, through the red. He wouldn't look at me. There was no world outside to see, only the diamond-studded spiderweb of the windshield.

I pushed open my side of the door as far as it would open, which was barely enough for me to slide out. I crawled away from the wreck over the glass on the pavement, which made a sound like ice dropped into warm water and seemed to crumble into dust under my weight. It didn't hurt at all. I was fine. I reached the wall of the storefront and propped myself against it, arranging my skirt modestly over my knees, and then I saw the blood streaked across my legs, the blood smeared across my lap. I wondered whose blood it was, where it came from. I looked at the shattered glass all around me, tiny triangles of it glinting in the streetlights. It was almost pretty. I clawed at my legs because they were suddenly unbearably itchy, and that was when I noticed all the shards that were ground into the skin along my shins, my knees, my palms.

By that time a crowd of people had gathered around. Concerned faces pushed in at me amid a sea of legs and an unintelligible chorus of low, freaked-out voices. When I saw that Aaron was still in the car, when I realized that I had left him alone in there, I stood to run back to him but I was too dizzy. I tried to crawl but the amoeba of people held me back. The sirens and the blue red blue red washed over me like forgetting and I couldn't see clear; the scene shifted in and out of focus like I was twisting the ring on a camera lens.

They had to open the top of the car up with one of those huge mechanical can openers to get him out. It made a sound like ripping the sky in half. It was then that I remembered to pray but my brain was all wrong. I couldn't remember my prayers. I could only mouth, "Please, Jesus," over and over and even that got fumbled up. My mouth was full of something that tasted like pennies.

The paramedics took Aaron away on a gurney and he was still slick and purple and streaming in blood like he had just been born. They cut his shirt open with scissors as they rolled him away.

They took me next to a hospital so fancy it was practically a hotel. The emergency room wasn't some decrepit free clinic like the ones I'd seen before, but instead it was nice and clean with warm colors and framed prints of the desert. Attractive nurses floated by in pink scrubs and clogs with clever patterned socks peeking out. It was near Easter. I remember little bunny socks. And I was all right, a concussion and two broken ribs and lacerations, a lot of lacerations. Pain stabbed at my side but I hovered somewhere far away from it in an opiate haze.

They told me I couldn't see Aaron yet. He was still in surgery. There was no way of knowing. It would be hours. I went over everything I wanted to say to him when he woke up. I'd apologize for everything and make it right. We would do better. We would start over. I succumbed to the brain rattle and to the morphine fuzz and faded away wondering how we would ever pay for it all.

I don't know how long it was before I woke up. Before I could slog through the heavy waters behind my eyes and find my way to a desk to ask where he was. Every breath I took felt like shards of glass had lodged themselves in between my ribs on my right side. The feeling was so convincing that I actually lifted my gown to check. And when I looked at my stomach, fish belly pale and mottled with strange bruises, I remembered a dream I'd had. I dreamed of the accident, except that when the paramedics came I was still in the car. I was entirely bisected by a pane of glass, straight through the stomach, straight through the seat belt. I knew they could never remove it because if they did I'd split in two like a magician's assistant after a trick gone horribly wrong.

Dragging my IV next to me, I padded down the hallway in my bare feet to see Aaron behind the last doorway on the right. The hallway wasn't long enough. I was at the last door on the right too fast. The hall smelled like floor cleaner and like cooked food in plastic lids and it made me gag a little. I walked in.

What I saw was, he was smaller, sizes smaller, shrunken. My Aaron whose feet hung off the bottom of every bed. How did he shrink?

He lay alone in a room so small it looked like a monk's cell. There were bandages all around his basketball-sized head and over most of his face. What little skin he had that wasn't bruised purple looked white. Not white like a white person but white like the dust on a red grape.

His bed nearly filled the room, which didn't smell of food like the hallway but smelled of nothing at all. He was attached to some mobile contraption—a fake set piece with mechanical breathing noises like Darth Vader and those green moving mountain range beeping lines. The front of his head was shaved and the few dreadlocks that were left escaped from his bandages like dark ropes on the white pillow. A child's drawing of a sun with the lines bursting out around it that means shining.

The sheet only covered him to his waist. His arm was in a brace and a block of white plaster encased his leg. His sunken, nearly hairless chest moved mechanically up and down. He looked uncomfortable, like they had laid him down awkwardly with his one good arm partially wedged underneath him. Everything was off kilter and too crowded. His eyes were slightly open, half-moons of white. He shook epileptically. The shaking is what you don't see on the TV comas. A thick breathing tube obscured his mouth.

First thing I did was stand there like someone had hit me in the face.

Second thing I did was I cried. I laid my head on his chest and cried and hoped my tears would spark him awake like the snow on the poppies in *The Wizard of Oz*.

I talked to Jesus a lot in those days. That was before I stopped bothering. So the third thing I did was I fell to my knees on the cold linoleum and prayed to Jesus like I never had before. I pressed my bandaged palms together and prayed with all my heart to Jesus Christ to please save his life. Promised Jesus that if he would only be with Aaron right then, if he would only wake him up, that we'd be spiritually reborn. Just save his life and we'll live in the light of God's love and never stray again.

When I talked to Jesus that was how it came out. It was etched into my brain that way after so many years at Zion Pentecostal. So when I wanted to talk my own way I sometimes talked to my pop. Because even though I knew that Jesus was boundless compassion, that Jesus was love, that Jesus was forgiveness, still somewhere I thought that maybe a dad who loved me crazy but still drank himself to death would offer forgiveness of a different sort.

So, I prayed to my dad. Pop, I fucked up. Pop, I'm sorry I did this to me. Pop, can you help save his teeth, can you help save his hands? I didn't mean to be this. But we're not just this. You should see us in our dreams. You should hear him when he plays. I'm unforgivable but forgive me, forgive me.

In my peripheral vision I saw a nurse come in and stop in her tracks, hovering there, unsure of what to do. Hadn't she ever seen anyone pray before? I looked at his trembling body then turned to her.

"He's cold."

"No, he isn't."

"He's shaking. Can we please have another blanket?"

"He's not cold."

I put my hands to his bare chest and could feel against

my wrists where my bandages ended that he was warmer than I was. I was so cold that furious goose bumps covered every exposed inch of my flesh. I placed one hand to his heart and one on his belly like I was a preacher with healing powers. Like I had seen work a hundred times before back home. You may doubt it; you may think it was some kind of a sham, but you'd be wrong. I know what I saw was real. Anyone could be a healer.

The nurse left the room.

The fourth thing I did was that when I was done praying to Jesus and my pop I talked to Aaron. I told him that I was just kidding what I had said. I told him that God was going to give us another chance. I told him that I would learn how to love better, that I wasn't sure how I had gotten it so wrong.

His thin frame shook and his rib cage moved up and down to the mechanical rhythm. Up and down. I can still hear it sometimes when I'm trying to sleep. I shake my head to make it stop. When I start to hear the ventilator, I get up, go downstairs, and turn on the TV.

After the strokes that stopped his brain, it was Aaron's mother who signed the paper to turn the machines off. She didn't speak much to me, but we sat together. We sat together with him when he died but that's the part I'd rather not get into now because that's the part that lives like an overhead projection superimposed over all of my days. When I first sobered up I actually tried banging my head on the wall to get rid of it, but the folks at the detox threatened to put me in a whole different level of lockdown if I didn't get a grip and anyway it didn't work, it just added a headache layer on top of the firebrand memory. Eventually what I figured out is that I can nudge it out of the way for a minute here and a minute there by pressing the rewind button and seeing instead the moment when I was on the pool table and my alive boyfriend stood in front of me and reached out his arms as if to say go ahead and fall. Fall and I'll catch you. And that was all I had ever wanted—someone to catch me.

Two

I was almost saved once, when I was baptized in the waters of the Maumee River on the outskirts of Toledo. I thought that the cold dip would do the trick but almost isn't enough. Look away for a minute and your faith will be gone and you may not get a second chance at it. That is what I think as I sit outside of Serenity in my shitty pink-that-used-to-be-red Honda with the sun-bleached hood and the busted passenger-side door. Not so much about faith but about second chances.

Serenity House is on the back slope of a hill in Echo Park. It is one of two state-sponsored halfway houses located in neighboring restored Victorians. I park the car on the steep grade and hope like I always do that the emergency brake will live up to its name. I got my beater car cheap from a lady whose son parked it out by the ocean and slit his wrists. She wanted it gone fast. She had it cleaned real good, though. You can only see a couple of the stains if you look. She told me the paint was faded because he was a surfer.

The downtown L.A. skyline looks like Brigadoon in the mist—a cluster of tall, fuzzy-edged buildings floating out of a low-slung sprawl of lights that stretches forever. Walking up the street, I pass by Chandra, our ghetto princess, the one who talked me into going to beauty school. Chandra just finished getting her cosmetology license, which, in the voc-rehab system, is like being premed in college—it means you really have a future. But tonight Chandra sits in the passenger seat of her boyfriend's white Lincoln Continental and cries, her hands in front of her face, her two-inch-long acrylics stretching to her hairline. It gives me a jolt to see her like that. She's a fighter, not a crier. I pull my jacket around me against the wet chill of the night and look away.

I throw my fast-food wrappers out in someone else's trash can before walking around back and climbing the few stairs up to the kitchen entrance. I opted for fries and a milk shake after Jake stood me up and left me hovering alone at the edges of an AA meeting where everyone was too bright and too loud and too pretty. I slipped out before the end and kind of felt like crying with frustration but instead stuffed my face in the parking lot of the Fatburger next door.

It's not his fault, really, that he rarely manages to show up for our dates. Jake lives in the men's house next door. He qualifies for housing in a dual-diagnosis facility because he was honorably discharged from the Marines due to a diagnosis of schizophrenia. His particular flavor of schizo is characterized by paranoid delusions and auditory hallucinations, neither of which was eased by his fondness for exotic psychedelics. By the time we met in a drug treatment center, before we both graduated and transferred to Serenity, Jake introduced himself as Jesus and really believed it until they got his meds straight. It's been a while since I've seen Jesus, but I know he's there, trembling underneath Jake's skin, waiting for life to squeeze Jake too tight so he can emerge again. So I try not to squeeze. I give Jake a lot of room.

Why would I date a guy who periodically thinks he's the Messiah and more frequently has an audible commentary going in his head? You'd have to meet him to get it. He has the most remarkable eyes, and by that I mean not the color or the shape or anything but how they see things. And besides, we who have been branded and filed away into the state mental health system, we have to stick together. Who else will have us?

My roommate, Violet, sits out on the back porch. She sits folded into the seat of one of the wire chairs with her knees tucked under her chin. The end of her cigarette glows with each furious drag. Violet is a goth girl with a baroque sense of style when she has the energy, but tonight she is wan and wearing black sweatpants so old they're gray. She tugs her sleeves down to cover her fingertips so only her cigarette emerges.

"Hey," I say.

"Hey. How was the meeting?"

"Jesus didn't show."

"Jesus stood you up *again*?"

"He has issues. I try not to get too attached. How was your night, Mistress of the Dark?"

She immediately goes listless and flat. "Fine."

Violet suffers from major depressive disorder in conjunction with a major suicidal ideation and a major fiending for methamphetamine. She turns inward, to her cigarette. I stand in the doorway for a minute. I wonder if there were constant awkward pauses before I got sober or if awkward pauses are one of the many new delights of sobriety. I can't remember. Violet can be jumpy, so when I go in I hold the screen door to make sure it doesn't slam.

Four of the girls are gathered around the old TV set in the living room. A couple of bowls sit on the coffee table smeared with the milky remnants of frozen yogurt. I go to the front foyer to sign my name and the time. We live by the chore wheel and the sign-in sheet. Every night the other girls sit in front of the TV but I rarely join them. I use TV time to get some hours alone in my room. Other than that, there's no such thing as alone. We share bedrooms and bathrooms and constantly talk behind people's backs about who left the crumbs on the kitchen counter and who dropped her bloody tampon outside the trash and who is a slut and who is on a trust fund and who has a stash of pills. Halfway house living is nothing if not cozy.

Mostly they watch *The Bachelor* and other such crap, but tonight they're watching the news. Even our little family of self-obsessed drug addicts has been watching the news lately. The girls seem unusually grave. I lean against the doorway and one or two of them give me a weak hello.

"What's going on?" I ask the general room.

"War," replies Althea, a pasty, somber girl who wears vintage hats and meditates on the tarot for hours every day waiting for guidance on what to do with her life. She pays the rent off her parents' credit card. She paid for her prescription habit with the same card before she got sober. "Again. Still."

Buck, whose real name is Becky, says, "These are the sacrifices we make for liberty, Al. We're guarding your freedom to be a freaky pagan and shit. Anyhow, it's their own fault. These people are dangerous psychos. Fanatics. Their religion tells them to blow shit up. They're going to nuke the free world if we don't do something about it. Like, I know it's terrible, but it's necessary."

"You smoked too much crack in your life, Buck," Althea mumbles. But no one wants to fight with Buck, the Republican dyke from Alabama who has a rebel flag tattooed in the center of her chest.

Missy sits in the ratty orange recliner and says nothing. Everyone pointedly avoids looking her in the eye. She's been having nightmares about her brother in the Air Force. A few nights ago, she clawed at the curtains that hang over her bed and woke as the rod crashed down on her head. Susan Schmidt said it was a result of Missy's post-traumatic stress disorder. PTSD, ADD, ASPD, ADHD, GAD, DID, MDD, BAP, OCD. On top of our substance abuse problems, we've all got some initials that qualify us for placement at a dual-diagnosis facility.

My initials are fairly unimpressive: MDD: major depressive disorder. CD: chemical dependency. ADD: attention deficit disorder. Mostly my problem is I like cheap chardonnay and expensive cocaine and vodka tonics and Vicodins. Or I did until the accident, after which a sympathetic lawyer helped me get into a treatment facility. The lawyer waited exactly three weeks before he started showing up with bunny slippers and cheesecake and tales of a Laurel Canyon hideaway with a killer hot tub. So much for philanthropic motives, but anyway I thanked him before I got him barred from visiting me, because I quit drugs and drinking and have stayed clean ever since and without that scumbag I'd probably be dead.

God is really a comedian because you pray to Jesus and a lecherous lawyer is the one who shows up to help. And then you diss the lawyer but wind up breaking the treatment rules anyway because you're so despondent and lonely you sleep with this mad handsome ex-Marine, artist guy named Jake, who's got a cool scar across his cheek and turns out to be totally bonkers. How is he bonkers? He thinks he's Jesus. See what I mean? Comedy.

After treatment I arrived here at Serenity. That was over a year ago now. Seems like yesterday. Seems like forever.

So now I am pretty much an ex-everything. Ex-Christian, ex-stripper, ex–drug addict, ex–pretty girl. Or rather I am half a pretty girl. I am mostly not so bad from the waist up, but my hands and my legs are a bird's nest of smooth, pink keloid scars. A bucket of worms is what my legs look like. I keep them covered and try not to think about them, not so much because of vanity as because they remind me of all that's irreparable.

"That monster. This is horrible," I say. Meaning our president. I like to blame him. Who else is there to blame? Me? I can barely stay off drugs and I am hanging on by a thread at vocational school. I have a dead boyfriend and MDD and CD, for Christ's sake. What do I know about war?

"He's a hero," says Buck, puffing her chest out toward me like a lezzy Napoleon.

"He's a criminal," I reply, leaning in the doorway.

Buck, who is actually one of my best friends here, snorts and turns back to the TV.

"Fucking communist hairdresser. Make up your mind. Last week you were practically ready to swipe the NRA sticker straight off my bumper. Don't go and get all peacenik on me again."

What she means is that last weekend I went and shot the handgun that Jake is in no way legally allowed to have off the back of his cousin's porch in Joshua Tree. Another reason I stay with Jake in spite of the fact that he occasionally doesn't show up for our dates is that when he does show up, he takes me places I've never been.

I had never felt the weight of a gun in my hand before, my face turned to the desert wind, my feet planted like I knew what I was doing. I could have told a whole other story of my life. I could have been someone else right then. I made the mistake of telling Buck the truth about it—it had been thrilling.

The guy on the news has the same suit same hair same studied inflections as always—dog show or wheelchair Olympics or war. It doesn't matter what I want for the world or what I want for my life. I try not to want anything, because I am convinced that, karmically, every prayer I enter in the logbook, every wish I make on a birthday candle, the exact opposite is fated to happen.

So I shrug and leave. I go upstairs to my room and hang my favorite denim jacket on its designated hanger. One thing these close quarters has done is make me tidy. Life gets small. Our closets are tiny, so we each have a neat row of shoes beside the door. We also have neat rows of labeled toiletries on the bathroom shelves and neat rows of labeled food in the kitchen cabinets.

The juxtaposition between my stuff and Violet's stuff is laughable. Violet's half of the closet looks like a vampire estate sale; mine looks like the closeout rack at Ross. I'm tall like a model except I'm not a model. Pant legs are always too short, shirts too tight in the shoulders, so I settle for whatever fits and is cheap.

Black fishing net covers the wall over Violet's bed. Spooky, white-faced marionettes hang from nails over her dresser. All her long necklaces and the latest lace skirt project hang off an antique dressmaker's form in the corner. I wish I could carry off a look like Violet does. She has a whole genre to live in. But I am not that committed to anything, so I am just me and stuck here. Just me in Chuck Taylors and black polyester pants and a white Moda Beauty Academy T-shirt every morning. Just me in jeans and a hoodie every night. A lame proto-hippie Indian bedspread hanging on the wall over my bed.

Aaron's and my old guitar leans against the side of the dresser, the only thing I kept of ours. His treasure, his trumpet, went with his mom and that was fine because I didn't want it anyway. Our guitar is the only lovely thing I own, and it is truly a lovely thing—a vintage Martin from the fifties, polished and golden with curves like a woman, a present to us from Billy Coyote. If my housemates had any idea of its value, they would've stolen it long ago. But no one would suspect I have anything nice.

I'm trying to teach myself guitar from a book. As of now, I know two songs, "Wild Horses" and "Dead Flowers," and I've been playing them over and over again the whole time I've lived here. Sometimes I try to learn some new chords or a new song but I don't get past the frustration. I go back to what my fingers already know.

The steel strings reverberate so loudly in the old house that I almost never strum them at full volume. I sit on the bed cross-legged with the guitar in my lap and sing softly. I barely touch the strings with my right hand while I move my left hand stiffly into crowded configurations of imaginary dots on the neck. In my enduring fantasy, I am someone who can pick up a guitar and make music into the dead air, out of just me, like magic.

Three

1528 hours down. 72 hours left to go.

I calculate it fresh every morning. I am a master of wasting time and learning nothing while earning credits.

Mornings we spend in theory class and afternoons we work downstairs on the floor. I slurp coffee from my 99¢ Only Store travel mug that leaks down the front of my lab coat if I'm not extremely careful. Violet is my classmate at Moda as well as being my roommate at Serenity, so she pretty much knows my life story so well that it could be her own, and vice versa. Between the two of us, the tragedy damage award is a toss-up. She prefers to wear hers on her fishnet sleeve. I prefer to wear mine in my choice of boyfriend.

So day in and day out for the last almost-year the Mistress of the Dark has been sitting on one side of me. On the other side sits the yang to her yin, the sun to her moon. On the other side of me sits Javier—my perfect angel, my basket of kittens, my cocoa on a snowy day. Javi is a not terribly young, not terribly thin queen with a Mohawk of constantly changing color and an unflagging optimism that I judge mercilessly but need like air. Javi and Violet are as close as I get to family, but don't tell my mom I said it. Or tell her. She's so gowed on pills she won't remember anyway. On a good day, Javi and Violet can convince me that there's such a thing as second chances because here I am living one. On a bad day I feel like I'm in that book where the guy wakes up and he's a roach or whatever. Like I'm something so ugly and transformed forever and waiting for the bottom of a giant shoe to come along and put me out of my misery. I feel that way mostly in the mornings at Moda.

Mornings are so slow. Afternoons go faster because we park ourselves in the back of the room and just hang out and talk while I pretend every day to roll a perm on the same doll head full of perm rods, unrolling and rolling the same curl each time a teacher walks by, a pile of decoy rods spread out on the station around me. I wouldn't admit it to many people, but I actually find the repetition soothing. So afternoons I can live with, but mornings are interminable. I lay my head down on the worn, checkered tablecloth and count off each five-minute pie slice of the big clock on the wall, calculating how many pies I have left to go. An eternity of pies.

Miss Mary-Jo is late today, so Violet doodles on the inside cover of her textbook: Tim Burton–esque sad-eyed girls holding blow dryers and dead flowers. Violet looks even more haunted than usual today because yesterday saw the end of a six-month saga involving some drummer who told her he was clean but turned out to be yet another junkie. This particular junkie's biggest interest in life was being a member of some dumb white gang that wore matching jackets—he was that kind of loser. Tears teeter along the lower rims of Violet's round green eyes. Her prettiest thing is those eyes. One fat teardrop falls onto the book and smears her drawing as she tells me about last night, when she found Jimmy slumped on the toilet with his works scattered on the tile around him. They fought, of course. Or rather, she fought while he nodded.

All around us the other women chatter to each other in Armenian. Moda Beauty Academy is housed in a stucco strip mall in Glendale, and there are only seven native English speakers in our class of fifty. The native English speakers are the three of us in my little clique, two horrid blondes from the Valley who transferred from another school that kicked them out, a big gal with terrible skin who Violet calls Shrek behind her back, and a scary stalker named Candy who also lives at Serenity. Candy has borderline personality disorder and keeps inviting me on dates to the Olive Garden. The reason that there's an overlap between Moda and Serenity is that Moda gets money from the State of California for being a participant in the vocational rehabilitation program, aimed at giving addicts some kind of marketable skill.

All the rest of the students here are Armenian and they mostly hang out with their own, with the exception of a goodwill ambassador named Vera and her sister-in-law Lila. Vera speaks perfect English and talks to me once in a while.

She could be my evil twin. She's as tall as me, but wears high-heeled boots every day, which bring her to around six foot three. She has ink black hair set in big sweepy waves with hot rollers, as if she's going to an eighties nightclub every day of her life. I'm in awe of Vera, always looking so slutty and polished. She's a big fan of the liner: eyeliner, lip liner. Her face looks like one of those coloring books where a little kid made a bold outline around the edges first and then colored the rest in lighter. Even her uniform looks sexy, subjected to the scissor and the sewing machine and remodeled with a push-up bra and hip-hugger pants. A silver Playboy Bunny pendant dangles from the ring in her exposed navel. Next to her, I'm nothing.

The Armenian women have a potluck lunch every day. Each one of them brings a heavy-looking dish in a Tupperware container. They dole the food out onto paper plates and turn the lunchroom into a homey, chaotic picnic. They brew sludgy Armenian (don't call it Turkish, I learned) coffee and drink it out of ornate, gold-leafed china that they store on top of the fridge. Lila brings me a cup once in a while and I feel privileged. When she does this, Vera will ask me questions and then translate for her friends. Like yesterday, when she asked, "Where is your family?"

"My mother's in Toledo. Ohio. My father died when I was a kid," I answered, sipping the bittersweet liquid out of the delicate cup, flattered by their curiosity.

She turned to the smiling audience of heavily made-up

faces and said a few words in Armenian. The women looked concerned.

"So far from family?" Vera asked.

"Not far enough."

But they didn't get the joke. They kept smiling at me with sympathy while talking to each other in Armenian.

"They are talking about you," said Lila. "They are saying that you are nice. They are sad about this. Your family. That you are so far."

Far. And this out of immigrants from Armenia.

I feel kind of special when they talk to me, but in the end I get tired of trying so hard. I usually wind up at a table in the corner eating pale sandwiches with the rest of the outcasts.

"Do you think I could get Jimmy to a meeting?" Violet asks.

"I don't know, honey."

She knows the answer. She looks at me, disappointed, then looks away at nothing.

I don't know anything. I definitely don't know how to help her scumbag boyfriend. I just know how to put one foot in front of the other along the balance beam. All day long every day.

"It's really over this time. I told him that this is the last time I'm going to listen to his lies," she says for the six-hundredth time.

I consider telling her that Jimmy isn't going to quit and that he's going to die and, maybe worse, stay alive and drag it out and drag her through it until she is as broken and deluded as he is and that's how it goes. But I don't because she already knows. Me and Violet both know that he isn't going to quit. That quitting is pretty much impossible. The two of us are here riding on some kind of miracle or some kind of fluke. I have no explanation as to how after everything I'm sitting here in Moda Beauty Academy awaiting a lecture on the dangers of nail fungus, complete with a delightful array of full-color photographs. My reprieve probably won't last long. But I take notes during lectures, and I roll my perms on my doll head, because what if it does last? I have to have a plan for that, too.

"I told him about San Francisco, Bebes," says Violet. "I told him that we're out of here just as soon as that clock reads five P.M. on our last day. So I was planning to leave him anyway. Dumb loser. We are going, right?"

"Of course we're going."

"You promise?"

San Francisco is our plan, home of the Church of St. John Coltrane. My dad always talked about how he wanted to go and walk the streets of North Beach, but he drank himself to death without ever making it farther than Indiana. Aaron was going to take me, but he never got the chance. So there's no one left but me and I haven't given up on San Francisco yet.

"I promise. We're going north as soon as we get out of this dump."

Miss Mary-Jo bounds into the room in a complete panic because she's late. She's the only teacher here who cares about the students, liberally doling out hugs and encouragement. The rest of our teachers use their thimbleful of power in the world as an experiment to see how much misery they can inflict in the course of an eight-hour day. But Miss Mary-Jo we all love. She's the absentminded beauty professor, constantly doing things like dropping her textbook. Then when she leans down to pick it up, her glasses fall off her face. She'll do that, like, fifteen times an hour.

"I am so sorry. So sorry. I had the much traffic. Take your notebooks out because we are too late."

Miss Mary-Jo is a stocky Armenian woman who barely comes up to my shoulders. When she reaches to give me a hug I feel like Godzilla. She wears rhinestone pins on her green teacher's smock: scissors on the left and *I Love Jesus* on the right. Her short, eggplant-colored mushroom hairdo bounces all as one unit as she begins the day's lesson, earnestly looking out at us from behind globs of mascara.

"Yesterday was the one for the plain manicures and we had a great success with this one. Today we will learn the oil manicures. Oil manicures are the very good ones. It is called to upsell."

Miss Mary-Jo writes "upsel" on the board, breaking the chalk in two, the errant piece flying into the room and bouncing off a table.

She goes on, "You can upsell the regular manicure to the oil manicure and it is for the more money. Always you want to make the more money, but only for a good one. Only for to help people."

With her remaining chalk stub, she begins to list on the

board the steps for manicure preparation, copying painfully from the book that we all have in front of us already. She quits after about three words, exasperated, and instead has Violet read aloud:

1. Sanitize the table.
2. Sanitize all additional equipment, tools, and implements.
3. Set up the standard table.
4. Wash your hands with soap and warm water.
5. Cordially greet your client.
6. Have your client remove all jewelry and place all items in a safe, secure place.
7. Have your client wash her hands with soap and warm water and dry them thoroughly with a clean and/or disposable towel.
8. Perform a client consultation . . .

This list of instructions continues for twelve pages, mercifully ending with:

39. Using long strokes, apply top or seal coat first to the right hand, then to the left hand. Brush around and under the tips of the nails for added support and protection. A UV topcoat can be used instead of an air-dry topcoat. Place both the client's hands under a UV lamp dryer (Figure 22.42).

40. Instant nail dry is optional; if used, apply it at this time. Apply it to each nail to prevent smudging and dulling and to decrease drying time. The oil manicure is now complete (Figure 22.43).

There is another whole page on "Cleanup and Sanitation."

I look around at the faces of my classmates. The fluorescent lights illuminate everyone's most damning qualities: lines and blackheads and brassy bleached hair and greasy skin and heavy features. We're none of us very pretty in this light. Maybe Vera almost makes the grade, but not even Vera looks all that hot in here. Pretty requires a more forgiving context.

There's this thing I do when I'm anxious or bored. Like now, for instance, when I'm near catatonic. I don't know why it goes like this or how it started even. I've always done it, since I was a little girl. I did it even before I joined Zion. Like a mantra or a counting game or something, except I use Jesus. I don't talk about it too much because I know it sounds religious and most people I meet around Los Angeles at least think that religious means creepy. Anyway, it's not religious. It's just a list of what I see around me.

Jesus is under my fingernails. Jesus is in the soap bubbles. Jesus is in the chalk dust.

Miss Mary-Jo always switches her words around and says the opposite of what she really means.

She says, "It is very important that you contaminate your instruments after the using. Everything on the sanitary maintenance area must be contaminated or exposed of or you will translay the fungus."

The mention of fungus elicits a somber nod all around. We've all been subjected to the photos of the yellowed, grossly twisted toenails going black around the edges and digging into the bright red, tortured toes beneath them. The word itself seems to carry infection in its wake. Mention it and I want to take a bath in Barbicide.

"We have now a quiz from the yesterday lesson. What are the five nail shape?"

As a group we easily get the first four: round, oval, pointed, and square. Then the rest of the class is stumped, but I remember.

"Squoval," I say.

Jesus is square. Jesus is pointed. Jesus is squoval.

"Yes! Squoval! It is the trick question! Good work, Bebe. Now everyone go and get your instruments and begin oil manicure with the partner."

Violet is my manicure partner, and she wants to mope about Jimmy the whole time. Javier sits next to us, partnered with Shrek and cheery as usual. I listen in as he chats with her about a recipe for a string bean salad with a touch of orange zest and about the wonders of Accutane. I forget my cuticles are soaking in oil and absentmindedly run a slimy hand through my hair. Now I am greasy on top of being eyeball-aching tired.

Valley Blonde #1 breezes by our table and nearly upends my oil tray with a sweep of her denim-encased hip.

"Oops, sorry," she says and reaches to steady the tray at the same time I do. She sees my hand and startles, her neon blue eyes (lined in neon blue eyeliner) widening with horror.

"Oh, my God! I think you got a fungus."

"Honey, are you high?" Javier asks Blonde #1. "You've been sitting in class with Bebe all year and you don't know yet that she has a few teensy scars on her hands?"

"Oh, my God, I forgot. I'm sorry. It just scared me."

"Well, at least it's good for something," I say.

"Huh?"

"Never mind," says Javi. "On your way now."

When people express horror at my mummy hands it hardly even bothers me anymore. Months ago I gave up on trying to incorporate gloves as a fashion statement. But the interaction with the Valley Blonde makes me think of Jake and our lunch date today. Jake is a lousy boyfriend for a lot of reasons, but he's a freak who thinks my hands are beautiful and that makes up for a lot.

At the end of the morning we bring our cards to Miss Mary-Jo, who sits at the front of the room like St. Peter at heaven's gates. She holds a felt-tip pen and signs out everyone's points. Violet and I hold out our poorly manicured, shiny-skinned hands for her to judge. One point each, practical manicuring. Three points' credit for manicure/pedicure theory. Pedicures come later in the week, the high torture of vocational school purgatory.

Miss Mary-Jo looks at my hands and adds an extra point to my card. Then she rubs my hands between hers.

"Your hands," she says. "There will be the healing."

This is what Miss Mary-Jo knows: beauty school is a doorway. It's not a school so much as a test. I envision a real job, or a career even, at the end of these sixteen hundred hours. And, more important, I imagine a life. One where I have a skill people pay me for and I wake up in the morning in my own little apartment and make coffee in a sunlit kitchen and maybe I have a cat or something. A sunlit kitchen in San Francisco. I don't know if there is that much forgiveness in the world, but that's the truth of why I'm here, in spite of nasty pedicures and regulation smocks and words like "squoval." If you want to know.

1532 hours down. 68 hours left to go.

Four

Jake comes to meet me for lunch. He picks me up in the Ghetto Racer, which is the shittiest car you've ever seen in your life. No, really. When he pulls up to the curb a general giggle erupts all up and down the sidewalk. People actually turn and point. Jake has to carry a book of vehicle codes around with him on the floor of the passenger side because he gets pulled over by the cops at least once a week and has to prove the car isn't in violation of anything but taste.

The Ghetto Racer is missing its front bumper. In the rear windows float demented doll and stuffed animal heads that stare out at you. The stick shift is a doll arm, tattooed with a Sharpie. Stickers for bands with names like Maggot Pus and Alien Sex Fiend cover much of the body of the car. The few parts of the paint you can see are badly rusted. Once it was a black hatchback Honda.

Jake looks as nuts as his car, if a whole lot more handsome. A wave cap with a grandpa hat over it covers his head. A still-pink, angry scar travels diagonally down the left side of his cheek from underneath his eye to his jaw. He has as many stories about how he got the scar as there are people who ask him about it, but I'm pretty sure I know the truth. I'm pretty sure he did it himself in order to let the poison out from beneath the spot where he was convinced he was kissed by Judas. That was during the psychotic episode that got him slapped into the detox where we met.

Today, he wears a filthy white T-shirt, covered with car grease and paint, and his jeans are stained green and brown from dirt and grass. There are multicolor brush marks all over everything, from his shoes to the ceiling of the car. He's wild-eyed and muscular and he moves like a spooked animal. He's the same age as me, but in the bright afternoon sunlight he could be forty. His twenty-five years on this planet have been long ones.

It's important with Jake to make the distinction between when he's going crazy, like clinically, and when he's just being Jake, which means eccentric in the impale-a-doll-arm-on-your-stick-shift way but not crazy as in you can literally see the fiber optics in the air that connect you to God. It's important to know the difference, but it can be hard, even for me, who might know him best. Even at his sanest, Jake still shines with an otherworldly quality. Talk to him for long enough and you may start to believe that he really is periodically privy to the conversations of angels and not just a victim of some faulty wiring in his brain.

"Hello and much worship, Divine Angel," Jake says as I get in the car. He takes both of my hands in his and kisses them. "To where do we travel?"

Jake's smile kills me, wide and sweet, with a chip in his front tooth. Like a little boy who went over the handlebars on his bike.

"We travel to the California Pizza Kitchen three blocks down on the left, unless you have a better idea."

I never meant things to get where they are with him because he's an obvious impossibility and also because I am not looking for love. I have no place left in me for love. But here we are.

Jake is the wild card in my mundane existence. He reminds me that things used to be more colorful than the ten-minute drive between Moda and Serenity, sliding by on barely enough gas in my tank. There has to be something in between that grayness and life in the Ghetto Racer, but I haven't figured it out yet.

I'm still kind of pissed off about last night but I can tell he doesn't even know he stood me up. I don't mention it. I'm too proud to admit that I was forgotten, even to the guy who did the forgetting.

California Pizza Kitchen is hideous, of course, but all the spots around here are like that. Everyone is on their lunch hour from the surrounding office buildings. Men with sunburned faces and too much gel in their hair lunch in their shirtsleeves. Women who wear nude hose and navy skirts like flight attendants pick at salads. I feature the ever-present, ever-humiliating school uniform. The purpose of uniforms, I figure, is to keep you from feeling confident. If you always feel like shit, you are more malleable. Or maybe that's only true for certain uniforms, because military uniforms seem like they would make you feel sharp. I've seen pictures of Jake in his dress blues and it's enough to make even me want to wave a flag.

After he was discharged, Jake made his way to New York, where he started doing these mega guerrilla public art projects. He erected statues overnight in corporate sculpture gardens and painted over commercial billboards with sci-fi worlds of zombies dressed in high fashion, incredibly crafted, criminal explosions of color. He paints like a deranged angel, so you can imagine that those New York socialites couldn't get enough of him—his rare talent, his genuine insanity, his incongruous military bearing. You know, very real-life. He spent his summers at swanky beach pads in the Hamptons and his winters in Central Park penthouses or chic SoHo lofts. He beat the husbands at chess, graffitied the bathroom walls, and fucked the rich wives. He stole the prescriptions out of their medicine chests and the jewelry out of their drawers and they ate it up. Where is there to go from there? That kind of success can ruin you. Lots of things can, I guess.

People stare at us when we walk into the restaurant, but not directly. Rather, they stare out the corners of their eyes, then quickly avert their gaze the minute I look back at them. Jake looks like what he is: a guy who took too many psychedelics and periodically thinks he is Jesus. He has *J-e-s-u-s* in

Cholo script tattooed on the top of his hand, wrapped in a snarl of vines that travels up his forearm. He got it when he was shooting acid intravenously. I didn't even know it was possible to shoot acid, but it is. Not recommended, but possible. He once told me he had gotten the tattoo when being God still felt good.

I order a salad, trying to make up for the milk shake binge last night. Life is a constant series of cleaning up the last mess.

"How is your day going in the palace of beauty?" Jake asks.

"You mean the pit of boredom? It's swell."

"It is a box inside a box for you, Angel. You're a princess in a tower guarded by zombie gorillas. But you'll prevail."

This is how Jake talks. You get used to it, kind of.

"Only sixty-eight hours left. Tomorrow we start the joys of pedicures. After your friend's gotten way too intimate with your feet, you get to put your closed-toe shoes back on your freshly painted nails."

"Surely the princess has some stockings or lovely lace ankle socks or, better yet, knee-highs with stripes she could wear to remedy the tragic problem of smudged toenails."

"You're a pervert," I say. Jake is something of a sock fetishist, obsessed with striped knee-highs. I have seen him stare at sock displays in shop windows for long, transfixed moments. At least it makes him easy to please. It also makes him the perfect boyfriend for a girl with lacerated legs.

I redirect. "How's the job going?"

"Me and money are not friends. I've decided I can't do it. I can't work for the monster boss people. I can't concentrate with real people concentration. I said it would take me five days to paint these rooms and now it's been eleven. One color, one color. If you break it down by the hour, I haven't made minimum wage. I'm practically paying them to paint their fucking house."

He looks around, distracted. I have brought his good mood crashing down. I can tell it disappoints him that I'm so boring, you know, asking about things like jobs when he wants to talk about zombie gorillas.

"Maybe it'll get better once you do it a few times."

This is my best attempt to sound supportive. Truthfully, Jake's noncooperation policy annoys me. I know he could do it, he just doesn't want to. He makes everything so difficult. I call it his civil disobedience act. The world shows up and he goes limp. I don't know how we're supposed to get anywhere if we're not willing to even try.

"Or maybe I'll reenlist. There's a war on now. They're not calling it a war, but it is and they could use me. I have skills," he says with sudden renewed interest.

"Good idea."

"I'm serious."

"What the fuck are you talking about? All you talk about is how much you hate this president. How stupid the war is. It's, like, your number one diatribe."

Sometimes it's hard to tell if he's serious or talking in metaphors or just joking.

"Politics means nothing. Politics is totally extraneous, beside the point."

"Whatever. They won't let you hold a gun. Sorry, soldier. Looks like you're stuck having to get a job."

"Politics means nothing," Jake patiently repeats, as if I haven't even said the word "job." "We laughed at the government. There were communists and fascists and fucking whatever in my platoon. We talked about it when we got drunk and we made fun of each other but it meant nothing. Politics means shit compared to the sense of self you get out there. I'm telling you that the weight of a hundred-pound rucksack, a thirty-pound machine gun, is nothing compared to the fucking weight of having to pay the fucking rent in the city of Lost fucking Angels."

He leans forward, his hands planted wide on the table, his gray eyes lit with clarity. It is a man thing, I think. I stare at the breadbasket and contemplate an olive roll. I put the breadbasket on the table next to us so I won't have to look at it. Jake takes it back, puts it in his lap, and bites off large hunks of a baguette, talking with his mouth full. Gooey dough balls stick to his teeth.

"Don't think it's about America. You think that's why guys go over there? It's not for George fucking Bush. I'll tell you that much. Anyway, what should I stay here for? Tell me that."

"For your art," I say, but it sounds thin. It's not the answer he wants. "For whatever's coming next," I continue. "What if it's something amazing? It could be. It has been before."

The truth is, I don't have anything near his brains or his conviction, with my Mr. Rogers aphorisms and my twelve-step meetings and my self-help books and my nothing real I believe in. One thing Jake has that I don't anymore is faith. He has the capacity to believe he's Jesus. To believe in joining the Marines. I can barely believe in the next hairdo.

"That is what you come up with, Princess? For my fucking art? For something amazing? You can't even ask me to stay here for you? And anyway, what are you staying for? I'm serious. Maybe not about the Marines, but let's go volunteer for the Peace Corps. Or I'll teach English in Bangladesh and you can volunteer, like, teaching prostitutes to give pedicures or something. You're not born for this drudgery."

"What are you talking about? This drudgery is actually exactly what I'm born for. I come from a long line of drudgery."

"I'm talking about purpose," he says. "I'm talking about daring to fucking exist. I'm talking about commitment. If you had ever had any, you'd know what I mean."

"Change the subject," I say, chastened. It's rare to get through an hour with him without either a catastrophe or a revelation. He's that kind of a dice roll. I feel like I got kicked in the solar plexus, but I try to remember to hold my head up, pull my shoulders back. *Milady's Standard Textbook of Practical Cosmetology* has a whole chapter on posture.

"You're right. You're right," he says. "I'm sorry. I didn't come here to add stones to the princess's prison walls. I came here to save you, even if it means painting all of Los Angeles one color, one color. I'm not enlisting in anything. I'm not going anywhere. I'm just talking. I'm just an asshole."

He kisses me in the CPK and a bored temp looks up from her Chinese chicken salad, her former judgment turning into a little stomach twinge of envy.

He's impossible. I'd bet my cosmetology license that he'll leave his job half-finished and will never even pick up the check. Me, I've always been good at showing up for work. That's the kind of girl I am. But I can't look Jake in the face and tell him that it's gotten me much further than not showing up for work has gotten him. Here we both are.

Jake drops me back at school and drives off in the opposite direction to stare at the unpainted walls of his unsuccessful attempt at a job. I'd say that I have the worst luck with men but when you make a choice like Jake you can hardly call it luck anymore, can you? Still, he saves me from the sameness of my days.

Jesus is in the polish on my nails. Jesus is in the stucco walls. Jesus is in the sun on my face.

Five

Before I clock in, the phone buzzes as soon as I slip it into my smock pocket. I take it out and look at the screen and the area code isn't Jake's as I'd hoped. It's Toledo.

I take a breath like how they teach us in group. They teach us to breathe. I decide to pick it up, hiding by the lockers in the back hallway to talk. Partly because I have nothing better to do and partly because I've got to talk to her sometime, don't I?

"Hi, Mom."

"Hi, honey." My mom tries to sound upbeat, to banish the sticky eternal glaze of need from her voice. The attempt makes her sound like one of those fascist Disney chipmunks.

"How are you?"

"I'm doing pretty good, Mom. Not bad. Could be worse." How many ways can I say the same nothing? "A little tired from school but all right. How are you doing?"

It's hard to explain why this is so agonizing. How can there be so much bullshit in just a "hello, how are you?" that it makes me want to stick my head in the oven? She is listening to see if I'm drunk; I'm listening to see if she's drunk. And both of us are broke and depressed and alone and hanging on to our respective life rafts by a pinkie nail. So you can see that the truthful conversation is not the one you want to have, either.

"Good, honey. Real good. It's getting ready to snow here. Can you believe it? You can smell it in the air. It's real nippy outside today."

"Huh."

"Still getting snow so late this year. The frost killed my early flowers already two days ago. Bet there's no snow out by you, though, huh?"

"Not exactly. How's work?"

"Oh, the same. The same. Pam took me to Red Lobster last night and I thought that was real nice of her. Those shrimp are just sweet as candy. Do you have Red Lobsters out where you are?"

"What's the occasion?"

"For what?"

"The Red Lobster?"

"It was her birthday."

"She took you to Red Lobster for her birthday."

"So?"

Someone closed a locker on her windbreaker. Someone dropped her box of wig pins and didn't bother to pick them up. Someone spilled something liquid on the floor of the hall. There's a Three Stooges moment in the making. I imagine Mrs. Montano walking down the hallway, slipping on the liquid, and trying to grab for the corner of the jacket. It slips through her fingers and she lands right on her ass on the wig pins.

I forget what we were talking about.

"Um. Yeah," I say.

Or I could just go ahead and stick a wig pin in my eye.

"Yeah. Well. How's your beauty school? Are you beautiful yet?"

"Ask another question."

Mom has been working as a receptionist at a doctor's office for about ten years now, which gives her perks like health benefits and free pens from pharmaceutical companies and unlimited stolen prescription pads. When we talk on the phone I hear the telltale fading in and out, the lazy consonants. She calls a lot less than she used to. She started drinking again when my stepfather, Rick, left her for some slut who had just graduated from junior college and was studying for her real estate license. At the time, I was bitter and dismissive. Said it was a good thing, that she was better off without him. That hasn't turned out to be true.

"Another question?"

"I'm almost done here. The pin curls are challenging but I think I've got a real aptitude for blow-dries. I'll have a big career any day."

"You can do my hair next time you come to visit."

"Sure, Mom." I never visit. I haven't visited once in four years.

"Eyes on the prize, honey."

"Eyes on the prize" is pure Rick. She still talks like him all these years later. He's still in her. In our family, it was always him with the "chin up" and the "early bird gets the worm" kind of shit. I remember Rick at my soccer matches: "Eyes on the prize, Bebe. Eyes on the prize, sweetheart."

I had asked my mother to tell him not to call me that and, while he was at it, not to come to my games at all, but my mother pointed out that it was his car and I should be grateful we had one at all. She said I should be thankful he took an interest in me and wanted to marry a widow with a six-year-old daughter.

Rick sold hot tubs. A luxury profession in a luxury-starved town.

"You shouldn't be able to sell hot tubs in Toledo," he said. "Not now. Used to be a different kind of place. Where there were plenty of men doing ordinary jobs for fine money and plenty also getting rich off them. Not anymore. But I'm a can-do guy, Bebe. And there are always people with money and if there aren't people with money there are people with credit and if there are people with credit than I can sell 'em something."

Mom met Rick at an AA meeting and they bonded over the fact that his son, Hunter, was the same age as I was. It was a valiant save. How Rick swooped in just before the house was gone and the car blew its last whatever it is cars blow. I remember Mom sitting up rod straight on the padded chair at the head of the polished oak dining room table that used to be Grandma's. She called me over and pulled me into her lap and then she told me about Rick. How we were leaving the house and moving in with him on the north side. They had only been dating a few months.

I felt panic. We couldn't leave. We lived in the only house with a hill in the whole town practically. A hill to roll down. A hill to lie across and look at the sky. Dad would have dismissed Rick with a snort. Dad would have called Rick a square.

"I don't want to go. I want to stay. Rick is a square."

Mom laughed at that. She pushed my bangs off my forehead to kiss it. I guess she once was the kind of mom who smoothed my hair.

"I know, sweetie. But Rick is an okay guy. And he can take care of you and Mommy."

My mom was a pretty lady. Prettier before she cut her hair off short and started wearing sweater vests, but pretty still. Why did she have to give up so fast? Our old chandelier threw little rainbow splashes onto the gray walls. There were no rainbows in Rick's house—no rainbows, no hills, no dad I wanted anything to do with. I held her hand, her nails always polished coral and filed to a tight oval. Then I put her index finger into my mouth and bit down, crunching the bony joint. She yanked her hand away and shoved me roughly off her lap. Her hand hovered in the air somewhere between suspended in surprise and wanting to give me a good whack. She never did whack me, though. I can say that for my mom.

"I swear, Beth Baker. I don't know what is wrong with you sometimes. What kind of animal are you?" She stalked off into her bedroom and I stood outside the door and heard her crying and was glad.

The last day of August we moved into Rick's house with the stone fence and the broken gate and the orange carpeting woven through with yellow dog hair. Rick lounged in his undershirt on the recliner in the living room that first night, with the cable box resting on his round belly, and showed me how to make the channel change, the fat, white buttons making a nice thunk sound when you pushed them in. I guessed Rick was okay, but I didn't like him to call me sweetheart.

Every night in that new house my mother lay next to me and sang when she put me to sleep, holding my hand in hers, her sweater smelling like perfume and dinner. My wallpaper was green and white with a fern leaf design that crawled and shifted in the dim light. She and Rick took me to pick it out myself. A seashell night-light glowed peach in the corner. We sang Joni Mitchell songs, "Big Yellow Taxi" and "Little Green." We sang the Beatles' "Yellow Submarine" and I sang "sumbarine" instead. When I want to hang up on her, want to put down the phone and never pick it up again, I try to remember that. When I hear her voice and it seems it belongs to no one I've ever met, I remember how we sang the song about the sumbarine.

I used to want her to be a mom who could teach me

something. Who would pass down a recipe for homemade spaghetti sauce, an heirloom necklace, and wise words about love. But I am her daughter—pretty like her and unlucky in love. And I don't have a pot to cook spaghetti sauce even if she did have the recipe to give me. So it's not just her who can't figure out how to live.

"Well, guess I should get back to my pin curls."

"Pin curls. How funny. Your grandma Betty used to set my hair in pin curls."

Six

I 532 hours down. 68 hours left to go.

After lunch, I clock in three minutes early and go to the back of the room, taking my regular station next to Violet. The room in which we spend our afternoons looks like a combination of a classroom and a beauty salon. It's called "the floor." Stations line up back-to-back in crowded rows and are lit blue-green with fluorescents glaring from the particleboard dropped ceilings. Everything here has a film of grime ground into it that dates from Paleolithic times. If Hercules went at it with a river of Clorox this place would still look dirty. All along the walls are posters from the eighties that are bad Nagel rip-offs meant to demonstrate an array of hip hairstyles. All the white girls in the paintings look like Sheena Easton and the white guys look like David Hasselhoff. The black people have their own separate poster and they look like the cast of *The Cosby Show*.

The Armenian girls spend their days highlighting each

other's hair until it breaks off in clumps. We've perfected the art of looking busy while we do as little as possible. We use the same doll heads styled with the same finger waves to get points every day. In all fairness, finger waves are seriously *hard*. Women have it rough, man. We do. I can't believe women used to do that to their hair every day.

Anyway, most of us, excluding Javi, are usually either trying to scam the teachers for our points or hiding in the bathroom or cutting the hair on our doll heads progressively shorter and shorter in random terrible haircuts until they look like butch dykes. At which point we paint tattoos on their necks and Violet makes facial jewelry for them out of paper clips. Violet and I duck beneath our stations when real clients show up, but Javi bounces up with enthusiasm every time someone walks in the door. We don't get all that many clients anyway. Mostly we just gossip, roll the occasional wet set, and stare at ourselves in the station mirrors that hang merciless in front of us all afternoon.

We've each named our favorite doll heads, the ones whose hair we don't cut but rather leave long to style into wet sets and finger waves and blow-dries and beehives. Javier's is a blonde named Lorelei Lee, mine is a redhead named Kitty Hawk, and Violet's is a brunette named Bella Donna. I'm not sure why I named mine Kitty Hawk, except that maybe something about her pert, shiny face reminded me of pictures I saw once of Grandma Betty when she was young. Grandma Betty, my mom's mom, was born in Kitty Hawk, North Carolina, and she maintained that there was an unusually high population of angels there. She told me that was why it was the place where the Wright brothers first took flight. She said they didn't just fly, they were lifted. My mom used to roll her eyes and say I got my religious streak from her.

When I get back from lunch, Javier is already at work directly across the aisle from Violet. He is in a particularly jovial mood because last night Paul dyed his Mohawk sky blue and new hair always makes him as giddy as a schoolgirl. Also, he's breathlessly excited about the extravaganza he has planned for his daughter Milla's birthday party tomorrow. Paul calls every three and a half minutes with cupcake disasters and complaints about Javi's bitchy sister and, I imagine, worries about whether Violet is going to pull off her all-important role in the festivities.

Violet has been cast as Snow White because of her vampire pale skin and her jet-black hair but mostly due to the fact that she has an incredible costume. She inherited it from her mother, who was Snow White at Disneyland for a record fifteen years—the longest-lasting Snow White in Disney history. Vi pretty much grew up at the happiest place on earth and you can see how far all that happiness got her. But she treasures that costume and it wasn't all that hard for Javi to talk her into carrying the torch for the day. I suspect she's regretting it now. I'm glad I turned down the role of Ariel with the excuse that I have a mandatory meeting with my social worker.

Javi drills Vi on the lyrics of "Some Day My Prince Will

Come" and criticizes her performance until she's almost in tears.

"Do it again. You're singing like an emotionally retarded turnip. Remember, you're it. You're the real thing. As far as these little girls are concerned, you're a genuine princess. I hope you fully appreciate the awesome burden of that responsibility."

"That really puts me at ease."

"I'm not interested in ease. I'm interested in magic."

"Javi, stop terrorizing her," I interject.

"Oh, you're right," he concedes. "I'm a psycho. I'm sorry. You're gonna be great, pumpkin. Even if the best you can do is stand there and look like you don't want to hang yourself, you'll still be better than last year's princess. Oh, my goddess, you should have seen the Sleeping Beauty they sent. Sleeping? Nodding is more like it. And ugly as a bucket of homemade sand."

Every day, Javier tapes pictures of Paul and Milla all around the mirror of his station. The teachers here make him take everything down at the end of the day, but each morning he decorates anew. A single daisy stolen from the farmer's market sits in a Starbucks cup next to his color-coded wet set rollers. Javi knows what starting over is about. Most of us do, here at Moda, one way or another. In Javi's case, he was married with a newborn and working a desk job for American Airlines when he wandered into Pottery Barn one day and saw Paul restocking the Fiestaware. It's hard to imagine—Javi in polyester uniform pants and a matching tie. Javi coming home to a pregnant wife and a town house in Simi Valley. It's enough to make your head spin.

Javi goes back to work putting the final touches on his black doll head. To set off her press-and-curl, the doll wears a leopard-print scarf on her head. For her face, Javier glues on fake lashes then applies dramatic liquid eyeliner. He's been working on her with fierce concentration for hours. He steps back as if done, then sees an invisible flaw and fusses again for a few minutes. Finally, he presents her to us with a flourish.

"Do you love her? She's Diana Ross circa the Supremes era. Can you tell?"

"She's fabulous, honey," I say, because she is.

A few of the other students gather around to ooh and aah over his work. He has the kind of talent that comes from love.

"I have a vision. She's the star of my new musical," Javier says, indicating the disembodied head stuck to the top of his station. The heads have a hole in the bottom of them. You set them on a short steel pole with a little vise on the bottom to secure it to the end of the table. The stand looks like a silver butt plug and is the subject of many jokes.

"What musical is that?" Violet asks.

"The musical I'm presently composing about our rich experience here at Moda Beauty Academy. It's called *Beauty School Massacre*. All the doll heads come to life and mutiny. They murder the owner of the school. It starts out with a scene where one of the students graduates. The doll heads sing for him . . ."

As Javi begins his song he mock-cries, dabbing at his eyes with a pantomime hankie. He acts out the scene of his musical, doing the pomp-and-circumstance slow step down the aisle between the stations.

One of the students is now moving on
To a Beverly Hills salon
When he leaves we will surely cry
That queen could style a great beehive . . .

Javier's semicircle of an audience all giggle appreciatively, though I know many of them don't understand the actual words he is saying. Still, he gets the point across. Violet laughs so hard at Javi's song that she has to wipe her tears with the corner of her smock. I think the musical is actually kind of a good idea.

As if on cue, a cloud rolls over our little party. The owner of the school, recently cast as the mutiny victim in Javier's new musical, waddles down the stairs directly behind us. She no doubt heard the laughter and aims to quell any merriment that might soften our daily misery.

Mrs. Montano looks disturbingly like pictures I've seen of John Wayne Gacy when he dressed up like a clown. She appears to be wearing a giant beach ball costume, with only her dwarfed hands and feet sticking out. Her hair is a lacquered auburn helmet, the exact shade preferred by beauty school teachers the world over. Her makeup looks like a mean puppet face, with white foundation, an angry gash of red lips, rainbow-colored arches of frosted eye shadow highlighting the crepey skin of her eyelids, and two perfect circles of blush that sit unblended on her cheeks. We hear her heavy breathing as she comes down the stairs, but not fast enough to reassemble and look industriously unhappy.

"Hello, students," she says real evil, as she passes us and walks to the reception desk.

Mrs. Montano looks at the books and gets on the intercom. She turns up the volume so the crackly loudspeaker assaults us.

"There is a perm client here. Javier, please come to the front."

Let me explain that this is meant as a punishment. Perms reek enough to make you gag, they take forever, and they're so toxic they peel the skin off your hands if for some reason there are no gloves, which sometimes happens in this chintzy pit.

"You have no power here. Be gone. Before someone drops their house on you, too," he says under his breath before sauntering, unshaken, to the front of the room. He doesn't hide from the clients and cheat on his credits like the rest of us. A devoted clientele of local biddies always ask for him. Javier offers his arm and chivalrously escorts the perm client, a deflated old Chinese lady, to his station. One of her gray, knee-high stockings has crept down around her ankle. A thing like a fallen stocking can make me so sad some days.

"How do you stay so cheery? And without meds even," I ask him, ignoring the client, who just sat down in his chair.

"Honey, I could have it a lot worse, okay? I could be in Guatemala farming sugarcane with my ten brothers and sisters."

"You grew up in the OC, so spare me."

"But I *could* have been born in Guatemala, honey. My grandma was. And you could be in Tolethal, Ohelpme, right now, so chin up. Only sixty-eight hours left to go before you start your glamorous new career in the vortex of vanity." His own phrase impresses him. "Hey, that's good. Maybe I'll name my salon Vanity Vortex. Or maybe it'll just be my new drag name."

The idea fires him up. He bounces up and down on his toes for a minute. How can he care about every little thing?

The old lady sits in Javier's chair looking dazed. He spritzes her thinning hair with water before sectioning it off in neat little rectangles with his rattail comb and then rolling each section onto a thin, hourglass-shaped perm rod. He works quickly with a little wrist flourish after he secures each rod. A fat drop of water runs down the client's nose and she makes no attempt to wipe it off. Javier sees it and blots it gently with a towel.

Javier pauses and turns toward where I slouch in the chair next to him and pull at a loose thread on the hem of my smock.

"Sit up straight," he says. "You're such a pretty girl and you go around slouching like you're wearing a fifty-pound hat on your head. And even if you are, honey, sit up straight anyway."

Mrs. Montano strolls the room like a chain gang foreman while I roll Kitty Hawk's hair in wet set number one hundred and eighty-five of the two hundred that are required. Closing in on the finish line, I tell myself. Eyes on the prize, sweetheart.

I look in the dingy mirror, sticky with a film of hair spray. My cheap black pants snag on the nail protruding from my station. My hair is greasy. Painful purple zits blossom along my chin. Remnants of last night's eyeliner hang on beneath my lower lashes. Huge caffeine- and exhaustion-dilated pupils nearly eclipse my dark brown irises and the effect is blankness.

When Javier finishes with his client, he styles her tight perm into a fluffy confection. Then he takes the daisy out of the Starbucks cup vase on his station and pins it above her ear. She looks like an ancient version of a WWII dance hall girl. It's transformative. Her head perks up and her eyes look almost alive and suddenly her stockings don't seem so sad.

After she leaves, Javier calls me over to his chair and throws some quick curls into my hair with the iron, then rolls each curl around his finger and pins it.

As he rolls and pins, rolls and pins, we talk with Vi across the aisle.

"What I don't get is, where in the story are you?" I ask. "Are you Snow White, like, already married and living happily ever after? Or are you at some other point where you still have that catastrophic apple thing ahead of you?"

"You don't get it," says Javi. "Snow White is a *magic* princess. She exists pre- and post-apple at the same time. Pre– and post–happy ending at the same time. And Milla gets to insert herself into the script any damn place she chooses or take them all to brunch with Goldilocks and the Three Bears at their summer place in Mendocino County. People get all blah blah it sends the wrong message that all the princesses get saved by men. Like these stories are going to ruin the rest of my daughter's whole life. It's bullshit. Milla knows that she can write another ending for the princess anytime she wants."

"You have to admit, though," says Vi, "Cinderella does suck."

I don't feel like arguing, but I don't agree with Javi. I think it can ruin you to think that some man is going to kiss you awake and that you'll open your eyes to a new world. Prince Charming or Jesus or whatever.

But at the end of the afternoon, Javier takes the pins out and runs his fingers through the waves and I am transformed into a poor man's fairy princess. It's that easy. And I remember why I'm serving out the remaining sixty-four hours of my sentence at Moda.

"Just sleep on a satin pillowcase and those curls will still be luscious tomorrow," he says.

I clock out with confidence. Stop believing in one thing

and you make room for believing in something else. Hopefully something that works a little better.

A hairdo can change the course of your whole day. Maybe your whole life, I tell myself, if you let it.

1536 hours down. 64 hours left to go.

Seven

Violet stands in the middle of our room in her Snow White wig and her underwear, a princess gone porno. I take the dress from its hanger on the back of the door and help her to navigate the sea of tulle and satin before zipping her snugly into the bodice. She pulls on her little white gloves, the final touch that changes her from porno into perfection.

She hollers, "Buck! Get up here!"

Buck takes the stairs two at a time and appears in the doorway. When she sees Violet, she's immediately hypnotized.

I toss the bag at her and she offers Violet her arm to walk down the stairs.

"Aren't you a vision."

Buck is Violet's escort to the party and she's dressed as some approximation of Prince Charming, in a white jacket with gold epaulets and a gold sash.

"Are you Prince Charming or a tuba player in a marching band?" I ask.

"That depends on which you think is hotter."

When I hear the door close behind them I settle back to read the weekly free paper and wait with resigned dread for my meeting with Susan, our resident social worker. I flip absentmindedly through the pages until I get to page seventeen.

What I see on page seventeen turns my stomach cold and causes dark spots to flicker at the corners of my eyes. I haven't seen that face in over a year now. I haven't seen it since the funeral.

It's an article about Billy. The headline is: *The Radical Reinvention of Jazz Legend Billy Coyote*. Some words I see are: *sober*, *new band*, *new sound*, *new vision*, *reinvented*, *reborn*.

The bees start to pump into my bloodstream every time my heart beats and then the rhythm speeds up and my breath catches as if there's a little door in my windpipe and it blows shut. I can't suck in enough breath. The dark spots in front of my eyes grow larger and the memory loop gets rolling and no matter how tight I hold my head there's no stopping it. The film runs through the machine making that flickaflicka sound. A shaft of light shoots the pictures out onto the world in front of me. It starts with the lie I told Aaron: that I was going to California.

I had been working at Rusty's four nights a week since the summer after I graduated high school. A summer job that turned into a year that turned into three years. We had jazz and blues at Rusty's. Mostly local guys and not too bad. Once in a while a small touring act came through. For bands on tour, Toledo was somewhere to fill in a show between Cleveland and Detroit.

I restocked the beer at around four the night Aaron's band showed up. I was already keyed up before they even walked in. They were an out-of-town band, a wild card. He ambled in the door first, trumpet case in his hand. I looked up. I hadn't seen anything like him in my life. I couldn't read him. Not a white guy but not a black guy, with a head of dreads and slow, brown eyes behind those Buddy Holly kind of glasses. Tall like me but all angles.

He strode up to the bar.

"Hi," he said. "I'm Aaron." He extended his arm, smiling a goofy smile with those pointy wolf teeth on the sides that I always liked.

I wiped my wet hand on my jeans and shook his. Long and dry and warm. No other musician had ever walked in and shaken my hand like that. Maybe he thought I was somebody I wasn't. But probably not. I didn't look like anybody. Kind of pretty in the face, maybe, but not like I was somebody.

The rest of the band and their one roadie filed in the side door behind him.

"Dressing room is around the left side of the stage," I said, pushing my hair back out of my eyes. "First door on the right."

He headed toward the back of the club. A couple of the other musicians nodded or mumbled hellos as they followed him. The last one in was the guy holding the guitar case, whose band I assumed it was: Billy Coyote. He kept his sunglasses on and his head down, with a lit cigarette dangling from his lip. He looked lost, like he couldn't find his way even through the simple geography of a bar.

If I had to be in Toledo, which I did until I could formulate an escape plan, Rusty's wasn't such a bad place to serve out the sentence. Most of the assholes from my high school went to the bar with classic rock cover bands. There was good music at Rusty's and a bunch of harmless, regular drunks who were sloppy but nice to me.

Mike, the real bartender, was a fat, laid-back guy with a bad mustache and an emergency Twinkie always hidden behind the bar. He had been working there for a hundred years and he had some good stories about my pop. His old lady died the year before from cancer and I think he knew something about me and something about a lot of things, though we didn't talk about it much. Instead he asked dumb stuff like when I was going to apply for college and maybe if I didn't like regular school that I should go to cosmetology school like his oldest, Janice, who had her own shop now and made a grip of money and didn't even live in the old neighborhood anymore but had a ranch-style house on the north side of town.

I always replied, "Why would I want to apply to school when I won't be in town long enough to graduate, Mike?"

Mike shrugged and didn't tell me I should be sensible and stay, like everyone else said. Get a job as a hairdresser and find a husband.

Mike was one of the reasons I drifted from Zion in the first place. Mike was a lapsed Catholic and his old lady passed away and she wasn't saved. How was I supposed to look that guy in the face and tell him that I believed that Sandy was burning in hell? For that matter, how was I supposed to look myself in the face and imagine my own pop there?

It was one of those things that I didn't get how important it would be until later. The being-saved thing. That it wasn't just about being saved, it was about all these other souls not being saved. Little babies in Africa with flies on their eyes who die of starvation and Gandhi and earthquake victims in China and my pop and Mike's Sandy. And in the end I couldn't hang. I just couldn't hang with that. I miss the rest of it every day, but I don't miss hell.

Anyway I stood smoking a Virginia Slim, one hand on the bar, rag over my shoulder, and watched the band as they sound-checked. Billy Coyote was too high or drunk or something. He never even stood up off his stool and he barely lifted his head the whole time, but still, you couldn't stop looking at him. The rest of the band was bickering and lackluster, except for Aaron. He stayed off to the side in a pool of calm as bright as a spotlight. When he put the horn to his mouth, for the first time I understood in my gut something my pop had always told me: playing the horn is really singing. Aaron played a killer solo in a nearly unrecognizable interpretation of "Dream a Little Dream," except I pegged it on account of I sat around a jazz club every night. And I could tell Aaron's performance was for me, the only audience. He was singing to me.

When they were done he took a long step off the stage, pulled a baggie of weed and a package of rolling papers out of his shirt pocket, and walked up to me.

"Smoke?"

The early evening was heavy with humidity, but we went outside anyway and sat sticky on the white vinyl seats of my mother's Camaro. We rolled the windows down and passed the joint back and forth. It was incredibly strong, not the Toledo dirt I was used to, and the world spun like a slot machine. I had to blink hard and will it to stop. I focused on the Jesus Loves You air freshener hanging from the rearview. It was my contribution, but had long since lost its scent.

"California," he said, meaning the weed. "Got it from some cat in San Francisco. That's where I'm going when we're done. To the Church of St. John Coltrane in San Francisco."

"That's funny. Me, too," I lied. But at that moment I felt as sure of California as I was of anything. "I mean California. That's where I'm going as soon as I've got enough saved."

"Oh, yeah? When will that be?" he asked, with a sarcastic edge I didn't much like.

"I'll let you know. So you can look me up when you get there."

The pot was too potent for me. I held on to the door handle. Breathe in. Breathe out. Brain like fuzzy sparkles. The church of who?

"Where are you going to?" he asked.

"What?" I was confused.

"Are you leaving?" he asked in a lazy kind of way, leaning his head back against the seat and smiling. "You're gripping the door like you're leaving."

"No," I replied. "I'm just hanging on."

"I get it," he said.

Later, after the show, he kissed me in the parking lot. I figured I was being a slut because he was leaving for Cleveland in the morning and I probably wouldn't ever see him again. I consoled myself with the fact that I wasn't going back to his motel room like some kind of hooker. But I wanted to kiss him to see what it was like to touch such a creature who owned all this music inside and carried powerful drugs in his shirt pocket and whose hands were so long. A guy who said he was going to California and probably would. Probably he wasn't the liar that I was.

He put his glasses on the hood of the car and placed his hands on either side of my face like I was someone he knew or cared about or something. I was wearing my Levi's tight on the hips then, red hair feathered over to the side and too long over one eye. I grabbed his wrist because I don't know what, and then let it go and let him be there and touched his shoulder blades over his nice, cotton button-down shirt, because jazz guys don't wear T-shirts even in dingy bars in drab towns. And kissing him was leaving Toledo right there. A promise of another side. Easy to lose myself because I probably wouldn't see him again and really I was just standing there in the gravel next to my mother's car.

I asked him with my mind, my psychic will, to take me with him to California, to Cleveland, to Chicago, to anywhere. Things you don't say out loud. He tasted like whiskey just turning to late-night sick sugar mixed with my own spearmint gum. Smelled like nice sweat and some kind of coconut hair oil. And we didn't kiss for too long and we didn't get sloppy sucky mouth open too wide and he didn't try to grab my tits, which made him the first in history.

That night I drove away with him still standing there. Always good to be the one who leaves first. Advice from Mom that she never took herself. But I went back. I went back the next morning. I went back with a bag packed and figured I was at the beginning of my own little fairy tale.

"*Breathe slow, now,* Bebes. It's okay. Just slow it down."

I'm on the floor with my head in my hands. Buck sits next to me and rubs my back. I don't remember falling. Another panic attack. They happen pretty regular since the accident but mostly in the car.

"Good thing I came back for Vi's headband," Buck says. In her hand is a bedazzled red bow.

Billy Coyote. Son of a bitch. Of course after all of it, he's the one who reinvents himself.

Eight

"*Hello, Beth,*" says Susan Schmidt, our director of counseling here at Serenity. Susan Schmidt insists on calling me Beth because my born name is Beth Baker. She has this theory that nicknames reinforce "old behavior," even though I've explained to her that my own mother calls me Bebe. It's not like it was my gang name.

Susan is always calling a meeting with me about some concern she has. "Concern" is her favorite word. I can't figure out why she doesn't like me. Why I don't like her is that she is a big rich phony who looks at us all like we're a bunch of derelicts and thinks of herself as some heiress Mother Teresa, when really she's a control freak with the tiniest sadistic streak. Like she enjoys it when she has to kick someone out of the house for an infraction. I've noticed a glimmer of pleasure in her eyes when she alters someone's life completely with a stroke of the pen. I saw it when she cajoled my friend Tammy into coming clean about her stash of diet pills and then gave her the boot.

"Come in, please."

The office is set up faux cozy. A framed print of a sunflower with a Maya Angelou quote underneath hangs over a wall of mismatched filing cabinets. I sit on a lumpy thrift store love seat facing a new brown leather chair. I can tell Susan Schmidt thinks her chair is very therapisty. All of this crowds into what may have been a walk-in closet when this place was a grand Victorian house, before it was a haven for half-crazy drug addicts.

I look around at the same crap I have looked at a hundred times—potted plants, a crystal paperweight, a wooden plaque that says *Keep It Simple*—just so I don't have to look at Susan. The air hangs thick with awkward static, like it usually does around the endless parade of therapists, social workers, and grief counselors. Does anyone feel comfortable in these tableaux of forced intimacy where you're meant to shine a light in your darkest corners for someone who is supposed to be nonjudgmental? As if there is such an animal.

Today, Susan Schmidt wears a blazer and riding boots and some kind of khaki leggings that might, God help me, be jodhpurs, but I can't tell for sure because she's sitting down.

She leafs through some papers in the manila folder on her lap. "I see here that you've been with us for over a year now and that you're nearly done with your cosmetology training. That's just wonderful." She crosses her legs, looks up, and smiles. "How do you feel about this accomplishment?"

When Susan Schmidt talks she gesticulates with her left hand, her chunky diamond engagement ring catching the light with dramatic flashes. I bet she sits at home in front of the mirror and practices making that ring sparkle.

"I feel fine. Grateful to be alive and sober today."

It's the truth, you know. I am. I mean, if I have to be the one left alive, I'm grateful to have at least done this one thing. At least I've looked life straight in the eye for a year and haven't once taken a drink or a drug. Maybe you think that's sad, if it's the only thing valuable I've ever done. Maybe you think that's pathetic. Like some people are born to win gold medals in the Olympics and some people go to medical school and then help little kids with cancer. But the truth is that was never going to be me, accident or no. Some people are just trying to learn how to not want to die all the time. Some people don't have a whole lot to be proud of, but I'm proud of me for this. I am. I just don't go into detail with the likes of Susan.

"You really have a wonderful tenacity, Beth."

Along with the word "concern," Susan is fond of "wonderful."

She shifts her facial muscles into a more somber configuration, indicating that the real reason for our meeting is coming up.

"You've been through a great deal. A profound tragedy. I suspect you have more feelings about it than you seem to be comfortable expressing to me or to your peers on a group level. I imagine that could feel terribly lonely," she says, swinging her shiny brunette bob around like a hair commercial as punctuation.

Wow. They give you a degree for such staggering insight? But what I say is, "I guess we all get lonely, sometimes."

"I'll be honest with you. I'm concerned with some of the things I've been hearing. Have you ever heard of the 'fear of success'?" she asks, making those little bent bunny ears with her fingers.

"No. What's that?"

"You're so close to completing this program and finishing up your schooling. You've come so far. It concerns me that you might be jeopardizing all of this wonderful hard work you've done with some careless behavior regarding one of the residents at the men's facility."

"Who do you mean?"

"You're only as sick as your secrets," she says. This is the recovery one-liner that she regularly uses to pump us for information.

"My heart is an open book, Susan."

Susan Schmidt sighs and shuts the folder in her lap, looking at me levelly.

"Consider this a friendly warning. I will not hesitate to take disciplinary action against you if I find out you're violating the terms of your contract here with us. You well know that your voc-rehab funding requires my signature. I like you, Beth. I really do, but you've got to work with me a little more here. I'm on your side."

"I appreciate that. I need someone on my side."

Jesus is in the veins on the leaf. Jesus is in the veins on my foot. Jesus is in the paint drips on the windowpane.

"Why don't you try to share some of your lonely feelings in group tonight? The hole inside you that you tried to fill with drugs and now are trying to fill with an ill-advised intimacy, that hole can't be filled by your self-destructive acting-out. There is only one thing for that hole and that's God, Beth. It's a God-sized hole."

"Thanks for this talk. I'll work on putting God in my hole."

She nods. "You may go. See you in group."

I stand, walk down the hall to my room, and toss myself onto my bed, where I curl into a ball on my side and lie there with my hands between my knees and my hair falling over my face like a veil. I'm not sure why these conversations with Susan Schmidt always pitch me down the ravine. MDD, PTSD, CD, ADD. Are the letters in your chart, the corresponding diagnostic numbers, supposed to free you? Are they supposed to make it easier for you to get better? Or do you walk around for the rest of your life carrying them like a sack of mail addressed to no one? Can I deliver this somewhere? Is there a doorstep I can drop it off on?

JAKE lights up the phone on the nightstand, the vibrations rattling the particleboard. I press Mute.

I am a loser, I think. I lose things. Aaron, love, keys, jobs, father, Jesus, earrings, cameras, bank cards, friends, sunglasses. And I could lose this so easily. This tiny thread of hope, this tiny foundation of a new life.

Jesus is in the hollows of my temples. Jesus is in the cracks in the ceiling. Jesus is in the dust in the corners of the room.

MDD PTSD ADD CD stop it stop it stop thinking stop thinking.

I don't call Jake back right away. I don't feel like talking. Instead I fall asleep on top of the covers with the early evening light fading on the other side of my eyelids as L.A. changes seasons as much as L.A. ever changes seasons, which is only by shades of blue and gray in the sky and sometimes by the rain and the temperature of the nights. It's warmer. Just slightly, but it is.

I dream I'm with Aaron on a street corner that looks like the ones in the black-and-white footage of the civil rights marches in the South in the sixties. We cross the street to order a soda from a counter at a drugstore. Behind the counter stands a black woman with enormous arms who says to me angrily, "What am I thinking? You think you know what I'm thinking? What am I thinking? What am I thinking?"

Poor me. Poor baby. What do I know about suffering? I'm such a victim. I'm all sick in the head. I had a tragedy. Poor me. I remember the glares I got from some black women when I walked down the street with Aaron. I imagined those glances said what the woman with the big arms said in my dream. They said you don't know shit about being a victim of anything. It's true I guess. I don't know shit about being a victim of anything. But still, this is enough. My suffering is enough.

I wake and the first thing I feel is fucking starving. I'm always fucking starving.

I walk woodenly downstairs and into the kitchen, hoping no one is in there to view the impending carnage. The house is alive with early evening bustle. I hear clomping around on the wood floors and voices echoing through the hallways and the shower running. The kitchen smells like someone recently heated up ramen noodles.

I park myself in front of the toaster oven with a package of tortillas and a tub of margarine. I eat, like, seven tortillas smeared with the yellow grease, toasting the next while I shove each one in my mouth. I only stop when I am nearly ready to barf.

Buck and Missy each walk in and grab a snack out of the cupboard and say hi and I say hi but pretend like I'm in another dimension and really they can't see me standing here with the wad of tortilla in my cheek and margarine on my face. They're too busy thinking about themselves to care, anyway.

Afterward, I sit with my legs tucked underneath me in the threadbare orange recliner while my housemates start to file in for group. I wish I could go and puke, but someone would hear and probably snitch and I don't really need them to add any more initials, any more twelve-step meetings to my regimen. Hi, I'm Bebe and I can't stop eating till I barf.

Some awards show plays on the TV. A dark-haired chick in a simple burgundy dress sings at a piano and she is lovely. She is curvaceous and her voice is earthy and she sings something like a jazz song except it is a pop song and the faces in the audience watch her, quiet and rapt. It occurs to me that there was something I wanted to do once, and it was to shine like that.

Everyone arrives on time and Missy begins the meeting by reading from a black three-ring binder. Then we go around the room reading a paragraph each from the Big Book. Today we read about some Native American guy who drinks too much, causes havoc, gets arrested on his reservation, then gets sober and helps little Indians learn to read or something. It's one of those later edition stories that try to modernize and diversify a book written by a couple of white Christian guys in 1939. Looking around the room you would deem it to be successful, or at least no one complains.

After the reading, we each check in about how we are doing this week; it's called "Here and Now." Then we pray and then we discuss house issues. All seven of us attend these weekly, mandatory meetings. We crunch in together on the nubby seventies couch and lean on pillows against the bookcase. Three seven-day candles with saints on the front from the 99¢ Only Store flicker on the coffee table and light up the room pretty cozy. I stare at everyone's feet or sometimes I stare at their faces until they look back at me and then I look away.

Buck kicks off the sharing.

"Hi, my name is Buck and I'm an alcoholic. Today I'm feeling fucking pissed. Today was really fucked. I ran into my ex-old lady while I was working. She was, like, getting a fucking frozen yogurt or something and she looked really pretty and really stoned and when I told her what was up with me, that I'd been out a few months, her eyes lit up all interested. Then I told her I was sober and living in a sober-living house and shit and she was, like, looking over my shoulder and couldn't get away fast enough. She looked at me like she felt really bad for me. That fucking bitch. When I was inside she wrote me, like, two letters in two years anyway."

Buck pauses and looks out the window even though the curtains are closed and I suspect it would be a crying pause if she was a crying kind of guy, but she isn't. Instead, she crosses her muscular arms, covered in dense sleeves of tattoos, and goes on.

"Then she tells me that she met someone. Some, like, documentary film director or some shit who got a prize for a documentary about a guy trying to make ferrets legal in California. Fucking ferrets."

Everyone laughs. Buck disappears further into herself, but only I can tell because I know her. From the outside it looks like she's squaring her shoulders for a fight.

"Anyway, I really hate you all right now. Fucking uptight weirdos." She always says this kind of thing. How much she hates us. "I am so out of here. I want out of here, okay. But I can't because of my fucking parole conditions. So I'm staying but I still hate you right now so fuck you all . . . Thanks for letting me share."

"Thanks, Buck," we all say.

Buck sits on the floor next to the recliner. She turns to

me and gives me a half smile, the candlelight glinting off her gold incisor. She picks at the loose shreds of denim edging the holes in her jeans. From this angle, it strikes me how handsome she is, in a redneck kind of way.

I sit directly to her left, so I pick up the sharing. "Hi, I'm Bebe and I'm an alcoholic. I don't have too much to say. Just want to check in with everyone."

"Check in" is a good thing to say when you want to say nothing.

"I'm finishing up my last hellish two weeks at beauty school." Everyone claps for me. Buck whistles through her teeth. "Thanks. I have a ways to go still with the State Board and all that but still, it's something. I guess I am afraid of what my future is going to look like. You know, how it's going to be when I move out of here and try to live like a real person. What I really feel is, I shouldn't be here. Not here like here in this house but here like here on this earth. But here I am so what do I do now?"

I said something real. Susan should put a gold star in my folder. I never know what to follow it up with, though. I say something that is true but is a bummer and then it just hangs there and I am supposed to offer a solution but there isn't one. "Anyway, glad to be here. Grateful to be sober today."

Susan Schmidt looks at me pointedly from her perch on a hard-backed chair she brought in from the kitchen. God, I loathe her.

"Oh, yeah, and I've been feeling kind of lonely lately. Thanks for letting me share."

"Thanks, Bebe," choruses the room.

Violet goes next. She sits cross-legged on a floor cushion. A deep purple, handmade velvet skirt pools around her legs. She hangs her head and her black hair falls like drapes on either side of her pale, sharp-featured face.

"Hi, I'm Violet and I'm an alcoholic." I can always count on Violet's share to make me feel like I am positively bubbly. I am a cheerleader compared to Violet.

"I just feel sad and I can't get rid of it. I'm grateful not to be smoking speed today and making decoupage lamp shades for ten days on end, but I feel so heavy from the minute I open my eyes.

"When I was tweaking I was so motivated," she goes on. "I never actually finished anything but at least I started. I started all kinds of artwork and I was so thin and I had so many ideas. I guess that's what I miss the most. That feeling like I had something to say." Violet sniffles back that first drip of teary snot, but she pushes the lid down. "Now all I can do is smoke and watch TV. And I want to kill myself. I'm sorry but I do. I think about it all day long, about how I would do it and who would find me and that I wouldn't want to do that to any of you and, y'know, ruin your life from having to see something like that.

"I know I was a disgusting mess before and that it's better now. But before at least I felt some relief, and this." She puts her hands out to indicate everything. It's her only gesture; other than that she's been a statue. "This is just relentless."

Violet folds her hands back into her lap and drops her

head even further so her hair almost entirely covers her face. "Yesterday I was looking at my sewing needles and I felt an overwhelming compulsion to stick one directly up inside my vein and let the ugliness flow out. I know that's totally gross. I want some relief, y'know? Just for a minute. I want to figure out a way that I can live sober like this and it won't break my heart. But I didn't hurt myself. Instead I used the sewing needle to sew up a tear at the seam of my mom's old costume so I could go and make those little girls happy. And I remembered my mom and how she used to dress up for my birthday parties, you know? All the other girls thought I was so lucky that I had a princess for a mom. I think she would have been proud of me yesterday. I think she would have loved to see me dressed up like that. I miss her."

The tears boil over. We all sit back and breathe and let her cry. No one holds her hand or jumps for the tissue box because it's not the way we do it in this group. In our group therapy they tell us not to interfere with anyone's expression of emotion; that if you hand her a tissue it's like asking her to stop because you're uncomfortable with her sorrow. If she wants a tissue she's capable of getting one herself, is what Susan would say. Which is pretty cool, actually.

Sometimes there are these Zion phrases that come back to me and reinsert themselves into my life. Like the one I think of here is "bear witness." We're here to bear witness to each other's sorrow. Because no one else cares about our poor-prognosis, likely-recidivist asses except us. To most people outside of places like Serenity, lives like ours are a statistic and the statistic doesn't tell a very hopeful story. So why listen? So why care? But we who are thrown here together by court order or probation requirements or various diagnostic criteria, we're here to bear witness to each other's lives, each other's stories, to make sure we don't disappear unheard, unseen. So it sometimes makes me ashamed, how Violet tells the truth and I'm so full of shit.

Violet adds, "Oh, and also I finished my third step and I guess it was okay. Oh, yeah, and someone's eating all my food and it's really pissing me off, but I'll bring that up after as a house issue. Thanks for letting me share."

"Thank you, Violet."

It is me, by the way, who eats all of Violet's food. Late-night compulsive binges where I sit on the floor with someone else's labeled jar of peanut butter and a spoon until there is no thought and no me anymore, there is nothing but eating. Every night I vow to stop and every next night there I am again. I don't confess.

Candy tells an inappropriate compulsive lie, as usual. This week she insists she caught a guy looking up her skirt with a shoe mirror at the library and had him arrested. She says that she plans to keep up a correspondence with him while he's in prison because she felt a mystical bond with him as the police were hauling him off. Last week she shared about having sex with a strange woman on the Zipper at the carnival. She tries to corner me at beauty school and tell the same kinds of stories. When I have nothing else to do, I listen.

Buck and I have started to bet whether Althea will mention Joseph Campbell or pre-Christian goddess worship in her share. Tonight she goes for Joseph Campbell. I win. Buck owes me a chore.

Missy, our doe-eyed, fragile blonde, shares about her brother in the Air Force and her boyfriend who is in his twelfth treatment center. Missy has Tourette's on top of about fifteen other diagnoses, so her sentences are peppered with a sound that is kind of like a hiccup mixed with a bark. She weeps into her hands. I can't stop looking at her. She's so cracked and beautiful, all crumpled like that.

Missy has worse problems than her tweaker boyfriend. She's a lifer in these kinds of places. I have caught her many times frozen in the middle of the upstairs hallway, her pupils dilated with terror. With a little prodding she admits that voices drive her out of her room. They speak to her through the heating vents. There are no vents in the hallway, so that's where she goes to escape them. The demons chase Missy wherever she goes, but she doesn't talk about it too much on a group level because she knows how it sounds. That's the difference between her being here and being in a lockdown facility.

Chandra is our equivalent of the captain of the cheerleading squad. Her being a black girl, ex-hooker cosmetologist is enough to make her the coolest person here, but on top of that she is our resident AA expert, with the most time sober (two years) and the most steps completed (all twelve). So Chandra is the one who settles disputes and doles out late-night tough love. She's the one you want on your side.

"Hi, I'm Chandra and I'm an alcoholic. I suffer from the disease of alcoholism and I am feeling it today. I am feeling the cunning, baffling nature of this disease like a worm in my brain. Because my disease is telling me that it's okay to be with Robbie, because he's supposedly clean and he supposedly loves me and I have been waiting all this time for him. But he tells me yesterday that he is dealing some weed on the side, just to help him transition into going straight, right? And my disease is telling me, what's so wrong with a little weed? He's just selling it, not smoking it. We all need to get by, okay? But I know that I got to be more vigilant than that. By God's grace and by the program of Alcoholics Anonymous I have a daily reprieve from my obsession to drink and to smoke crack cocaine. And I'm not going to be fucking with that. I know I can't be fucking with no weed dealer."

I wait for Chandra's shares. I count on her. I count on her to believe in this.

"I love him," she goes on. "I do. But I love myself more. I love God more. And God will put another man in my life who isn't a drug dealer. I have faith. I am grateful to be sober and to be here with all of you beautiful, strong women today. Thank you for letting me share."

"Thanks, Chandra."

I think about how I saw Chandra crying in Robbie's car the other night. She pulls it together quick.

Everyone's always sharing about love in group. It's the golden ring and it's the suicide mission. Me, I'm not on the prowl for love like everyone else here. I've done my time with wild love and I used it all up, I think. I tried with Aaron but never could figure out how to live with love pressing in around me all the time. I was shot through with poisonous jealousy every moment. Now he's dead and I wish it were me.

Living with a bunch of mental patients on parole is its own kind of safe wavelength. But love is treachery. Love is Aaron and my pop and everything already lost before I figured out what to do with it. First few months after Aaron was gone, I rolled out of bed onto my knees every morning with my fists pressed into my belly, unable to stand. All my support beams tumbled. Nothing held me up anymore. I was like one of those babies born with no bones.

Now I get up every morning and stand on my feet. No, I am definitely not hunting for love. But when the phone vibrates in my back pocket, I have this feeling that it's probably Jake and my chest gets a little tight and my big toe starts twitching and I know it's foolish, but there it is.

Nine

I 536 hours down. 64 hours left to go.

I remove the rollers I left overnight in Kitty Hawk's hair: wet set number one hundred and eighty-six of the two hundred required. I tease and spray, tease and spray, one section at a time, attempting to sculpt a peak of record height at the crown of her head. As I tease and spray, tease and spray, I meditate on Jake and our date tonight, which he may or may not remember to show up for. Things he said blindside me at unguarded moments and I think about him more than I mean to.

My boobs seem to be in the way of my arms as I style Kitty's hair. They're sore and swollen. The new meds are probably the reason I feel all tilted: ringing in my ears, occasional tunnel vision, shaky hands, fucked-up hormones. The list of possible side effects is about ten pages of microscopic print, so nobody really reads it, but you can safely assume that any disturbing physical development is a side effect.

Next to me Javier also teases and sprays, teases and

sprays, until we are enveloped in a haze of Grand Finale. At least once a week Javi comes to school wildly hair inspired by late-night TV. Last week he convinced us to style our dolls like *Charlie's Angels*. Today we're doing *Valley of the Dolls*.

His doll is Sharon Tate; mine is Patty Duke; Violet's is that other girl what's-her-name. Javier fusses at his station and makes frustrated little snorts as he tries to create realistic-looking mascara tear streaks down Sharon's face. He is a true perfectionist. When he is satisfied he removes the glamorous yet trashed doll head from her stand and holds her up.

"They love me," Javier slurs like Sharon after swallowing thirty Valium. "They *all* love me, Goddammit."

Violet and I scramble to finish our far inferior attempts.

"Fine," says Javier. "I don't need you. I don't need any of you. I'm going to make art house films. Now give me some damn quaaludes."

"You don't do art house films. *I* do art house films. You get breast cancer and kill yourself, remember?" I say.

I've spent my share of sleepless nights in front of the TV. I know my *Valley of the Dolls*.

"Oh, what do you know, you lezzy lush? I want to do the dirty movies."

"Was she a lezzy?"

"Patty Duke? Oh, honey, please."

"What is my doll's name?" Violet asks, spraying a liberal coat of shellac on her sagging bouffant. Violet has little natural talent in the hair department, but she has resolve, she has determination.

"No one knows that other actress's name except for obsessed queens hiding under a rock of crystal somewhere in West Hollywood. Reasonable people only know the name of the actress who was gruesomely murdered by sociopathic hippies on bad acid."

"And the one who played Helen Keller."

Miss Mary-Jo surprises us, sneaking up on us from behind. "What is it that you are doing back here? You are supposed to be doing the work. Not as much the talking for playtime. One point each for the wet sets, now we are moving on. Why don't we open our books for the studying?"

She's good-natured about it, though. She looks at our doll heads before marking the points on our cards, her head tilted quizzically.

"What is wrong with her face?" she asks Javier.

"She's been ravaged by fame. Plus, she's a drug addict with breast cancer," he says gravely.

"You are the very naughty one," Miss Mary-Jo says, pinching Javier's cheek and then giving him one of her hugs.

Sharon and Patty and what's-her-name go on the shelf and we sit with our books open in front of us and talk about *Sex and the City*. Violet prefers true-crime specials. Javier is adamant that Carrie's new love interest isn't worthy. I am adamant that a writer could never afford that apartment, much less that shoe collection. Javier is genuinely disgusted with me.

"You're missing the whole point."

When Miss Mary-Jo comes by, we act like we're quizzing each other from the questions at the back of the chapters.

"How many processes are involved in double-process hair coloring?" Violet reads from the book. I think she's making that one up, actually.

"Uh. Wait. I've got it. Two," says Javi.

"What is the difference between off-the-scalp lighteners and on-the-scalp lighteners?"

"Uh. One is applied on the scalp and one is applied off the scalp?" I offer.

"What is the role of ammonia in hair color formula?"

This one stumps us.

"You see?" says Miss Mary-Jo. "You should do more of the studying and less of the yakking. The State Board will come to you before you know it."

The thought of the dreaded State Board exam sends us into our books for real for about three minutes before I get restless and stare at the clock again. Let me explain about the State Board. The State Board is like the beauty school bar exam. It's a looming storm cloud: a full day of sadistic torture with your fate in the hands of embittered public servants. One wrong move and you may fail and if you fail you don't get your license and if you don't get your license you can't work in a salon. All these hours of your life, a whole year spent staring at these walls, and in one afternoon it can all be fucked. It would be a sobering thought, if I weren't so sober already.

Lunchtime we clock out and walk out of the fluorescents and into the sunshine, which always makes me want to take off running, but I don't. Instead I stroll with my friends along Brand Boulevard toward the falafel place a few blocks away. Glendale looks like a city in a different state. There's no Hollywood trendiness, just a combination of generic Old Navy–ish stores and small Armenian clothing boutiques with window displays that look like Stevie Nicks's garage sale. There are mysterious-looking used bookshops, cell phone stores, and hair salons, none of which you would ever go into. They look like fronts for money laundering or drugs, but they probably aren't. Or maybe they are.

And then there are bars. Weird bars with stone facades and names hung over from another time like Dante's or the Cave. Sports bars and Armenian restaurant/bars and vintage tiki bars with Polynesian murals on the walls. Now, there may very well be cell phone stores I'd never walk into but the same definitely does not apply to bars. Anyplace you can get a vodka cranberry feels like home to me. Every time I pass one of the bars on Brand, I have an overpowering impulse to turn in to it and shift my trajectory in a whole other direction than this life of meetings and school and trying so hard to change. Easy as that, just turn left instead of walking forward, and have a glass of white wine, a vodka martini, a Bloody Mary. Or do it just once and don't tell anyone and show up for groups at Serenity and for school and live with a little lie on my conscience. What's one lie? Who would care?

But today I don't. Sometimes I'm not sure why I stay sober except that I suspect it is my only chance. Sometimes I'm not sure why I stay sober except that I want to drink so bad I know it must be the worst choice. Instead of taking a drink, I put one foot in front of the other and wait in line for my falafel sandwich. The tables at the restaurant are too crowded so we order our food to go and bring it back to school in greasy paper bags.

When I pass back under the stucco archway and through the door of Moda, I see a little girl wearing red clogs, funny sunglasses, and Snoopy barrettes. She colors quietly at one of the stations. Her mother must be a student here. She gives a little wave as I pass by her and I think about how I used to play beauty shop with my pop.

For some reason my beauty shop was called Mrs. Jones's Beauty Parlor. I was Mrs. Jones. My pop would sit on the floor as I sat cross-legged on the couch behind him with a hatbox full of plastic barrettes in the shapes of pink flowers, yellow butterflies, orange teddy bears, and red apples with tiny green stems. My pop made funny faces in a hand mirror while I covered every inch of his head with the barrettes, clumps of hair sticking out all over. He made me laugh so hard it was a struggle not to pee my pants. When I was done, he always acted thrilled with his hairdo and walked around with it for hours as if he was so fancy. I remember him putting me to sleep with the barrettes still in his hair, the light from the open doorway behind him framing him, casting him in silhouette. The silhouette of some crazy Muppet with clumps of hair sticking out crazy all over.

We would hold our hands out as far as they could get from each other.

And he would say I love you this much.

And I would say I love you this much.

And he would say I love you as much as the whole ocean.

And I would say I love you as much as the whole sky.

I love you all the way to heaven.

I love you infinity infinity infinity infinity.

Maybe it was stolen from one of my baby books or maybe we made it up, I don't remember. I don't care.

One time I decided I wanted to give him a DA, like dreamy John Travolta in *Grease*. I applied nearly a whole jar of Vaseline to his hair until it was gleaming and perfect, my finest creation. He was so handsome.

He couldn't get the Vaseline out for weeks. He tried dish soap, floor cleaner, anything to cut the grease. Nothing worked. He got scabs on his scalp. He had a fight with my mother about it.

"You can't go to work like that."

"What would you like me to do about it exactly, Jean?"

"You were too drunk to notice she was using Vaseline? I mean, Vaseline? You let her do whatever she wants. She could have been shaving your head. You spoil her. You don't notice anything. You're a menace."

She was right. He was a menace. And then he up and died and left us alone. So I had a pop who disappeared but there was one man who never left me. My love, my soul mate. John Travolta.

Later, when we moved into Rick's house I kept a poster of John tacked up above my white wicker headboard. My love for John spanned years, withstood the changing houses, schools, fathers. John's smiling, dimpled face floated on a background the color of a sunlit Caribbean Sea. Or not John Travolta exactly, but Danny Zuko. The real John Travolta wasn't half as cool, though I forgave him for *Saturday Night Fever*. It wasn't that there was anything wrong with John, but he wasn't Danny. Every night before I lay down to sleep I pressed my lips to the cool, shiny paper of the poster. Staring into the dark, I silently moved my lips and rehearsed the words to our duets. *Summer lovin', happened so fast.*

Then I'd imagine how it would happen. I'd round the corner of an aisle at the Kroger and I'd see him standing there at the end of it—black T-shirt with the sleeves rolled, hair so greasy it glimmered in the harsh lights over the deli counter. Or I'd be standing next to my mother at the Kiwanis Carnival and would slip into a crowd of sticky-faced children so stealthily that she wouldn't even notice I was gone. Then I'd see Danny operating the Tilt-A-Whirl, his hand on the rusty lever.

I kept a knapsack packed and hidden in my closet—a sweater so I wouldn't get cold, an extra T-shirt, a pair of socks, my special folding travel toothbrush for sleepovers. I was ready to leave at a moment's notice for a world where there were dance numbers and saddle shoes and bell skirts that rustled when you walked. A world where when you were sad you sang your heart out wearing a nightgown in a moonlit backyard.

I loved Danny for his smile and his "Stranded at the

Drive-In," but mostly for his flying car. Because even Rydell High wasn't high enough for Danny, and that was the perfect boy for me. He would know it the minute he saw me. There weren't enough roads. Roads were too slow. I needed the boy who sang and had a magical car. That way there would always be music and we could always fly away.

I'll always be grateful to John Travolta for never really showing up in the first place. That way I never have to say that he left.

After lunch, Violet pulls out her personal collection of nail polishes that span a decade. At least fifty different bottles of every size and color, tiny to huge, new to crumbling dry, some shaped like Christmas bears or Halloween skulls.

We wash the morning's makeup off our dolls before embarking on our new project: transforming them into rock stars. We use Violet's nail polish to paint crazy makeup on them, à la Ziggy Stardust. I paint sky blue wings on either side of Kitty Hawk's neck, a star around one eye, a moon on the other. Javi looks at her and sings: *Don't tell me not to fly, I've simply got to.*

At the end of the day, the rest of the students noisily crowd the back hallway, chatting and slamming their locker doors. Javier straightens his compulsively organized equipment before locking it up. Jake is meant to pick me up out back in a few minutes, but I have money for the bus in case he forgets. I cross my arms across my chest and press the sides of my hands into my breasts, testing the strangely amplified tenderness that has been bugging me all day. The ache pulses through me and nearly churns my stomach. It must be the stress, the PMS, the meds.

One rule I have learned: never bring your doll head home at night. The disembodied head will scare the shit out of you in the dark, even if she was your salvation from boredom during the day. I put Kitty Hawk into my locker before we clock out. Shut the door on her unblinking stare. Tick off one more day of school. One more day of my life.

1544 hours down. 56 hours left to go.

Ten

I walk out the back door to the alley. The sun is setting and it has turned chilly—chilly like I imagine San Francisco, with the sky twelve shades of gray. The red of the brick wall looks darker in the moist air. I lean against it and the cold penetrates through my hair to the back of my head, through my jean jacket to my spine.

I check a voice-mail message that was left while I was doing a haircut. I don't recognize the number.

Hi, Baby.

The voice makes me sick. He always called me Baby instead of Bebe. The whole band did. It used to make me feel like I was part of something.

Francesca got your number for me from some friends . She heard you're clean now and living in Echo Park. It's been a long time and I think—

I hang up. I don't want to hear. I can't believe he tracked me down and I don't want to hear what he thinks. Actually,

I can believe it. Because Billy is like the devil that way. He never gets tired of fucking with your life.

I decide to forget he called. And if he calls again, I'll forget again. I'll forget as often as I have to until he leaves me be.

I wrap one arm around me and smoke a bummed cigarette with the other, half expecting that the night will get even worse and Jake won't show. But I look to the right and spot, with a rush of relief, the unmistakable bumperless Ghetto Racer trundling down the alley toward me. Of course, he's driving the wrong way down the one-way street.

When Jake emerges from his prized bucket, I can see from his face that he's having a good day, which probably means he quit his job and did whatever he does all day when he doesn't work. Paint. Drive around. Who could guess? Or it could mean he's seeing signs and the signs say good and holy things, but I try not to think that. I try not to look at him all the time and wonder if he's going crazy again. Because that's no way to look at someone.

For now he looks like some kind of supernatural messenger. It's a unique thing he has. It's why he slides by, fucking up all his life, and he remains afloat. These moments when he is scrubbed clean of the film that living leaves on you. The muddy haze we carry around from doing dishes and coming up short on our bills and eight and a half deadening hours a day of blob brain, like I have. Jake is free of it. He's pure and electric, his slate gray eyes alive with light. He lifts me off the ground, no small feat for my size, and nearly crushes the breath out of me. Then he sets me down and kisses my eyes and my earlobes and my cheekbones and my mouth. He acts like he hasn't seen me in ten years, and not just since yesterday.

"Angel," he says, "I have plans for us." He takes both my hands in his and kisses them. "But first, we have to attend to our healing. You and me, Angel. We're the least likely prophets. If we can heal, there's hope for this race that's otherwise turning fast into zombies."

I don't say much. I don't need to when he's on a roll. He talks the whole drive and keeps going without a pause as we park and walk up the street to the United Methodist Church, complete with steeple, nestled among the soaring property values on the corner of a rapidly gentrifying street.

We descend the side stairs to the rec room where they hold the AA meetings. Along the back wall people gather around a table set with large, stainless steel coffeepots and foam cups and trays of cupcakes and carrot sticks. This particular group of alcoholics is fashionable and smiling and some say hello to us, but most of the pretty ones are otherwise occupied. I notice they favor the carrots over the cupcakes. I notice that even the ones who do say hello avoid looking Jake in the eye. I wonder if maybe I'm just so accustomed to Jake that I miss the first signs of another episode, because other people definitely edge away from him as soon as he starts talking. Like they're thinking, oh, crap, I don't want to get verbally held hostage by this crazy guy. Like they're thinking, oops, that's what you get for trying to be inclusive, for trying to be friendly.

But they don't know him. They're just squares.

We find seats and thirty or so people file into the rows around us as the leader of the meeting and the speaker take their places at the front of the room. It's ironic or comic or something, that after walking away from church here I am in yet another church, a member of yet another congregation. Here I am trying again to change my life, trying again to have faith in myself or in other people or in Jesus or whatever, sitting in a horseshoe of uncomfortable metal seats and attempting to look open in the eyes. As if I'm part of the thing, whatever is going on. And if I had to compare the two, well, church was more fun. I always want to suggest, to the twelve-step powers that be, that they should have a little band, that the speakers should testify with a killer soundtrack, that we should all sing and lay hands on each other, that we should believe in miracles. But if I had to compare the two, this is not as much fun, but there are less roadblocks.

The woman testifying—except we don't call it testifying, we call it sharing—is about fifty years old with wildly curly hair, conservative clothes, bright red lipstick, and simple gold jewelry. She looks like she smells good. She sits at the front of the room and tells one of those really human and inspiring stories that can make me believe in people or at least make me believe in stories. I look down at Jake's hands. They're the most gnarled hands I've ever seen—punished and cracked and stained. I take one of them in mine for a minute and it feels like an ancient piece of a tree, a mystical organic fossil that has weathered the elements for two thousand years. I listen to the end of the story, the readings, the clapping, and, finally, the praying. I tick off one more hour of paying my debt to I don't know what. One more hour of trying, but not hard enough, probably.

My stepbrother, Hunter, was the reason I got almost saved the first time. Hunter with the bony wrists and the constant Coca-Cola and the yellow dog hair all over his clothes. It was just as the summer ended the year I turned twelve. In the six years we'd been stepsiblings, we had gone from pitching tents in the backyard and riding our bikes through piles of dried leaves at the curb to playing Atari and listening to the Police in Hunter's room. Hunter lived with his mom most of the time, but came to stay with us on the weekends.

Hunter was effortlessly popular. Me, I was a head taller than everyone my own age and was only popular when it came to picking sports teams. I played center forward on the soccer team, pitcher on the baseball team. I was the eye of the hurricane. Everything spun around me, party games and school plays and playground soap operas, and I was the still center with nothing happening to me except I kept growing.

I counted days between Hunter's visits, when he would grudgingly show up with his duffel bag over his shoulder. He barely unpacked, except for the perfectly pressed church clothes he brought with him already on hangers. His church clothes were the only thing in his closet except for a few winter coats and my mother's overeager photo albums of a new, ready-made family. No pictures of my father anywhere.

One Saturday afternoon, Hunter came into the garage where I was peeling off my soggy shin guards after a soccer game. Hands in his pockets, he asked about the game and then, looking out the open garage door at the nothing special outside, he asked, "Do you want to go to church with me tomorrow?"

I flushed hot to the edges of my hair, pulled tight off my face into two neat braids.

"Do I have to do anything?"

"No. No. Just come check it out. You'll be surprised. You'll have a good time."

And for a moment I heard the salesman in him, inherited from his father.

After much wheedling and cajoling and finally a grudging assent from my mother, that Sunday I got dressed to attend Zion Pentecostal Church. I wore the only dress I had: navy, buttoned up the front, with a drop waist and puffy sleeves. I pulled on my white tights and stepped into my ballet flats and stood in front of the mirror feeling prim and shiny.

I wanted a glimpse at the source of Hunter's rare self-assurance. He knew something I didn't and I was finally getting let in on the secret. Mom tentatively knocked on the door, then came in and stood behind me, both of us looking in the mirror. She looked tired. I felt bad for her that she didn't get to do things like get dressed up and go to church and go to ladies' clubs and those things that my friends' moms did. I was kind of pissed that she didn't seem to want to.

"You look lovely, honey. I want you to know that it's okay to go and see what other people believe, but I don't want you to feel pressured into anything, okay?"

I just wanted her to disappear. All the ways she was sad. What did she have to teach me about anything?

When Hunter's mom pulled up, we left a tense Mom and Rick behind and slid onto the vinyl seats of her sky blue Chrysler that smelled like cherry air freshener. Before that I had only ever seen her through the glare of the car window as she dropped Hunter off. Margaret had long brown hair, thick like a horsetail, tied back by one of those fabric scrunchies. She wore a cardigan sweater and a simple jersey skirt and looked uncomplicated. She had an oddly shaped purple birthmark that crawled out the top of her sweater and up her neck to peek over the edge of her jawline. It made me like her right away.

"Hello, Bebe. I'm Margaret," she said. "I'm so glad to finally meet you. I'm sorry it didn't happen sooner. And I'm thrilled you can join us for church this morning. What a nice surprise."

While Margaret drove, I watched the familiar terrain along the Anthony Wayne Trail: the blocky skyline of downtown and the cramped aluminum-sided houses and the blue high-level bridge. But, unlike most low-sky, gray Toledo days, it all shimmered with a kind of sunlit warmth. I was on the inside of something. I felt a prickle of hope that maybe church would feel like home, as it clearly did to Hunter.

The church was a little stand-alone stone box crowded

in between a beauty supply shop and a storefront with paper over the windows with a For Rent sign hanging in the doorway. Out front a sign read:

HOW DO I KNOW HE LIVES
HE LIVES IN MY HEART

It wasn't much to look at from the outside, but inside it was like walking into a party. I was introduced to what seemed at the time like hundreds of welcoming people, but, thinking back, it was probably more like eighty. On the tiny stage a band was setting up, a small drum set and an electric guitar and a bass. The band looked like kids from the high school. Actually, I think they were kids from the high school, two black guys and one white guy with a Flock of Seagulls haircut. In front of them was a pretty, fat gal with nice makeup and an acoustic guitar.

The thing that surprised me was that it was white people and black people together and all acting like that wasn't unusual or something. As if maybe they'd go home and be neighbors, which would be unlikely, considering even the working-class neighborhoods were split up pretty neatly—white people over here and black people over there. Of course the high school was all integrated in theory but in practice it was like two parallel worlds floating around next to each other and occasionally bumping into each other and fighting for space. I had a couple of black girlfriends because I was in sports. So I guess the trick was to have some kind of common goal, like winning. Or heaven.

Something pressed up against the back of my throat as I shook their hands. It might have been hope, hope that I could be one of these people with the luminous smiles and the light in their eyes. I sat down next to Hunter and took a Bible from the back of the pew in front of me. It was dense, bound in faux leather, its thin pages crammed with tiny writing. On the front it said, simply, *Holy Bible*, in gold, embossed letters. Most of the people around me had their own dog-eared copy. I opened it to a random page and looked for a sign from God. A secret message I would instantly understand. I read this in the red writing:

Because straight is the gate,
and narrow is the way
which leadeth unto life, and
few there be that find it.

It seemed more like a fortune cookie than a sign from God, except fortune cookies are cheerier. Kind of a letdown, but there it was. Maybe the meaning would become clear to me later.

I knew from Hunter that the preacher, Pastor Dan, was an ex-biker who had left his criminal life when he found Jesus. He still had his bike. I had seen the massive chopper in the parking lot. The service started and there was music and then more music and every time I thought it was going to end there was still more music and I kind of wavered between being bored and wanting to sit down and thinking that if I wasn't so self-conscious I could be having more fun. Because everyone else seemed to be having fun. I knew my mom would have rolled her eyes. *Not exactly the Mensa convention, now, is it?* she would have said. In front of me a woman with a salt-and-pepper afro danced with a tambourine in each hand. Hunter sang and closed his eyes but Margaret and many of the other people there held their arms or turned their palms to the sky. They closed their eyes and swayed and smiled and by the end of the twenty minutes of music a handful of them had tears on their cheeks. I kind of swayed. I clasped and unclasped my hands. I felt like I was betraying someone but I wasn't sure who.

I craned my neck around trying to spot Pastor Dan, but when he finally took the stage, he wasn't much to look at. I had expected some burly biker daddy with a gray ponytail, but Pastor Dan was a slim guy, head shaved bald, soft-spoken at first. He had eyelashes so blond they were almost invisible and close-set, watery blue eyes, which made him look like he was always on the verge of tears.

The sermon that day was about redemption.

"What does it mean to be redeemed? Have you truly been redeemed? Do you recognize the covenant that you've made with God, here? A covenant is a commitment, right? Right, Shirley and Bob? I just married those beautiful children last Sunday so they got an earful from me about what a covenant is. A covenant is a sacred contract. A contract where God says I will give you all that I have. I will give you grace."

Amen.

"I will give you peace."

Amen.

"You will be born again of the spirit and you will have a new life in me."

Amen.

"But a covenant isn't just a one-way contract, folks. Sorry. God loves you so much he gave his firstborn son so you could enter into this contract with him today, but you have got to give your life to God, too. At each fork in the road if you listen, if you quiet down and you pray, the Holy Ghost will move within you and will tell you which path God wants for you."

Yes, he will. Amen.

"But here's the kicker. You can say no. You can say, no, God, this other path looks better. I said no. I said no for years. I said, no, God. I like the drugs down this other path. I like the women down this path, Jesus. And Holy Father, I'm real sorry but there sure seems to be a whole lot more money down this other path for me. Now, you all are smart folks and I don't need to tell you whose path that was. I really thought I could walk down that flashy path and have a little fun and I could confess later. But I had my motorcycle accident and I was in a coma for six whole days, folks, and I almost got to take a trip way farther down that path of selfishness than I ever intended to go.

"But I heard the voice of Jesus while I was in that coma, and do you know what it said? It said, I love you, Daniel. It said, I'm waiting for you, Daniel. I'm here for you, Daniel, when you want to open your heart to me. I woke up and opened my mouth and the words that came out were, Lord Jesus, forgive me. Say it with me now if you want to. Lord Jesus, forgive me. I'm a sinner, Jesus. Come on into my life and forgive me and all I am is yours."

Amen.

Everyone was crying by then. The hairs on my arms were standing up and I felt a little sick and something started humming in me.

"So, folks, you can say no and no and no to Jesus and Jesus will still love you. Jesus will love you always because Jesus is love and he will wait, he will wait until you see, like I did, that Jesus is everything he said he was. He is the way. He is the truth. He is the life.

"Now, is there anyone here today who doesn't know Jesus yet? Who is ready today, right here, right now, to let Jesus into your heart, to accept Jesus as your Lord and savior?"

I did want to be saved. I did want to be forgiven. Who doesn't? And why not. Why not there. Why not then. Saved from every sad thing I had known and reborn as someone else.

I stood. I was the only one that day. I stood and Margaret put her arms around me, her face glossy with tears. People sang and touched me and I stood in front of Pastor Dan and he laid his palm on my head and prayed over me and the whole world got brighter, like it was overexposed. And then it was over and I was born again. I had a new life, a new family, a new father in Jesus who wouldn't drink himself to death.

Two weeks later I was baptized. It was a windy Sunday in late fall. The congregation filed out to the parking lot and into a caravan of cars. Margaret's friend Ruth rode shotgun and Hunter rode in the backseat of the Chrysler with me, holding my hand between both of his and smiling warmly. I tingled with the exquisite and unfamiliar feeling of actually getting something I wanted.

There was a turnoff near a picnic spot in Water City, on the banks of the Maumee River. We arrived last. Everyone already stood by the side of the road waiting for us. I stepped out of the car and it was only a short, gravel-crunchy walk to the river's edge, which was muddy and strewn with fallen leaves. We could hear the cars rushing by on the highway behind us.

Margaret helped me on with my white robe and it felt nice to have my hands over my head and her pulling the robe down around me. She smoothed my hair out of my eyes and smiled like she was proud.

Pastor Dan and me and Stacy-Ann, the kid from the band's girlfriend, slipped together down the small incline to the river's edge. And all I could think of was the cold, cold, cold water. Like a bath I took once when I had the measles. My mother sat beside me and sponged my forehead and the water felt like needles and I wanted to get out but I was so tired and I guess I almost died that night, is what my mother tells me. And when I look back on it I can see that right there, right in that thought, was the thread that would catch on a nail and unravel my whole cloak of faith before too long. Because I thought, just randomly, I'll be in heaven with Jesus but where will my mother be, who sat by me, who doesn't know Jesus, who probably never will because she's had plenty of opportunity by now? In hell? And my pop? What kind of a God am I giving myself to? But the thought didn't fully gel until later.

Pastor Dan beckoned to us with his arms theatrically wide, calling us his children. Behind him the river was alive with sparkles of afternoon sunlight. He turned and waded in, smiling and undaunted, until he was waist high. Stacy-Ann went first. The temperature of the water stopped her in her tracks when she was ankle deep; then she set her face and propelled herself on by sheer will. She stumbled to the reverend's side. He spoke a few words to her I couldn't hear. Then she pinched her nose shut and fell backward and he cradled her in his arms until she was fully submerged. Stacy-Ann stood up, raised her arms to the sky, and ran for the shore into the elated cheers and warm blankets of her new brothers and sisters in Christ.

I went next. I left my shoes and ran in without being called, my stocking feet partly numbed against the sharp stones of the riverbed, the cold water going straight to my bones. When I reached him, Pastor Dan put his arm around my back like how I imagined you would for a dip in a slow dance. He looked me in the eye and I felt like I was in the arms of John Travolta or something.

"Because you believed with your heart and confessed with your mouth that Father God raised Jesus Christ from the dead and that Jesus Christ is now Lord of your life I now baptize you in the name of the Father, the Son, and the Holy Spirit."

It was that fast. And back we went.

I held on to him and looked up into his eyes, blue as the glass marble blue of the sky behind him, the kind of blue that means heaven, right before the water splashed in around my face. And what I thought was, Here we go. My old life, my old fears, all my doubts and sins are being washed clean and I'll emerge not perfect because only Christ is perfect and only a crazy person thinks they're Christ, so not perfect but new. New.

When I emerged, the drops of water on my eyelashes caught the sun and made swimmy starry spots in front of my eyes and Pastor Dan released me. But when I got to shore all I felt was blue cold. Not new.

Fuck, I thought. There it still is, that square of wormy scared dark in my heart.

Violet gets all fascinated by my born-again past and she asks me, what did it feel like? And I tell her, it didn't feel like I thought it would. I didn't feel new. Not at all. But I tried not to be disappointed. Because there was something I very definitely did feel. I felt love. I knew my church family loved me. I believed Jesus loved me. I didn't stop believing that until later.

Me and Jake walk out the door and navigate the sea of socializing bodies and the fog of cigarette smoke. The meeting quieted Jake. He reaches for my hand as we stroll through the clear night back to the Ghetto Racer.

It makes me want to laugh sometimes. I thought I cut the cord with God the day we pulled the cord on Aaron. I was sure I was done with God forever. And here I am in church. I traveled two thousand miles from Zion to sit in another church.

I guess some people have to be born again and again.

Eleven

"Where do you want to go now? We still have a couple of hours before curfew."

Jake doesn't answer but raises his eyebrows enigmatically as he pulls out and turns south down Vermont. We slide past gas stations and fast-food joints and Korean strip malls with their mysterious ciphers advertising boba coffee shops and karaoke clubs. I settle back, contented. I like driving at night, moving through shifting puddles of light, in between here and there.

Jake hits Wilshire and makes a right. When they built all these beautiful old hotels and apartment buildings on Wilshire, they thought it was going to be the heart of the city. They didn't know it would wind up just another long, long street in a town that can't be said to have a heart.

Wind rattles the bushy-topped trees growing out of their holes in the sidewalk. An impossibly huge and beautiful moon hangs dead center in front of us, lighting up the sky midnight blue, and it's a right-place-at-the-right-time-on-the-right-side-of-the-earth's-face kind of heartbeat. And I don't wonder where we're going; I don't even care.

Ahead of us, the ruin of the Ambassador Hotel peeks out from behind twelve-story glass boxes stuffed with staffing services and catering companies and temp agencies and bartending schools. In L.A. there are two kinds of people—servants and the people they serve. Somewhere on one of these blocks is the dreaded edifice where, in thirty-seven days, I will meet my fate at the State Board exam.

Jake turns left on a street that flanks the fenced-off Ambassador grounds, then turns again onto a dead end. A low, crumbling brick wall stands between us and the hotel property and in front of each wall is a row of grand palm trees standing their ground. Things like tall palm trees, haughty old things with knife blade fronds that catch the sunlight like camera flashes, can almost make me like L.A. Can almost make me feel a pang of nostalgia for some glamorous hazy past that never existed anyway. Everything looks better in black-and-white, and the Ambassador, with its history of celebrity scandal and splashy tragedy, is definitely black-and-white. Jake parks, grabs a Maglite from under his seat, comes around my side, opens my door, and pulls me out of the car.

Spirals of razor wire crown most of the tall fencing around the grounds, but Jake leads me straight to a gate that has a clean shot over the top. I hook my fingers through the metal diamonds of fencing, wedge my Chucks on a crossbar, and pull myself up. I swing my leg over, reposition, and in three graceful moves clear it and land with a quiet crunch on the grass. My head rings with adrenaline. I wonder if there are cameras, if there are guards, but I guess the only way you really know is if one catches you. I wouldn't normally mind the risk, but I am one week from graduation and this kind of trouble could be Susan Schmidt's ideal ammunition. Jake scales the fence so fast I barely see him climb it. The tricky thing about Jake is that he can seem like an incompetent lunatic, but really he has all these crazy skills.

What I hear is a billion crickets and a late-roaming ice-cream truck with a warped soundtrack and some people screaming with drunken laughter up the block. Jake takes my hand again and we are off like *Mission: Impossible* super-stealth spies across wide-open ground until, lungs aching, we reach the grand, ruined behemoth that looms over us at least ten stories high. Heading toward a service entrance, we pass under an overhang that looks ready to collapse. Behind us lies a massive, empty pool with weeds pushing up through cracks in the concrete.

Jake opens the door without so much as a jimmy of the lock and pulls the flashlight out of his waistband.

"I fixed it yesterday." He explains the ease of our breaking and entering. "It gets better."

I feel like we're in a movie except the genre keeps changing. When it opened, we were getting ready to enter the Cocoanut Grove, where Ginger Rogers would be waltzing with Fred Astaire. Then we had to break in and we were in a spy movie. But now, as we follow the dancing flashlight beam through a maze of corridors until I completely lose my sense of direction, it's like the scariest horror movie you ever saw. I make Jake walk in front of me because he has the flashlight, but then I change my mind and make him walk behind me because the darkness is thick and creeping up my neck and I would run screaming if I was alone.

Switch genres again and we're in a sci-fi time travel movie because we turn a corner and find ourselves in a wide, red-carpeted hallway lined by shops that look as if they were abandoned yesterday, except yesterday was in 1952. The shop names are painted on the windows in gold lettering. There is a flower shop, a barbershop, a travel agency with intact Art Deco posters advertising other cities: a dainty Chinese girl in front of the Golden Gate Bridge to advertise San Francisco, an old man with a white beard on a boat in front of the Statue of Liberty. Jake shines the light around slowly, illuminating one circle at a time of the lost world.

"It's still so perfect."

"We're then and we're now. We're in two parallel dimensions at once. You can slip through the wormhole if you want. If you choose it. Would you go or would you stay?"

"Huh?"

"Stay or go. Quick. Would you rather be in this hallway then or now?"

"Then. Anything but now."

"Too slow."

"What?"

"You hesitated. Hesitate and the universe closes the window. You're stuck with now. But you're stuck in now with me so allow me to make your now a mystical thing."

We continue down the hall until we reach what was once the lobby and it looks like something from *The Shining.* The ceiling opens up huge and high, and dark wood and wide red carpet stretch in all directions. A white fountain with a tall spire stands in the center of the room. Behind it a grand stairway unfolds to the upstairs. Chandelier after chandelier, each made of a thousand glittering crystal teardrops, hang from the ceiling.

"Oh, my God," I say, in a normal tone of voice that fades to a whisper because my voice sounds like a reckless violation, as if we are going to disturb some cranky, sleeping spirit.

"Can you hear them?"

I can't. And normally I'd worry about him hearing voices. But I can feel them this time. There's something here that wants to be heard. Maybe that something counts on people like Jake, with a fragile brain chemical cocktail. Maybe when he gets somewhere so clearly heavy with stories the weight of it tips his scales just a hair, just enough.

But no. We're subject to suggestion. Our brains play tricks on us. I'm in a perfect horror movie set so of course I imagine I feel ghosts. And my boyfriend hears voices when his brain isn't metabolizing adrenaline or something, so he isn't exactly the best fact-checker.

"Don't be scared," he says. "Go on up the stairs and then come down again."

"Why?"

"Because it's your big entrance. You have no idea what an audience you have."

What the hell. I climb the dramatic staircase and when I hit the top I turn right back around and glide back down, my hand grazing the smooth banister. And in my mind I have a dress that grazes the stairs. In my mind I'm a movie star. I'm a princess. I'm unscarred and lovely and whole. He's right. It may not be much but it's the biggest entrance I've got. Jake waits at the bottom, shining the flashlight on the staircase in front of me, and when we meet he turns it off and lays it down on the ground. The room is bathed in milky moonlight.

There, at the foot of the stairs, he unwraps me, first untying the laces of my sneakers and slipping my feet out of them, then removing my jacket, my sweater, my jeans, one piece at a time, leaving only my striped kneesocks. He bought me three pairs and all I have to do is wear them. What better boyfriend for me?

He picks me up romance novel style and carries me over to one of the dusty, floating white couches, where he lays me down. He runs his hands, ridged and tough as baseball gloves, from my sock-clad ankles over the hills and hollows of my scarred body and up to my face, as if he is testing to see if I am really there, that no part is a hallucination. He smells unshowered as usual but not bad and he looks at my body, transfixed, with eyes pinwheeling backward into some deep blackness that feels oddly familiar. His mouth hangs open a bit, revealing that chipped tooth, and what I feel is unashamed. When he puts his head between my legs I am lost and unashamed. Because what is there to be shy about with a lunatic sock fetishist who is most at home among specters and voices.

We slide off the couch and make love there on the ancient carpet, him with his pants and boots still on, which is how he does it mostly. It is a Marine thing, he explained to me once. He is always on the ready to protect us. But I think it is something else, though I can't say what. I can't say I understand him at all, but here we are.

We lie there next to each other on the floor for a minute, staring up at the chandelier, which sparkles even in the dark. Jake gets up and brings me my pile of clothes. While I pull on my underwear, he sits down next to me with his back against the couch and one sturdy arm resting on his bent knee.

"They're tearing it down," he says. "Fucking animals. This whole place is scheduled for the wrecking ball."

"They can't do that."

"Oh, they can. Real estate, Angel." He runs his hand through his hair and it stands up all crazy. "First they took the land from the Indians and now there's no more land to take and no one left to rob from, so they're taking history instead. They're stealing their own history from themselves."

"But look at this place." A gob of emotion catches in my throat. "It's a palace. They keep their palaces in France and shit."

"We're here to document it. To brand this moment into

our organs and then carry it with us like braille on our hearts and kidneys and skin."

He stands up, ready to move on.

"And now for a vital historical expedition. We'll still make it back to our home of a prison of a home under the wire."

I throw on my jacket and pull my tangle of hair out of the back of it, feeling that kind of proud disheveled that makes you want to walk out on the street with your hair still in a fuck knot just so everyone knows that you're loved. Jake is back in stealth mode. He leads me down a pitch-black set of concrete service stairs, moving quickly, without a pause or a word.

We go through a doorway into what seems like a ballroom. There's no ambient light downstairs and I see only what hovers in the tight, shaky circle of the flashlight. The darkness all around is dense and crazed with movement, atomized into a million particles. My insides feel the same, like my every cell is shivering.

We cross the ballroom. In the middle of the floor, Jake stops abruptly and whirls me around a few times in a furious waltz. I stiffen uncontrollably. I never dance with anybody because dancing reminds me of Aaron. The images flood me, quick and complete, like a morphine IV, except it doesn't feel good. It can double me over if I'm not expecting it. Maybe he can tell, maybe he knows without my ever mentioning Aaron's name. And I'm sorry for that but it's not like there's anything I can do. I'll always at least partly belong to someone dead.

"Can you tap-dance?" he asks.

"No."

"Too bad. I love a good tap dance."

We climb onto a small stage shaped like a clamshell, then through a backstage door and down some stairs until we are in a big storage room or pantry or something. A door opens into a cavernous kitchen with hulking columns that scare me as the flashlight moves over them. Stainless steel ovens and ranges and sinks line the far wall. I walk into the kitchen ahead of Jake, but he pulls me back into the pantry. Jake shines the light on the floor and there is a triangle shape, like an arrowhead almost, about six inches on each side, where chipped tile exposes the concrete underneath.

"That's the fateful spot. If not for that spot, the world might be a different place. Or that's what we like to think. That it could have been anything other than what it is."

I look at the dust-blanketed floor and say nothing. I'm used to his non sequiturs.

"By that I mean that this is the spot where Robert F. Kennedy hit the ground," he explains.

"How do you know?"

"I know things. I read things. I feel things," he says. "This is a vortex of profound tragedy right here."

"I guess it is."

We stand for a minute, in our own warped tribute to a guy who was probably a rich scumbag in some ways but was probably kind of a hero in others. And for how things get broken. We were here. And when they knock it down we'll remember.

We walk back out the way we came and it isn't as much spooky this time as it is sad. When we reach the ghost town of shops, Jake stops in front of one called the Jewel Box. He takes my face in his hands.

"If I could I would buy you a rock the size of India right in this shop. Right now."

I laugh it off and turn my face, hoping he'll let go and keep walking but he doesn't. Instead he pulls something out of the front pocket of his jeans. He sinks down on his knee and holds out a ring he clearly got out of a quarter machine at the grocery store.

Fuck.

"Change the future, Angel," he says. "Marry me. I'll take you wherever you want to go. We can be in San Francisco by morning."

I stand there, everything gone suddenly wrong. I'm glad they're bulldozing this pile. They *should* knock this place down, this shabby ruin. And here I go throwing another boomerang of hurt. I'm sick of him and these grand gestures that mean nothing. I'm sick of being so fucking careful all the time because poor crazy Jake needs special mommying or else he might go thinking he can fly and go jump off a cliff.

"Get up," I say, because there is nothing else I can say. "Get off your knees. Married? You mean like grown-ups who know how to live? You mean like people who can actually count on each other? San Francisco? You mean with all the money you didn't make on your last job?"

And then I say this, but I don't realize until it comes out of my mouth, until I hear it, that it's the same thing Aaron once said to me.

"Why do you need to ruin everything?"

Jake should know me. It is not the future I'm compelled by; it's the past. He should know better than this.

Twelve

The car ride home is silent. I try to apologize, try to explain, but he is seething somewhere deep and far and he is beyond apology and maybe I am beyond forgiveness, but still. Was I that bad?

Jesus is in the cool, metal buttons of my coat. Jesus is in the fist of the baby doll arm. Jesus is in the dust on his boots.

Jake drops me off around the corner of the house, which is what we do so no one sees us together. I step out of the car and lean down to say good-bye.

"I'm leaving tomorrow," he says robotically, looking straight ahead, both hands still on the wheel.

"What are you talking about? The Marines again? You already know they won't let you back because you're how you are. Come on. You'll get over this. We'll get through this. This is your home."

"Because I am how I am? Maybe I am just what they

want. They aren't you. Now go home. *Adios. Sayonara. Je t'aime.* Boo hoo."

I slam the door behind me, but I hear it crash shut and I am sorry that I did. When I turn around he's already pulling away without a backward glance.

I sign in twenty minutes late. There's no getting around it since compulsively honest Missy signed in fifteen minutes late right before me. Missy with the PTSD and the OCD and the paranoid psychosis and the touch of Tourette's. How can you get mad at her? I'll get a reprimand for tardiness at the very least, if not a write-up. No way Susan Schmidt is going to let this one slide.

I look at the sign-in roster and automatically know what everyone did with their evening. We wing nuts at Serenity House are often credited with things like "unpredictable behavior," but it isn't. It's so predictable. For instance, I know Missy (11:15) probably went to a meeting and then out for a coffee with some people afterward, including at least two predatory men who dig her *Rosemary's Baby* vibe. She's in bed now, but she'll get up again to check all the locks and all the lights and all the appliances. One unpredictable thing about Missy: you never know when she'll sleepwalk into your room and pee in your trash can.

Althea didn't sign in because she never went out. In a

pool of light thrown by the standing lamp, she hunches over the coffee table studying a spread of tarot cards. This house is like the waiting room of the cursed.

"Hey, Madame Zora." I walk past her toward the kitchen.

"You want a reading?" she asks, looking up from the cryptic tableau of princes and knights and swords and coins and suns and moons and queens and devils and hanged men and hermits. "For some guidance?"

Everyone else is in bed already.

"I want a fucking vodka tonic for some drunkness."

"We choose our reality by the language we use."

"Well, then, I want a miracle."

"How it works is, you say, 'I am a miracle.' Are you sure you don't want a reading?" She pulls her limp hair out of her face and secures it with a band from around her wrist.

"Thanks anyway."

"Namaste," she says, bowing slightly, her palms pressed together at her chest as if in prayer. I do the same back because it seems like a nice thing to do, before I pass by her and into the kitchen. I don't turn on the light but I can make out the blanched shapes by the moonlight coming in through the bare windows.

Starving hungry, I open the fridge. Inside it is packed with Tupperware containers and pickle jars and ranch dressing and milk cartons, all labeled with names written on masking tape. Violet labels all of hers with a purple marker. I take out the jar of Violet's crunchy peanut butter as desperation overrides any sense of personal integrity. I barely buy any food for myself because I try not to eat so much, though I always fail miserably. I start a new diet every morning and by noon I have hit the pretzels, the Starbursts, the caramel macchiatos. Whatever anyone has at school and offers me to snack on. Impulse control is a symptom of one of my mental illnesses; I can't remember which one.

I take a commemorative Elvis mug out of the cabinet and scoop four large tablespoons of peanut butter into it. I filch someone else's unlabeled maple syrup off the top of the microwave, drizzle it on top of the peanut butter, then stir it all together. I squat with my back against the sky blue cabinets—some resident project paint job—and lick the concoction off the spoon, heavy and sweet. I close my eyes and my body dissolves until I am nothing.

This is the last time I do this, I resolve as I get up for more. I grab a bag of chips from the top of the fridge and I swear to myself, I start a diet tomorrow. Then I put one after another into my mouth and I'm unaware of chewing, unaware of swallowing, I'm aware only of disappearing.

Only when my stomach churns so badly that I can't stuff anything more down my throat do I stop and sit there, staring blank eyed at the wall, holding Chandra's decimated Kettle Chips. Like always, memories of Aaron wipe my brain clean of anything actually happening in the present. Thoughts of him stab at me every quiet moment. And most loud moments. And most times in between. The periods when I momentarily manage to forget him are the exception.

These memories justify my sitting here on this kitchen floor with this bag of chips in my lap and this life that I have. They justify the fact that I chose a boyfriend who is very likely to respond to our fight by going downtown to start recruiting apostles. I had a tragedy. Stronger people don't crumble under the weight of regret, but me, it crippled me.

I think about how it was when I first got on that bus with him and left Toledo behind. I was so sure there were greater things in store for me than I could even imagine, with the California sunshine on the not-so-distant horizon. I was bursting with possibility. Wanting to know the future and not wanting to know. Holding out for the surprise.

And I was. I was very fucking surprised.

"Someone's been eating my porridge." Buck's voice startles me from the darkened doorway.

I look up, busted. I am the food thief. Someone was bound to find me out sooner or later.

"Can't sleep?" I ask.

"Rarely sleep. That is what I miss most about getting loaded. Those dreamless sleeps. Twelve, fourteen hours of nonexistence."

Buck sits down beside me, her back against the cabinets. She reaches in the bag, grabs a fistful of crumbs, and funnels them into her mouth.

"Tonight I even fell asleep, but Mia Farrow woke me up shuffling around the hallways and flipping the light switches. I was, like, Shut the fuck up, creep show. But now I'm awake. So do you want to make out or what?"

"Not really."

"Don't break my heart, now, kitten," she says, crunching another handful of greasy shards. "Now, what the hell you doing sitting here munching alone in the dark?"

"I had a bad date."

"A fatter ass ain't going to cheer you up any."

"Thanks for this little chat."

"Aw, I'm sorry. You know I love you. You can steal all the food you want, I won't tell. But seriously now, I want to talk to you about your spooky, sultry, sad roommate up there. Do you think there is a possibility that she might be somewhat bisexually inclined, if given the proper motivation?"

"Like what motivation?"

"Me."

"You like Violet?"

"No, ma'am. I think I love Violet."

Prison, rehab, halfway house—there are no greater crucibles for the alchemy of love. There is no more combustible fuel than desperation. What else are you going to do while you're doing time? But Buck, Buck is a rare find. You have to get past the first line of defense to know it, but she'd make a great boyfriend.

"I'll see what I can do."

I trudge upstairs, sick with myself, and find Violet lying in leopard print jammies on top of her leopard print comforter, staring at a flickering votive candle on her bedside table. Five others burn in different places around the room. Violet carves her intentions onto the surface of the candles with a safety pin and then lights them. Powerful witchcraft, she assures me. And I have tried it a time or two, I admit. Once, shortly after I arrived here, I just wrote "help." It was the next day when a bunch of us were hanging out on the front porch that Jake handed me a drawing of wild roses.

"I brought you flowers," he said.

They were the prettiest flowers. Jake can do things like draw flowers and make them not cheesy at all.

Tonight, leaning against one of the votive candles is an index card, across which Violet has written "Help Is Not on the Way."

"What does that mean?" I ask.

"I got it from a Buddhist book I was reading earlier. I meant it to be an inspiration."

"How's it working?"

"About as well as anything. How was Jesus?" Violet asks, without moving.

"You know. A ray of sunshine in a dark world," I say, sitting down on the edge of Violet's bed. She moves her legs to make room for me and rolls over onto her back with one arm behind her head. She nods to show she is listening. They teach us these things in group: (1) nod to demonstrate active listening; (2) take a breath and pause when agitated.

"Bad?"

"Bad. But it started out killer. You would have loved it. We broke into the Ambassador."

This stirs Violet to a sitting position.

"Oh, my God! I'm so jealous. He's a freak, that Jesus, but he truly is so cool."

She's right, I think. He is cool. And I'm an asshole.

"Did you see ghosts?" she asks.

"Yeah."

In Violet's excitement she forgets to conceal her forearm and, where her pajama sleeve has lifted, I see the raw, fresh, cigarette-sized burn marks. Five of them in an angry circle.

"Oh, Vi." I grab her wrist and pull her arm toward me, assessing the damage. "Bad?"

"Bad."

I go down the hall to the bathroom and return with hydrogen peroxide, a cotton square, gauze, and tape. She doesn't protest when I wipe down the wounds and they fizz up white. I tape a clean square of gauze over the area and pull back the comforter. She slumps down again and wedges herself under the blanket. I crawl behind her on the bed and lie down, shaping myself around her rigid bends and putting my arm around her.

"It's okay. Just go to sleep now."

"We're getting out of here, right?"

"Of course."

"You swear?"

I link my pinkie with hers.

"I swear."

I lie there until she sleeps, exhausted by her own misery. Then I go back to my own bed, where mine keeps me awake and staring at the ceiling until the curtain is seamed with the electric blue of the dawn and I finally drop off to sleep.

Thirteen

I 544 hours down. 56 hours left to go.

We have a guest lecture on Charm Gels today and everybody is upstairs in the lecture room—maybe fifty or so people crowded around the long tables. Javier and Violet arrived late, so they perch on the high stools in front of the mirrors that span the perimeter of the room. Candy sits next to me, too close for comfort. She thinks that because we live in the same house we are meant to be BFFs at school. I try to avoid eye contact. She likes to start fistfights, ask everyone out on dates, and give people her accessories. On any given day she'll either accuse you of stealing her box of hairpins or give you a cheap bracelet off her wrist that she says was her grandmother's. Candy offers at least once a week to take me to Italy or Ireland or Israel when her disability check comes in.

For my breakfast this morning, I gingerly drink black coffee out of my busted travel mug and eat plain cereal out of a ziplock bag.

“Diet?” Candy asks, pointing to my bag of cereal.

“Always,” I answer, not looking at her.

“I can help you. I have fen-phen hidden at the house. I got a boatload of it before it was illegal, but it doesn’t agree with me. Bad for my skin. I can give it to you,” she says, scratching the back of her neck and loosening some white flakes that float down to the shoulders of her black Moda Beauty Academy T-shirt.

Shit. She hooks me. I turn toward her.

“Really?”

I suspect that Candy really does have the pills, and that I’ll have to pay for them in hours of conversation. I know it’s a mistake as I say it, but I can’t resist the idea of getting some help on my quest to not keep growing and growing like one of those tiny capsules you put in a bowl of water and it turns into a spongy dinosaur, which seems to be the way things are going. I am a tall, big-boned girl to begin with. Doesn’t take much before I start looking like a pro wrestler instead of the hairdresser I am aspiring to be.

“Do they make you speedy?” I ask. “Are they, like, speed?”

Would I be sacrificing my hard-won sober time by taking the fen-phen? Or is it a free pass to the land of thin people? Fen-phen is shaky ground, and until now I have been a perfect sober angel. Really, I have. Except for my meds, but they’re legal says Susan Schmidt. And I agreed to keep taking them if I want to stay at Serenity.

“No, no. They’re not speed. Mostly they just make you not hungry, is all.”

I wonder if there truly is the miracle product in this world that could make me not hungry. I am hungry all the fucking time. All I ever am is hungry.

"I'll get them for you," Candy offers. "I'll bring them tomorrow. You'll love them. You'll see."

If I know anything, I know there isn't a pill for what ails me. Plus, I hate that diet pill feeling—not butterflies in your stomach but rather wasps in your blood vessels. Unbearable without a drink to take the edge off.

"Thanks anyway. I hate diet pills. I'd rather be big and beautiful."

"Okay, okay. Tell me if you change your mind. Hey, what are you doing later?" Candy asks.

"I have to go meet my sponsor," I lie.

"What about tomorrow? Or any night this week? I know this really great Italian restaurant near school. We could go on our way home. Maybe you heard of it. It's called the Olive Garden. I just got my check. I could treat."

"Okay, Candy. That sounds great. I'll check my schedule."

I am rescued from Candy's advances by the huffy entrance of a sunburned queen in a silk shirt, pleated trousers, and shiny shoes. He has perfectly frosted blond hair and carries a cardboard box, which he slams down on the table in front of him. He tapes onto the blackboard an unwieldy chart that lists the names of the Charm Gels semipermanent color gels and the corresponding hair color results. When he is done taping, he turns around to face us.

"Hey, kids," he says ironically to the room of mostly over-thirty women.

Javier is the only one who replies with a "heee-ey" and a little wave as if he just spotted a friend across the dance floor. The guy shoots him a brief, peeved look.

"I'm Ray," he says so slowly that I almost expect him to start doing sign language. "Before I talk to you about Charm Gels," he begins, making a game show gesture toward the chart, "we are going to do a little personal motivational exercise. But first, let me ask you . . . how are you all doing today?"

Violet dabs at a coffee stain on her white smock. Someone blows her nose. The room stares at him blankly. Candy and one or two other people give him a disunified "Good" or "Fine"; Javier chimes in, "Peachy." This doesn't satisfy Ray.

"Let's try that again." He is the gayest, most annoyed counselor at Camp Cosmetology, and that's saying something. "How are you all doing today?"

Ray hurts Javier's feelings by ignoring him. I can tell, because Javi pouts silently with his arms crossed over his chest. Three or four more people answer this time, with an unenthusiastic "Fine."

Our lack of bubbliness personally affronts Ray.

"This is your *life*, people. Right now. So participate in it. Is that how you want to live?" He mocks us with a lethargic tone: "Fiiiiine."

Ray raises his hands to the sky, like a preacher, I think.

But not a very good one. The best preachers don't bully you into participating. They make you feel like you can't hold yourself back.

"One more time. How *are* you today?"

This time even I answer to stop him from asking a fourth time. *"Great."*

"That's better."

Ray reaches into his box and pulls out stacks of Post-its, which he tosses onto the tables in front of us. They land with purposeful little thuds.

"Now. I'd like to play a little game with you. I want you to pick a favorite mantra," he says, opening his mouth wide to enunciate each syllable as he writes "mantra" on the second blackboard, the one that isn't covered with the Charm Gels chart.

"A mantra is a saying that you find inspirational. You can also pick a little theme song if you want to. Like, the theme song of your life!"

Native English speakers and English language learners alike look at him baffled. He puts his hands on his hips and sighs, as if he has just made total sense but we're all mentally challenged so he'll charitably explain it again. Poor, long-suffering Ray. I can imagine the self-help books on his nightstand, next to the seashell from Miami Beach and the scented candle.

"I'll give you an example," he says. "For instance, when I watch TV, I like the Nike ad that tells me to 'just do it.' When I'm going through my day, if I get worried or afraid,

I think of that commercial and say to myself, *Just Do It*, and it gives me the strength to conquer the obstacle in my path. *Just Do It.* That's my mantra. Now, an inspiring example of a personal theme song is the classic Whitney Houston ballad, 'The Greatest Love.' *I've found the greatest love of all inside of me.* Get it? Good! Moving on! Now, for the first part of the game, I want you to choose either a mantra or a theme song and write it on a Post-it."

This stumps us.

"Now. Write. Go ahead. Write," he prompts, while making a pantomime of writing on one of the Post-it stacks. I grab a square and scribble the mantra *Another Day in Paradise*, but I change my mind and crumple it up. I go instead for the theme song and choose Freddie Mercury's "Fat Bottomed Girls (You Make the Rockin' World Go Round)." Javier covers his and won't show it to us. Javi and Violet come over and perch at the end of our table. They're on about Carrie and Big again. Javi argues for moving on and living in the now and Vi argues for true love conquering all. I cast no vote.

For twenty minutes the rest of the class confers with each other about the assignment or about what to make for dinner or maybe about Carrie and Big, until finally Ray is overcome with annoyance. "This is not rocket science, people. Let's move on."

For the next part of the game, Ray instructs us to stick the yellow Post-its to the pockets of our smocks. Then we are supposed to walk around and look at what mantras or theme songs our classmates have chosen and remember our favorite to share with the class afterward. Not much of a game, but there it is.

These are some of the cryptic choices I read stuck to the smock pockets of my classmates:

Rocky Theme Song

Carpe Diem

Be All You Can Be

You Can Rest When You Dead

Beat It

Survivor

If I am not work out people will think am old and fat

A puzzling, even disturbing, drawing of an elephant from behind.

We Will Rock You

About ten *Just Do Its* from the people who didn't understand or couldn't come up with one of their own.

And Javier's choice: *Don't Rain on My Parade.*

It's unclear to me what the connection is between mantras and Charm Gels, but Ray makes the transition seamlessly and without explanation.

Javier interrupts, "Oh, Ray? May I make a suggestion that we each do a performance of our personal theme song?"

I think it's an entertaining idea, but, of course, Ray ignores Javier. Instead, he does a semipermanent maroon gloss on Lila's hair, making her olive skin look startlingly chartreuse under the fluorescents.

A wave of exhaustion overwhelms me and I lay my head down on the table along my outstretched arm. Violet has forgotten to remove her Post-it, and I read sideways that it says *Here Comes the Sun*.

"Here Comes the Sun?"

"So what?"

"Nothing. Just unexpected."

My meds must be messed up; I must have wicked PMS; I must be sleep deprived, because, thinking about that song, my eyes well up with tears, and one or two even drop onto the plastic red-and-white-checked tablecloth before I can reel them back in.

And that's when the thought hits me. It would knock me down if I wasn't down already. Then the thought starts a chain reaction, like a hundred dominoes followed by a hundred others and on into eternity, so that I have to shake my head to stop it but it doesn't stop. It isn't possible. But it is. It is possible.

Fourteen

It's a short walk to the Rite Aid from school and I head in that direction as soon as I clock out for lunch, with no explanation to Violet or Javier as to why I'm not going with them for SanSai sucky sushi. They're used to my fluctuating moods. It's not unusual for me to wander off once in a while.

I enter the drugstore and circle around and around the labyrinth of aisles, which contain only a handful of customers and the possibility of a troll popping out and posing a riddle that you have to answer or live with him forever next to the scented candles. Didn't there used to be employees in stores who wore little vests with name tags, carried price guns, rolled carts stacked with canned peas, and pointed you toward the aisle with the Scotch tape or the nasal spray? No one.

I pass the candy aisle without even a thought, which never happens, but right now I'm on a mission. I have tunnel vision, literal, not metaphorical, which may or may not be caused by my medication. At the end of the tunnel are stacks of tampon boxes and I follow their blue beacon. Next to the tampons loom the pregnancy tests—cheery-colored, shiny boxes ranging from $9.99 to $21.99. I settle for one that costs $16.99. I glance at the ovulation kit nearby, with the fleshy baby crawling right at me on the front of it, caught in a moment of impossible cuteness. It is natural selection's way of giving babies a chance, this cuteness. So we don't leave them out in the middle of the woods somewhere when things get tough. But I'm not fooled.

I buy the test, my tunnel vision shifting in and out, making me seasick. On the walk back to the school, I'm completely devoid of past or future, totally unable to contemplate either. My breasts bulge in swollen crescents over the top of my bra. I thought I was just getting fat. I put shoe to pavement, right shoe, left shoe, head down as if I am leaning into the wind but I'm not because it's an L.A. sunny seventy-two-degree day with clouds like spun sugar and I fucking hate weather like this sometimes. Like God designed L.A. weather for the very beautiful and very successful and very rich. If you're not all of those things or at least two out of three this weather is like God laughing in your face.

Jesus is in the wind that isn't here. Jesus is in the meringue peaks of cheap stucco. Jesus is in those shoes in the window shiny red shiny red.

I reach school and walk down the aisle with empty stations on either side of me, then upstairs to the back bathroom. I pass the lunchroom, where the Armenian women laugh and talk loudly with each other. They always seem to be having fun even though I know their lives must suck, too. They are in this same decrepit school as me, on top of immigrating from some former communist country or whatever the hell is going on in Armenia that they all came over here to wind up forty years old and trying to be hairdressers. But they don't seem to walk around all day long needing a bucket of pills or a boatload of heroin or the lit end of a cigarette held to their forearm flesh. They do things like cook lunch and share it with their friends. Vera calls after me to come and eat, but I motion to my belly and make a face like I'm not feeling well. I motor past the door.

The bathroom smells of sulfur from the old pipes and of shit covered up with freesia air freshener from the hundred people in here before me and of perfume from the same. And if I was feeling like retching before, now I actually start to gag.

The bathroom is wood paneled and strictly seventies, like this whole building. Even the toilet seat is that wood kind. They warn you against cutting boards made of wood so who thought it was a real good and sanitary idea to make toilet seats out of wood, I wonder. The room is so small that when you sit on the microbe farm toilet seat your legs hit the sink. Mrs. Montano would never consider a renovation without a direct order from the Department of Public Health, which I am amazed she doesn't have already. Tacked to the door is a poster of a cat wearing a nightie, with a silver dryer bonnet on her head as if she is setting her curlers. The caption: *"I'm too pretty for mousework!"*

I open the box and unfold the directions, but they basically say to pee on the stick, which is what I assumed. I maneuver in the small space, hold the absorbent tip of the white plastic stick in my pee stream for the allotted three seconds, then put the pink cap neatly back on and leave it facedown on the back of the toilet so I won't watch it while I wash my hands. A bar equals a negative result; a cross equals a positive result.

Someone knocks on the door and my surprising reaction is fury. I could open the door and punch her in the face. I could throw her to the ground. I could knock her head into the floor like you see in the movies. Grab her by the hair and bash it again and again. I want a fucking toilet to sit on in my life where no one can knock on the door.

But what I say is, "Sorry, I'm sick in here. Could you please use the downstairs bathroom?"

The footsteps fade away. It's the longest, smelliest three minutes. I crumple the box and cover it with toilet paper so no one will see it in the trash. I don't bother with dread or hope. A profound tiredness saturates my arms and my legs. I could curl myself into a ball and go to sleep on this filthy floor.

I watch the second hand go around the Minnie Mouse watch Jake bought me at Disneyland a couple of months ago. The hands of the watch are Minnie's arms and her big white balloon hands always make me think of bandages.

I hadn't wanted to go to Disneyland. I had always thought it was, like, some corporate plot to take over the world by brainwashing kids. I was surprised when Jake contradicted me, because he's usually eager to jump on any brainwashing conspiracy train that passes his way. I dreaded the eternal lines and the inedible food and the twelve billion kids wiping their boogers on every possible surface. I dreaded interactions with their fat, miserable parents, who probably came in the day before from my hometown. Just kill me.

But Jake had promised Milla that on our next babysitting day he'd take her to see some fairies. So we went to see the fairies. And the ghosts and pirates and princesses, and in every new land he had a new story for her. And when she got tired he carried her piggyback.

One of the fairies we saw was so bogus and bitchy that Milla called her on it.

"You're not Tinkerbell."

Jake took her aside and said, "You're right. I think that fairy is a fake fairy. But where there are fake fairies, there are usually real fairies, too. You can't always see them but you can tell because if you listen really close, you can hear them sing. And you can be sure that somewhere there's a fairy who's watching you and who thinks you're the greatest little girl anywhere. And she can't wait to meet you. She's just waiting for the right moment."

If you were Susan Schmidt you'd say that I'm with Jake because I'm so fucked up and I think I deserve someone headed on an obvious crash course. She'd say that my own guilt and self-hatred prompts my self-destructive choice in boyfriend. But Susan Schmidt never looked at that little girl's face when Jake told her about the fairies.

When Minnie's hand hits the twelve for the third time, I turn the stick over and face my fate.

What I see is a cross. A cross equals positive results.

It's a mistake. I can't possibly grow anything. No seed would take root here, in this poison ground.

I hold on to the stick and slide down the wall, where I sit for a minute with my knees tucked under my chin.

Jesus is in the cross. Jesus is in the cross. Get it? It's funny.

I don't eat lunch, which is appropriately dramatic but leaves me starving hungry.

I clock back in, sit at my station, and stare into the mirror, but not at myself, through me to somewhere else.

Jesus is in the buckets of bleach. Jesus is in my hungry belly. Jesus is in the wide, wide windows.

"You are feeling unwell?" asks Vera, towering over my station with a concerned look on her impeccably made-up, glamorous face. She puts her hand over mine, which I hadn't noticed was gripping the edge of the table. There is the line of demarcation at her wrist that you get from a spray-on tan. Vera works evenings at Wet Seal in the Glendale Galleria. She should be a Transylvanian countess who feasts on the blood of virgins, not working at the Galleria with a fake tan.

"I'm okay. Little stomach thing," I say, starting to set up my station so I don't have to look her in the eye.

"You are needing some cola?" she asks.

"I'm good, thanks," I say. She mercifully moves on to her own station and begins meticulously prepping her foils to do Lila's highlights. Lila and Vera are inseparable. They married two brothers and live in adjoining condos. Each carries a wedding picture around in her purse. Vera was Lila's maid of honor and vice versa; the pictures are nearly identical with the roles switched around. That's a different kind of family than I know anything about.

Javier and Violet saunter back in. Since we have been upstairs learning about Charm Gels and the Meaning of Life all morning, we first set up our stations now. I put my rollers and clips and combs out in front of me, arranging and rearranging them, forcing a fake smile at Javier and Violet. Javier raises his eyebrow at me, then goes on about the elaborate task of his daily decorating.

With tiny pieces of Scotch tape, Javier attaches pictures of Milla and Paul and their fat, well-dressed Chihuahua, really named Zuzu but nicknamed Butterball, around the perimeter of his mirror. Since it's nearly spring, Butterball features pastel bonnets and matching capes. I guess Javier couldn't find a real flower today, so he puts a silk flower studded with rhinestones on the corner of his station. He sings under his breath: *"Don't tell me not to live, just sit and putter . . ."*

"I have a surprise for you," he says as he fusses, setting his doll head on her stand and preparing to sculpt his latest creation. Lorelei Lee must be the luckiest doll head in the world. Whatever impoverished teenage slave in Burma shaved her head so that we could have real human hair to practice on has had justice of some sort done for her lost locks.

"No." I stop, lean back in my chair, and look at his reflection dead in the eye. "*I* have a surprise for *you*."

He grabs my hand and leads me into the back shampoo room, which is still empty from lunch. We sit in the shampoo chairs next to each other. I rest my elbows on my knees and hold my head in my hands.

"Okay," he says, cheerfully. "You first. Does not look good. Looks decidedly ungood. What are you, pregnant?"

I stare at him in astonishment.

"A mother knows, honey. You've been a weepy pain in the ass for the last week. Plus, your ta-tas are positively voluminous. I merely observed your look of hopeless devastation and connected the dots."

"Shit." I lean my head over onto his shoulder. "What am I going to do?"

That's what you say, right? You say, What am I going to do.

"Well, honey, that would seem to be the question of the hour, now wouldn't it? Wait here a sec. I still have my surprise for you."

Javier leaves me sitting alone.

The thought blindsides me that if I had gotten pregnant when I was with Aaron at least I'd have some piece of him still. It wrenches my already wrenched gut even further. I'd have something more than an old guitar. But I didn't and now I have nothing. Not nothing exactly, but almost nothing. I can barely imagine a life for myself. I never think further than hoping to pass the State Board and get a good job in a salon. So I should get rid of it, right? Because I'm unfit. In some countries they sterilize people like me. MDD, CD, ADD: potentially genetic and definitely no good for a baby. I had a father like that myself. I was crazy about him. He didn't last long.

Javier walks in holding a modified Barbie doll and sits back down next to me. Like Kitty Hawk, the doll has a tiny star painted in nail polish around one eye. Her dyed red hair is styled into perfect Farrah Fawcett feathers. She wears a rainbow tube top and sparkly silver shorts. Her tiny heels are painted silver to match. Around her shoulders are little rubber band straps that hold a pair of pink construction paper wings, covered in iridescent glitter.

"Milla wanted me to give you this. We were doing makeovers on her Barbie doll collection all day Sunday. She asked me to tell her a story about the dollies at school and I told her about the adventures of Bella Donna and Kitty Hawk and Lorelei Lee. Anyway, she made this for you." He hands me the doll and I take her gently by the spindly plastic legs, trying not to rip her wings, which sprinkle glitter every time she moves. "She wanted to give it to you herself but she's with the Cuntessa this week."

"Milla made this for me?" I turn it over in my hands and

look at her fragile paper wings. This is the most precious thing. "Why?"

"You're Milla's fave babysitter fairy ever. She asks about you all the time." Javier sighs and leans back in the shampoo chair. I lie back, too.

Javi goes on as we stare up at the ceiling, "You think you're the only loser trying to change your life? I'm a fat, broke, thirty-eight-year-old faggot who goes to beauty school and lives in a Woodland Hills cardboard town house with my boyfriend. True, he's gorgeous and, true, I'm fabulous, but still. Milla's the one who saves my life."

"I don't know."

Could this save me? A baby doesn't save everyone's life, does it? Some people it ruins their lives and then they ruin its life right back. And haven't I learned my lesson yet about trying to get saved?

"I guess you got to tell Mr. Handsome, is the first thing." Javier thinks Jake is dreamy handsome in a bad boy kind of way, which he is.

"Me and Mr. Handsome got into it last night. Want to know the funny thing? Can you believe there's a funny thing?"

"There's always a funny thing," he answers, sitting up straight now and fluffing his Mohawk.

"He asked me to marry him."

"I hope you said no. He may be handsome but that man is nobody's husband."

"Of course I said no. He can't keep a job for five minutes and when he gets stressed he tends to talk to spirits and thinks the zombies are coming. Which brings me back to What am I going to do?"

We hear the creaking of the floorboards over us, followed by the unmistakable labored steps and wheezing of Mrs. Montano coming down the stairs.

"Quick," Javier says. "Look miserable."

Javier and I stand and pretend to be getting some setting gel down from one of the cupboards. Mrs. Montano walks into the room and stands at the door like a battleship. Her upper lip curls into a sneer and her makeup sits on top of the poreless, crinkled fabric of her skin.

"Bebe," she says, "you have a phone call."

"I do?"

"Please come up to the office. And Javier . . ."

"Jes, Meeses?" Javier says in his Mexican maid accent.

"Do something useful, please."

I hand Javier the Barbie and follow Mrs. Montano up the stairs.

The beauty school office is decorated with generic, bargain basement office furniture and walls of filing cabinets. On the desks sit ancient phones that actually have cords. There are little souvenir shop plaques around that say things like *What part of "NO" didn't you understand?* and *A Woman without a Man Is Like a Fish without a Bicycle.* A calendar from the Pechanga Resort and Casino hangs on the wall.

I perch on the edge of a mammoth metal desk and pick up the cradle of the archaic receiver.

"Hello, Beth. How are you?" asks Susan Schmidt. I can tell she is trying not to sound pissed at me.

This whole therapist thing really involves being a studied, manipulative phony, if you think about it. And that's who's supposed to help people get better?

"I'm fine. Is everything okay?"

"Beth, I'm going to ask you some questions, and I need you to answer me honestly because it concerns the safety of one of our residents here with whom you are close. I want to express to you that you will in no way be penalized for anything you reveal to me right now. Do you understand?"

"Susan, you're freaking me out."

"Jacob Hill is missing. I stress to you that we're concerned for his safety and for the safety of those he may come into contact with. This is very important. If you have any ideas as to where he might be headed, please tell me now, Beth."

I have some ideas where he's going. I almost consider telling her, but she'll sic the cops on him for being a danger to himself and others. He'll get arrested and then slapped back in the hospital so fast, and who knows when he'll get out.

"I have no idea where he is," I say. "I haven't seen him in days."

My cell phone vibrates in my smock pocket. I check it and the screen lights up: BUCK. Calling to warn me. Too late.

"Beth," Susan goes on in that reasonable voice, "we all care about Jacob. He's a unique and fascinating man, but he's deeply troubled. We have access to the resources that may be able to help him. If Jacob winds up hurt and there's something you haven't told us, you'll regret it for the rest of your life. Is that a risk you're willing to take?" she asks in a loaded way. Bitch.

"I'm sorry I can't help you."

"I'm sorry, too. I truly am. Please call us immediately if anything comes to you."

"I'll do that."

As I hang up the phone, one thing is as clear to me as a rare L.A. day when the smog blanket lifts and if you stand on top of a tall hill you can see the whole city glitter all the way out to the ocean. I've got to go find him. Before he does something reckless and they lock him up until forever.

I look at the intrepid hulk of Mrs. Montano at the desk across the room, thumbing through a stack of papers. I immediately revert to the fake crying face, which never loses its effectiveness on most normal people; but this is not your average foe. Mrs. Montano is a perfect example of what Jake calls a zombie.

She looks up at me with one drawn-on eyebrow arching sharply, like a stretched rubber band that could snap and shoot straight off her face. At least three pictures of the same mean, yellow-eyed cat stare out at me from ornate frames on her desk. A ray of light breaks through the water-stained ceiling—the perfect excuse.

"My cat is sick and she needs to go to the vet really badly. May I be excused for the day?"

Mrs. Montano casts a sidelong glance at her nice secretary sidekick. They're Tweedledee and Tweedledum, if Tweedledee and Tweedledum had been huffing bleach fumes for twenty years. The secretary is a little dippy and, I suspect, a little tipsy most of the time. She likes to gamble on the weekends and the Pechanga calendar is hers. She looks to Mrs. Montano and then to me, her fleshy face creasing with concern.

Mrs. Montano looks back down at her work and moves a few pieces of paper from one pile to another. I watch as a drop of sweat trails from behind her ear down the side of her neck. I stand there, conscious of my hands hanging awkwardly at my sides. The tight skin itches around the scars on my palms.

"You'll have to come at night," she says finally. "Miss any more hours and you won't graduate with your class. You'll have to wait another month until the next group graduates."

She sizes me up, as if looking at a spider on the floor and deciding if she is going to step on it. But I have already seen the flicker of weakness behind her eyes. I found the key to the zombie heart. She spares me the sole of her shoe and instead she says, "Go, then. I hope your kitty's okay. Don't forget to clock out."

"Thank you," I say, nearly trotting out the door and down the stairs, thinking that she's not so bad; she loves something.

I stride to my station, maniacally wrap all my equipment

in a towel, throw it over my shoulder like a sack, and lug it toward the back bays of lockers. Javier and Violet look up at me, surprised, and then follow me. They stand there as I attempt to force the unwieldy mound into my locker.

"Slow down, crazy," Javier says.

"I've got to get out of here. Drama. Big. Bad," I say, shoving on the locker door until it is mostly closed then kicking it and fastening the lock.

"That was the uptight socialite social worker."

"And?"

"And Jake's gone missing."

Javier puts his arms up as if in surrender and then starts to fan himself with one hand. "It's getting hot in here," he says. "What are you going to do?"

"Well, honey, that seems to be the question of the hour, now, doesn't it? I guess I'm going to find him."

"This isn't your crisis, doll. You've got your own crisis to deal with."

"I'd say this crisis and my crisis are kind of related."

"You can't just go running out into the world trying to find someone. What are you going to use, a dowsing rod?"

I pause. I hadn't thought much beyond leaving.

"Wait," Javi says. He grabs me by the arms. "Just wait one tiny, tiny second. It's important."

Javier runs to the other room, leaving Violet and me staring at each other.

"Bebes, stay. This is a terrible idea."

Javi returns, holding the Barbie that Milla made.

"Take her with you. She'll be like your little fairy."

"*You're* my fairy," I say to him, but I take the doll.

Javier wraps his arms around me and kisses me on one cheek and then the other.

"Go on, then," he says. "Go get your man."

1550 hours down. 50 hours left to go.

Fifteen

What I think is that Jake's probably gone to try to re-enlist. Where do you go to do that? There must be a million places and I don't know one. It was ridiculous, my revelation that I have to go and find him. How do you find someone?

I park out in front of Serenity, sag, and lean into the steering wheel. Buck stands on the front stoop talking to Jake's roommate, who gives me an uncomfortable little wave. Hardened criminals who have spent most of their lives in prison are so awkward around women it makes me want to cry for them. The roommate, who Buck likes to call Himmler, is actually a nice guy, even though he's done a lot of time and as a result has a giant swastika tattoo covering his entire back and he really does things like kill people. One or two. The story changes.

One thing about ex-cons is that they are the tidiest guys

you will ever meet. The women's Serenity House is often a sty, but the men's Serenity House next door is neat like an army barracks. Jake's roommate saw our kitchen one day and actually offered to clean it for us. And our resident reformed Cholo stood with me out on the back porch one Saturday afternoon and taught me how to iron. He showed me how to press razor-straight creases into a pair of khakis. Not that I've ever used it, but it's a good skill to have if one day I make a life where I do things like iron.

Buck bounds down the front stairs and slides into the passenger seat.

"I made you a sandwich and shit for the drive," she says. "Himmler over there knows where he's headed. I got it out of him."

"Why didn't he stop him?"

"How was he gonna stop him? The road was calling him. You gotta go, you gotta go."

Buck smiles at me, her gold tooth catching the sunlight.

"And?"

"He went back to the motherfuckin' Marines, that nut," she says.

I open the bag. Buck packed me a sweater, jeans, water, a sandwich, and carrot sticks.

"At least we know they won't take him. I just want to find him before they lock him up."

"You never do know. Maybe they want a nut like him to go in there and blow some shit up. Probably not, though.

And I don't know what the fuck he's going to do then, because they're not letting him back in here after this stunt. Maybe he'll stay up north with his mama for a while."

Buck looks forward through the windshield and visibly winces at how dirty my car is. She takes the sleeve of her flannel shirt and tries to wipe some of the dust off the dash.

"That's where he went. To go kiss his mama good-bye. That's what he told Herr Himmler, anyway. She lives in a trailer near Solvang, a couple hours north of here. I heard him talk about it once."

How I said that convicts are with women: that is how I am with moms. I'm incredibly uncomfortable around moms. But it's not just me. Moms will fight you for their boys.

"Really? By the way he described his mom's trailer I thought it would be further. Out in the middle of the desert somewhere."

"This is the middle of the fucking desert. We just pay the Mexicans to water it so you can't tell."

"Buck."

"What?"

"Never mind."

"He's got a head start on you, but you never know. He might still be there. Then you two can have a touching reunion."

"How do I find it?"

"His mom works at the casino. There's always signs for the casino, right? Never too hard to find a place that wants your money. What's this?" she asks, picking up Milla's Kitty Hawk Barbie from where she's lying in the well under the emergency brake. "Aw shit. This reminds me of my little cousin."

She gives the doll a kiss on the head and lays her back down.

"Himmler said he stopped taking his meds weeks ago," Buck says, looking in front of her toward the downtown skyline.

"I suspected something like that. He hates the way they make him feel."

"You shouldn't go, you know. You want I should come with you?"

"No. Thanks."

She wishes me luck and lurches back toward Serenity, a slight permanent limp on her left side. She never told me where she got it.

In the car, I quickly change out of my uniform and into the clothes Buck packed for me. Follow the 101 north and look for the casino signs. Not much to go on, but it's what I've got. I secretly hope for an arrow in the sky. Even when you don't believe anymore, how do you stop looking for signs? How do you stop listening for God? I turn the key in the ignition. I like long car rides. You sit in the traffic white noise of womb-like nowhere as if time isn't happening and you're at least not doing any damage you'll answer for later.

Unless, of course, you're this car's previous owner, who slit his wrists while he looked out at the ocean and died where I'm sitting. I think about him sometimes, like he's almost here to talk to. Thinking about the surfer suicide doesn't creep me out; it's more like having a friend in the car with me—a surfer dude who was so, so sad, a boyfriend I could have had. A blue-eyed gentle boy with a tangle of long blond hair and beach tar on his feet. Where he is now he might have some more wisdom than what he left with. He might know the thing that could have saved him. Maybe it could save me if I could get through to him. Listening for God and dead surfers and looking for signs in the sky—am I any less crazy than Jake?

The 101 freeway cuts a swath through the San Fernando Valley, and alongside it lie a hundred towns you don't want to visit. People say it's the suburbs but I'm from the Midwest and I know suburbs and this isn't them. This is something different. There's a faster rate of decomposition here; it's a big compost bin between the mountains, an endless grid of roads choked with sun-baked traffic jams. This is houses and more houses, box after box, richer or poorer, fancier or shittier. The poor just want to be the rich and the rich never get enough and everyone is driving these monstrous blood-bloated ticks of debt called things like Hummer and Escalade. This is tanning salons and nail salons and corporate coffee and cute coffee and strip mall yoga studios and storefront Scientology. This is the land of think it and you can buy it. This is window display after window display of ugly clothes and pretty clothes and the same slaves in China making all of it.

Welcome to the land of the living. That's what people say to you when you get sober. Uh, thanks.

And what do they say to you when you have a baby? Welcome to the land of living in the Valley? Welcome to the Valley, where you can breed and eat and buy until you die.

My phone rings and the display reads: DON'T ANSWER. It's the name I programmed in for the number Billy called from the other day. Billy again. Always Billy trying to pull me off the path when I have somewhere to go. I don't answer. I keep driving. What does he want? Same thing as ever, probably. To ruin my life, probably.

Sober, reinvented, reborn. My ass.

The Valley opens out onto rolling green and gold hills and this is where I start to breathe a little more and hate the world a little less. In summer these hills turn to kindling, except there are always those green broccoli trees that crawl up and around the mountains. I don't know how they stay green with no water. No water in summer at all, but there they are. I slip in and out of the fast lane, in and around the other cars. Always since that night, I'm aware of the steel and the velocity, the potential for destruction. The sound of metal on metal is engraved on my every cell. I wonder if it ever goes away or if I'll forever be like those vets who get hurled into a panic by loud noises for the rest of their lives. Exaggerated startle reflex. That's what it's called. It's one of the symptoms of PTSD. PTSD, ADD, CD, MDD. And still driving, folks. Come and see her. The amazing rubber girl. From the darkest reaches of Ohio. Watch as she falls again and again. She should have gone splat long ago but she just keeps bouncing.

I push forward, attempting to force the traffic faster with my will. I blast the radio, hoping the sound waves will cancel out any thought spirals infiltrating my brain. The thinking will get me exactly nowhere; the trick is to move without thinking.

The road takes a turn and I look to my left and, on the other side of a row of shaggy palm trees, the ocean appears. I open the window. The air is glorious. It smells like real air. The hazy sheet of ocean fades into the cloudless blue sky so that I can't see the edges of either one.

The trick is to move without thinking but I'm the world's most inconsistent magician. Because I see the ocean and that's how it starts.

I remember how Aaron and I rolled into California and then it rolled right over us. I try not to think about it but I don't try very hard. I just let it come. Because sometimes I'd rather be with him, even if it sucks, even if it hurts. Regret perches like an umbrella over all of my days. All I do is look up and I see its spiny inside. An invisible hand grips my heart just a little too tight and squeezes every time a memory washes over me. And, yes, Jake is my right now but Aaron is my always. Always gone and always here.

I have throbbing pulses of regret embedded in the sidewalks around L.A. I imagine them sprinkled across the grid of the city like red dots on a map. On the satellite map, take your finger and follow the freeway south instead of north and exit by the airport. You'll find a big bleeding splotch at the coordinates where Hawthorne intersects with Lennox. For some reason today that's where I go in my mind.

Jet Strip, all gray concrete and purple neon, was where I first got to know Billy's ex Francesca, my first stripper friend and my first real friend in L.A. I remember it all in soft focus, because that's how I lived then, the outlines of everything bleeding into each other. Unlike now, when everything is too sharply defined—blackheads and spider veins and gum on the asphalt.

One thing about me is I'm brave. I do things like wade into a freezing river and give my life to Jesus. I do things like pack a bag and step into a bus with a musician I kissed one night and never go back home again. I do things like sling a bag with a new pair of Hollywood Boulevard heels over my shoulder and step through the heavy velvet curtain that obscures the doorway of an airport strip club and act like it's nothing. I was always the one on the front of the sled, the first to try out a bigger hill on my skateboard, to cannonball off the high dive with a running start.

The dressing room was alarmingly small—a walk-in closet lined with lit mirrors. If you bent over too far, when you leaned in to curl your eyelashes you would bump bare asses with the girl facing the opposite wall. That's how tight the quarters were.

There were about six girls crammed in when I arrived. Their reflections eyeballed me suspiciously while I stuffed my bag into one of the tiny lockers. I looked for a spot on the ledge in front of the mirrors where I could wedge my makeup caddy. They ignored me, deep in their own coded conversations about parties they were at or customers who were in there last night or guys who would install a car stereo for a lap dance. Everywhere you go has its own special language—beauty school, AA meetings, strip clubs. Until you catch on, you won't make any true allies. And let me be clear, your first night working at a strip club you must have an ally. If you don't, the other girls will spill Diet Coke in your makeup and steal your shoes and make your life a worse hell than any junior high playground torture imaginable until you leave for good, clutching your remaining belongings to your chest. But I had a stacked deck, because I came in already kind of knowing Francesca. I had only met her briefly once in person, but Billy had put in a call to her about me needing a job and for some reason everyone fell all over themselves to help out Billy.

She breezed in five seconds later, a petite rockabilly girl wearing only red cotton hot pants with a pair of dice, showing seven, printed on the back. She dropped her flame-painted makeup case down on the counter and then moved it over to make room for mine on the end. On her cue, the other girls easily shifted to make space. The lid of her open box was plastered with a sweet collage of photographs and stickers. I wanted to look at the photographs, but I didn't want to be too nosy.

"Hey, Francesca."

"Hi, sweetie. I'm Betty here," she said, smiling at the mirror. "Who are you gonna be?"

"I'm Bebe. I'll just stay Bebe."

"Suit yourself."

I don't know why I used my real name. I was caught off guard. I didn't know I was going to have to make something up. Plus, my name, I like it. My pop was the one who started calling me Bebe in the first place.

Francesca was tiny and high waisted, with blue-black Betty Page hair and saucer-big, turquoise eyes in a sharp pixie face. There were seams of cherries tattooed up the backs of her legs and she looked oddly spiderlike in her tall, tall shoes. She was older than me, eyes surrounded by fans of lines in the dressing room light.

There are angels everywhere. Francesca was an angel to me. I never saw her after the funeral. I wonder sometimes where she is now.

I changed into the one costume I owned, a neon pink bikini from a Hollywood Boulevard sale rack. Then I surreptitiously checked out the competition and discerned that my ass was by far the biggest one in the room, its dimpled curves pushing the tiny pink shorts far into my crack. I figured that was why Francesca was being so nice to me. Because of Billy and because my ass was bigger than hers.

The dancing was not so jazzy or romantic as Aaron and

I imagined it, but it wasn't so bad at first. It didn't take a genius and it wasn't exactly fun but there's no need to be all victimy talk show dramatic about it. It wasn't horribly humiliating or anything. You put back a drink or two and the lights get starry and you can almost believe that you're truly pretty up there. It all gets normal fast. So after a while when some customer whips it out and comes on your bare ass during a lap dance, you just go to the dressing room, wipe it off, touch up your lipstick, and head back out. It isn't how you'd thought it would be, but what is?

Francesca had a fifth-floor apartment in Koreatown with French doors opening up to a balcony and almost no furniture save a canopy bed and a huge old steamer trunk that she said her grandmother brought over on the boat when she came from Austria. We went to her place after that first night and sat outside smoking and drinking wine poured out of a box. I wore her too-small sweatshirt and we laughed hyena laughs that got absorbed in the constant traffic buzz of the street below. There wasn't a view of anything very spectacular and far away, only the surrounding buildings, but even that seemed rare in the amber glow of the streetlights.

"You have to pretend like your true love is in the audience," she schooled me. "Just to the left of the stage and slightly out of the light so you can't see him. Imagine like he's watching you and dance for him. It'll soften you up. It'll make you care. You'll do a better show."

"Who do you think of?"

"My true love? Tom Waits. No contest. Well, Billy gave him a run for his money for a minute, but now I do all I can *not* to think of Billy."

"So why do you still keep showing up for him when he calls?"

"Because Tom Waits is unavailable, as far as I know."

In that moment my life was okay. I was floating there between the sky and the pavement and I had a drink in my hand and money in my pocket and I had made a friend.

After that I tried imagining that Mick Jagger was out there watching and then when that didn't feel quite right I imagined Chet Baker, who I always thought would have loved me if he ever knew me. But that didn't work, either, because Chet Baker kind of reminded me of my dad and you really don't want your dad in the audience when you're stripping. Then it becomes, like, the world's worst nightmare. I even tried imagining John Travolta once but that was just too little girl.

So in the end it was Aaron. I always imagined Aaron in the audience when I danced. Of course that's just a game you play with yourself. You don't really want your true love in the audience when you're stripping. There are things that are meant to stay between women. Francesca could understand that really I was dancing for Aaron, but Aaron would only ever see the other men there. I only know this now. I didn't know it then but I wish I had.

I learned it when Aaron came to pick me up at Jet Strip

one night. He usually waited in the parking lot out back, but I told him to come in that night because I wanted him to see my show for real and not just in my imagination. Francesca warned me not to, but I ignored her. I wanted Aaron to see me shine. And maybe I also wanted him to be a little jealous but mostly I wanted him to be one of them for a minute. I wanted to work the magic on him, too. I thought it would be fun. I thought he would think I was glamorous, powerful, sexy.

He thought it might be fun, too, so he agreed to come but he showed up a little earlier than he was supposed to. I had planned to be on stage right when he arrived but instead I was on one of the purple velvet couches that lined the club, milking the last lap dance out of a customer with his face buried in my tits, when Aaron walked in. I saw him before he saw me but not soon enough. I watched his expression darken and harden as his eyes found me on the lap of an insulation salesman in town from Duluth.

It wasn't as if he didn't know what I did. It wasn't as if he'd never seen a lap dance before. I didn't think it was a big deal.

I looked for him when I was on stage but he'd left the room. He didn't even come back at the end of the night to get me and he wasn't home when Francesca dropped me off. I don't know where he went, but I know some shadow grew in him after he saw me working. I didn't know who to be angrier at, him or me, but it doesn't matter because the important part is that I know he never looked at me the same again. It was one of those mistakes. It's one of those regrets.

Jesus is in the slow sparkles of the water. Jesus is in the quick glitter of the doll wings. Jesus is painted on the wall of a roadside church.

But Jesus doesn't stop it. Jesus doesn't make it better.

Sixteen

Somewhere after the trailer park with the big sculpture of Santa Claus at the entranceway, I pull over for gas. It's one of those whatever places with the terra-cotta fake Spanish-style strip malls and that's pretty much it. I always wonder what the people do who live near these places. Not what do they do for fun but what do they do for real.

My hands freak people out. The palms of my hands look like a million-year-old mummy, but more pink. When cashiers get caught unawares by the sight of my scars, it always gives them a visible jolt. So I'm careful to buy my bottle of water and pay for my gas palms down. The doctors always tell me—everybody always tells me—I'm lucky. I'm lucky I lived. I'm lucky it was just my legs and my hands and not my face or my insides that got all fucked up. I'm lucky I didn't sever any nerves or I wouldn't have my bright future in cosmetology to look forward to.

Refueled, I roll up the coast for another hour, the browns and grays and greens of the coastal cliffs rising to the right of me and the vast glossy expanse of ocean folding out on my left. This is the kind of thing they photograph and make religious calendars out of. Fuck, it's nice here. I wish Jake were with me because he'd probably paint it even prettier than the real thing. He sees things so pretty.

Have I told you about Jake's painting? As far as professionally being a famous painter and all that, he's kind of through. I don't think he has to be, but he refuses to finish anything, refuses to try and sell anything. He always gives his best stuff away to, like, some waitress he thinks is nice or some guy who works at the Jamba Juice and has acne so bad that his face looks like an angry relief map. Jake will think he needs a painting. He says that something just tells him who needs paintings. There's no talking to him about it so I don't try.

Most of his paintings are bizarrely twisted, ugly but still beautiful. His latest series was of ravaged Hitler clowns advertising whatever corporate thing Jake was hating on at the moment. Which makes it hard to believe that when Javi and Paul moved to their town house, they hired Jake to paint Milla's room. Not with Hitler clowns, of course. He agreed to keep it positive. But even painting a castle, he was impossible. He changed his mind a thousand times about every detail and took a whole week to find the right green for the grass and ate all the food in their fridge and some days didn't show up and some days showed up at ten or noon or two or whenever he damn well pleased and before the whole thing was done Javi and Paul were ready to get a divorce or kill Jake or both.

But in the end, the room was the most incredible masterpiece. It was a fairy kingdom, with the ceiling as the bluest sky and the walls decorated with hills and a castle and wood nymphs and birds and a giant oak tree and fantasy animals that Jake just invented as he went and angels and bunnies sailing in nutshell boats and cows with wings flying across the sky.

I had a dream after I saw the finished room. I dreamed I saw Jake in heaven and he was so handsome and he had this quality about him that was different from how I usually know him, and when I thought about it later I thought it was probably peace. He was peaceful. And he had no scar on his face and he wasn't wearing a hat.

He said, "Isn't it funny how we were so hidden from ourselves?"

I laughed and I knew just what he meant. And I wished there was a mirror because I wanted to see what I looked like in heaven, too. The Jake I saw in heaven is the Jake I can see in his paintings.

So I search each freeway marker and billboard and cardboard real estate enticement but they all lead to nowhere I want to go. Half an hour after I think I've gone too far, just when the desperation sets in, I spot the 246 that leads east off the main highway. Tucked into the bend in the road is a little green sign: *Chumash Casino 6.*

Here is where I should turn inland and lose the ocean but instead I pull onto the shoulder. The nausea I've been staving off all day creeps up the back of my throat and into my tonsils. I'm already sitting on a dry embankment with my head in my hands when Vi calls. The phone rings on the seat next to me and the screen lights up: VIOLET.

"Where are you?" she asks, like a worried parent.

"Nowhere."

"I know where he is, but you can't get there now so come home. There's no point in both of you getting kicked out of here."

"They caught him?"

"Apparently he walked into a recruitment station. Susan had already reported him to the police, so now he's on a seventy-two-hour hold."

"Fuck me."

"Better than prison."

This is what I was afraid of. I'm losing him. I'm a loser.

"There's something else. There's someone here waiting for you."

Of course there is. I can tell by her voice who it is. She knows the story of Billy Coyote.

Don't worry, I'll find you. That's what he said last time I saw him, before I went to detox.

Don't I always take care of you? That's what he said on the phone before he never showed up.

"Should I get rid of him?" she asks.

"Of course you should. How does he look?"

Pale, pale and blue veins and slippery hands.

"A babe. No doubt. He's a babe. But, Bebes . . . ," she says. She doesn't finish the sentence.

Seventeen

When you're from somewhere else, you think there's a promise to California. I don't know if it's some cellular thing—like your ancestors in the wagon train only made it as far as Ohio and you're completing the journey—or if it's the Beach Boys or the Beat poets or *Baywatch*. You get in that car pointing west and you think the answer is at the end of the road. You really do. But here I am at the continent's edge, jagged and final, and there is no West left to go to and I still don't have what I want.

I look down at Kitty Hawk Barbie next to me on the car seat and wish I could hold her up like a dowsing rod and she would point the way, just like Javi said. When I wanted a sign and I was back at Zion I would have dropped to my knees and prayed. I knew some people there who had clear visions from God pretty regular. But I never did. I thought it was because I was further down the scale from God, but I didn't know why. Just born that way, maybe. Just born a little dead inside—dead in the place that some people heard God. So I was reduced to seeing signs in the way the rainwater dripped down the window, in the number of Ford Crown Victorias I passed by in a day. But then you wonder—I'm making them up, right? I'm seeing the signs I want to see. I'm making the world reflect what I want, and I'm calling it God. And what bigger sin is there than that kind of pride? You can't think about it too long; it spirals down and down. So I kept praying, kept praying, until I got sick of not getting an answer.

I know Milla's Kitty Hawk Barbie is meant to be a talisman or a charm, but she isn't working. Instead she just lies there like the stiff piece of misogynist plastic that she truly is deep down inside, even with her glitter wings, silver shoes, and retro hairdo. Underneath it all she's still an impossible ideal that worms its way into little girls' heads and haunts them all their lives with what they aren't. I think it again, looking down at the doll. This child in me, I hope it's a boy child.

It's there all the time now: the baby, the thought of the baby, the possibility of the baby, the tiny glowing presence. There's no unknowing it now that I know it's there. There's no going back to being myself alone and separated from everything and everyone by the impenetrable membrane of my skin, this skin that's so resilient you can slice it to bits and it will still grow back tougher than before. Hold my scarred hand and you'll see what I mean.

But now there is this thing, this not even a baby yet, this

wisp of an idea, and suddenly I am not alone at all. Everything changes, without my thinking about it. Like, for instance, I am driving down a four-lane highway with only a double yellow in the center, and a road like this one used to inspire an overpowering urge to swerve the wheel and careen into oncoming traffic. The first few months after the accident, the impulse was so strong I often had to pull over, lay my head down on the seat next to me, and wrap my arms around myself until it passed. But now, I face the drive back down the coast with no good news about Jake and evening fast on my heels and I do not think it once. Or I do think it once, but it's just habit. I don't think it twice.

The late afternoon fog sweeps in over the coastal mountains, turning the sky and the ocean into shades of shifting, misty churning gray.

I drive for hours.

When I hit Thousand Oaks, it's nearly six thirty and I have to get back to the house. Am I going to give up and go home and sit in group and pretend like nothing's happening? I listen to the radio and watch for shapes in the clouds. I look for a sign. Where to go next. You never know when you'll get one. Even the most faithless among us are waiting to be proven wrong.

I set my trajectory for Serenity and creep along in the snarl of humanity that is the freeway as the red sticks of the digital numbers on the clock rearrange themselves to make me later and later. I screech off the exit, race up and down the neighborhood streets.

Jesus is in the thirty-two, three, four.

Sprint for the door of the house and get there exactly thirty-four minutes late for our mandatory Friday night meeting. I half expect to see Billy waiting for me on the porch, but he's already gone. I notice that I'm disappointed, which is my first clue that the next time the phone rings and says DON'T ANSWER, I probably will anyway. But the thought is a fleeting one. I have bigger problems than Billy right now.

I gingerly shut the door behind me and shrink as small as I can as I slink into the room and sit down against the wall. Everybody looks at me for a second and then looks away. I feel the judgment shimmering in the room like heat waves rising off asphalt in summer. And from Susan it's more than heat waves, it's laser beams. Laser beams of condemnation. Objective laser beams, of course. Nonjudgmental laser beams.

Violet gives me a tight-lipped smile that's meant to be reassuring, but just looks anxious.

After group, Susan calls me into her office.

"Please sit down, Beth."

I sit on the lumpy love seat that makes my knees stick up funny in front of me.

"I'm worried about you," she goes on, an off-center deep wrinkle of concern etched between her eyebrows. The wrinkle always fascinates me. I can't stop staring. Why is it pushed off to the left that way?

"It is not about an isolated incident. I'm sure you're upset about the situation that occurred today with Jacob Hill. I want to let you know that we located him and he is being well cared for. But such an emotional investment is hazardous at this stage of your recovery, which is why it's against the rules."

She pauses and I wait for her to go on, but she just looks at me so I assume it is my turn.

"I'm really sorry I was late. I had an ugly mishap with a chemical straightener."

I look her straight in the eye with what I imagine is a neutral facial expression.

You have to be careful around Susan. She can try to bluff you into showing your hand. It drives her crazy that I won't emotionally flay myself for her and let her stick Post-its on my every memory. She takes it as an insult that I don't welcome her into my most intimate, wet heart spots.

Jesus is in the water stain. Jesus is in the walls. Jesus is in the halls.

"Beth, I'm forced to take disciplinary measures. I don't want to, but I think you need to be aware that there are consequences for your choices. I'm writing you up for your tardiness at the meeting today. I need to bring your attention to the fact that this is your third write-up. This is it. One more and we'll be forced to terminate your residency here."

"I understand."

"Beth, I urge you to look at yourself. Try to see this as an opportunity to change your habits, to change your choices, and to therefore change the outcome of your choices. You are so close to achieving what you have worked hard for.

Stop being your own worst enemy here. Let us help you help yourself."

Trying to keep a hold on my running brain exhausts me. I don't have any fight left. I feel like I walked to the reservation and back. I have to press my hands down into the seat next to me just to prop myself up straight.

"You're right. I'll meditate on that."

"You can go now."

With my last scraps of energy, I shuffle down the hallway to my room. When I get there I find Violet and Buck sitting cross-legged next to each other on Violet's bed. They look up at me anxiously.

"Nice hair," I say to Buck, who sports a freshly shaved head.

"I feel like a new man."

I shut the door behind me. There are no locks on the doors here. There are no carpets on the hardwood floors. If you stand outside a door you can hear every word said inside. It can make you crazy. But if it doesn't, you get used to it.

Buck holds Violet's delicate, pale hand in her square, calloused one. This is a new development. Not terribly shocking, but new. I lie down on the bed facing away from them.

"We got rid of him for you."

"He'll come back."

"What's going on? What happened today, Bebes?"

"You found out more than I did. What did I think, I was going to catch Jake and have some big reunion scene? I'm so sorry cry cry. I love you cry cry. I'm having your baby cry

cry. Like it's my fault. It's not. Like I can stop him from going crazy again. I can't. I know that. I read. I'm not stupid."

I roll onto my back and gaze up at a hairy spider on the ceiling, wondering if it is poisonous. If the spider turns right, I tell myself, Jake will get out and everything will be okay and we'll be happy. The spider stays frozen there for a minute and then decidedly turns left and runs along the seam between the ceiling and the wall. It's childish anyway, how I'm still looking for signs. From who? Signs from who?

I look over at Vi's handmade Buddhist placard. *Help is not on the way.*

Vi says, "Are you, like, using a metaphor I don't understand right now?"

"Nope. Not a metaphorical baby. A real baby. Help is not on the way."

Buck startles me, leaping up from the bed and putting an arm up as if in victory.

"Yes!" she says and runs over to where I'm lying on my bed. She grabs my whole skull in her hands and plants a big kiss on my forehead. Then she leaps back across the room, topples Violet, and sticks her tongue in her ear, making her squeal.

Violet rights herself. "Stop it, Buck. It's not funny. What are you going to do, Bebes?" she asks, twirling a black snake of hair around her finger and blinking her wide brown eyes with lashes so long they look like zebra eyes.

Buck sits up and gets serious, with her legs wide apart and her elbows on her knees. "I'm not trying to be funny.

Help is right here. We're havin' a baby. If it's a boy, will you name it after me?

"Listen here," she continues, laying on the Alabama accent, which waxes and wanes and is definitely waxing. "Me and Vi, we're meaning to tell you that I'm coming with you guys to San Francisco. My parole conditions are nearly complete. I've got less than a week. And if that nutter can pull it together, bring him, too, and if he can't, hell, I'll be your baby's daddy. We're gonna blow this town. We're gonna start over."

"This has always been the plan, Bebes."

"Start over," I repeat. I look for the spider, but it's gone.

San Francisco. It was where we were supposed to go. I don't know how we wound up here. Aaron promised me San Francisco. Fog that rolls over the hills like cappuccino foam. Little pink and white and blue houses. Silver towers that sparkle in the sunlight like Oz.

"But I can't go now. What am I going to do about Jesus? I'm not leaving him."

"Only Jesus can get Jesus out of that place," says Buck. "It's not up to you."

Violet says, "I suppose you should at least go down there tomorrow and see what the damage is."

I have no doubt the damage is significant. No one does damage with quite Jake's flair. When I first met him in detox the scar on his face was still an angry gash crisscrossed with stiff black stitches. I was sweating as the dispensary nurse slowly decreased my Dilaudid, but not slowly enough, because I gripped the phone between my two bandaged hands and called Billy Coyote from the pay phone and wept and begged him please please come visit. Please please smuggle me some pills, some anything.

Billy said, "Of course. Of course, Baby. Don't I always take care of you? It's me you come to. It's always me."

He never showed. And that night my eyes just leaked tears, didn't stop for anything, and I woke crying in the pale predawn and wondered if I could somehow shred the sheets to hang myself. Wondered where I could hang myself from even if I got the sheets shredded. I wanted to gnaw my wrists open with my own teeth. If I could break apart a ballpoint pen in such a way that I could sever my jugular vein with the jagged plastic.

I went to the group room and there was Jake, awake and watching *Jesus Christ Superstar*.

Every spare moment, he watched *Jesus Christ Superstar*. I thought it was so funny how he was completely obsessed with that movie, with its groovy, multiracial, seventies cast dancing against a background of white sand, their hair blowing wild in the desert wind. Unable to sleep, covered in the cold sweat of a nasty detox, I stayed up all night with him that night, watching the bare-chested and bell-bottomed apostles look on as a wide-faced Mary Magdalene anointed a movie star Jesus.

Since he still claimed he was Jesus then, I asked him, "Doesn't it bug you to watch that? Isn't it like being a gangster and watching *The Godfather* or something? It must get on your nerves that they're getting it wrong."

"No, no. They're getting it right. There's so much music and golden light. My hands hurt; they're throbbing and cold and hot."

My hands. It was my hands that felt that way.

"Somewhere not so far is an ocean you can't hear yet," he said. And then he held me as I wept and the sunrise shot the dingy room through with clean, rosy light.

A few days later, he wavered about being God, and in a week more he said he had just been crazy. Anyway, it was the worst morning of my life and I lived through it with Jake and a bunch of bell-bottom-clad hippies singing in the desert. As we stumbled through the next few weeks, he tried to teach me to play chess in between group therapy and grief counseling. By the time we each graduated to Serenity, I wouldn't allow that I loved him. It was far too soon for that. But I knew he'd saved me nonetheless.

So maybe I can't save him back, but I can't just leave him, either.

I go to the bathroom to give Buck and Violet a chance to say good night. I wash my face twice and mechanically brush my teeth. I open my toiletry bag, eye the amber bottles of my meds, and then zip it shut again without taking my evening dose. Because when you're going to have a baby you stop taking truckloads of psychotropic medications designed to balance your tilted brain chemicals. Pills are bad for babies. Pills are bad for babies, but then what happens to moms?

Eighteen

I wake up and Violet is still sleeping, breathing softly with her covers pulled up nearly to her eyes. My breasts seem to be growing exponentially bigger by the day. I lie in bed and push my fingertips into the sides of them to test the soreness. Waves of ache shoot through me. I sit up slowly, expecting nausea, expecting something. But there's nothing. I'm waiting for symptoms, becoming hyperaware of every subtle itch and twitch and shift in my body.

I get out of bed with a renewed sense of purpose. At least Jake isn't at Camp Pendleton like he wanted to be. Though I do feel sad for him when I think of him striding into that office expecting his life to change, expecting a dramatic splash of transformation, and what he got instead was slapped into another hospital. He must have felt so betrayed.

I'm rolling the dice by missing another morning at school. I'll have to attend two nights next week to make up the hours for missing yesterday afternoon and this morning, which means twelve-hour days. Miss any more than this and they may penalize me by pushing my graduation back a month. I can't let that happen. I don't think I have another month in me at that place. I am only living through it right now because the finish line is so close.

Be a can-do guy. Eyes on the prize, Bebe. Eyes on the prize, sweetheart.

Like Rick used to say. And maybe Rick was a scumbag, but he managed to be successful selling hot tubs in Toledo. You can learn a thing or two from scumbags about getting what you want.

I get all brisk and directed. I take a shower, put on a somber sweater, and tie my hair back in a ponytail. I try to imagine that I'm someone a doctor might take seriously, someone to be trusted, someone who'll be allowed to visit the patient. I'm a can-do guy. Eyes on the prize.

I creep into the room Buck shares with Missy and wake her. She always sleeps with her boots by the side of the bed for an emergency or an earthquake or just out of habit in case she has to run. She reminds me of Jake this way, who takes it a step further and often doesn't take his boots off at all. The house around us starts to stir. Someone showers on the other side of the wall. I shake Buck and drag her silently back to my room and we both wake Violet for a conference.

"I need you to call the hospital and say you're Susan Schmidt. Tell them that his sister is coming over and that he should be permitted to see me."

"There's some kind of number," Violet says sleepily.

"What do you mean?"

"There's a number that she uses to identify herself. I've heard her call before. It's, like, her license number or something. It's on the pad by her computer. You need that."

"And this is why you want a felon as your friend. Who's your daddy now? I'll get into that office and Vi will make the phone call. How long do you think it'll take you to get over there?"

"VA hospital is, like, in Westwood. Crosstown rush hour. I don't know. An hour? Six hours?"

Buck makes a salute. "Done. We got your back here, soldier."

I pack my school uniform into the same bag Buck packed for me yesterday, then walk out of the house and down the three blocks to where my car is parked. I slide into the driver's seat and throw my bag on the floor of the passenger side because I don't want to smush Kitty Hawk Barbie, who is still in a seated position riding shotgun but has toppled so that one of her wings bends dangerously underneath her. I sit her up straight and point us west.

I pass through Westwood's tall corridor of doorman buildings to where it opens onto a stretch of wide, clear sky. The blue canopy hangs over a military cemetery—a bright green field with rows and rows of white tombstones and plenty of room for more. Flags flutter from the lampposts. Past the cemetery, a sign says *National Veterans Park*.

I drive through the gates. The VA looks like a huge college campus. I pass dormlike, Spanish-style buildings and a church with peeling white paint that appears to be abandoned. There's a wall painted with a mural of soldiers and helicopters and cryptic seals with acronyms on them: POW/MIA, SAR, AWG.

CD, MDD, ADD, PTSD.

On the other side of the wall I see what must be the hospital. It looks like a white square pushed up against another white square stacked on top of another white square and a white square with a door in it shoved on the front. I park on a wide expanse of asphalt parking lot, put Milla's Kitty Hawk in my purse for luck, and mechanically walk toward the entrance, trusting that Buck stole the license number from Susan's office and everything will go smoothly.

Stenciled on the tinted glass of the tall doors in white letters it reads:

THE PRICE OF FREEDOM IS VISIBLE HERE.

Jesus is in the letter V. Jesus is in the door hinge. Jesus is in the right foot, left foot.

On the wall of the entry hallway is a framed picture of our bloodthirsty esteemed leader. The hall leads into a small lobby with an empty reception desk, some seventies sofas, and a bunch of blown-up vintage soldier pictures on the walls. There are military seals all over the place and it looks official except there's no one around. A sharply dressed old black couple follows me through the door. The man looks like Cab Calloway, in a tan linen sports jacket with an ascot and a fedora. His wife is twice his size and wears a snazzy patterned dress and shoes with purple suede flowers on them. We stand in the middle of the lobby together, looking around, before they finally walk over to the desk where no one's sitting.

An elaborately cornrowed woman wearing a starched white uniform shirt walks out from a door behind the desk and sits down. The couple ask after a patient and are directed to a floor and a room. They walk away slowly toward the elevator, holding hands as if they have been walking together forever.

As I take their place it hits me. My oatmeal comes up hot from my stomach and pushes at the back of my throat. My head swims so badly I want to lie down and put my skull to the cool floor. I summon all my will and stare the woman right in the computer while I ask for Jake. Something she sees on her screen makes her ask for my ID. She festers and looks at my license and talks on the fucking phone and I want to grab it out of her hand and split her face open with it. I really do.

When she finally points me in a direction I barely hear what she says and head instead toward the bathroom, where I only miss the bowl a little. I sit there on the tile floor wiping up the puke with wads and wads of thin toilet paper and hoping that the nausea will pass and I'll be able to stand again. My body betrays me, the bones in my legs dissolving, my brain shaking loose of its moorings.

It's a good fifteen minutes before I can stand up. I wash my mouth out in the sink, dab my forehead with some wet paper towel, and look at my bloodshot eyes and no-longer-neat hair in the mirror. I am really pregnant like you read about, like you hear about. This is the thing that happens to other people. Happens to real people, not to me. But here it is.

When I venture back into the hospital world, I've forgotten the directions. A few stray souls wander around, but it feels cavernous and empty and without logic. I find a map and discern that I have to find the third floor of the West Wing to reach In-Patient Psychiatric. I get lost a million times doubling back past oncology and radiology. I wonder where the other people walking by are going: the old Korean guy; the chubby highlighted blonde with the big, flat ass and the baby in a sling; the old codger with his age-spotted hands and his shirt tucked in and his blue VFW baseball cap on.

At the end of a hall, finally, I find a nurses' station behind thick, smudgy glass with one of those metal circle grates to talk through that never seem to work. A blue, metal cage surrounds the station on the inside. A sign above the door says *High-Risk Elopement Area*. I've found it. Paper butterflies and flowers decorate the walls. It's nearly Easter.

The Asian, pink-scrub-wearing nurse with plates of hair frozen in hair-sprayed layers seems annoyed with me before I even say a word.

"Hello, ma'am. How are you?"

She nods and looks at me.

"I'm here to visit my brother, Jake Hill. I believe his doctor called ahead of me."

"What?"

I repeat myself.

"Who?"

I repeat myself.

"Who?"

I pass my ID through and there's a bunch of clucking and shuffling and conferencing with other nurses and yet more typing and typing and a phone call made while looking suspiciously over a shoulder at me. At any point on this chain someone could just say no and that would be it. The possibility that I won't be allowed to see him flutters right behind my heart. I clasp my hands together in front of me to steady them from shaking.

When she comes back, I put my ear to the grate to try to hear what she says. I think she instructs me to go through the door to my left. There's a loud buzz. I push and the door opens so that I am in a corral, with another locked door in front of me. When the first door clicks shut behind me, the next door buzzes open and I walk through. I know how it works. I have been on a lockdown ward myself. Me and Jake, together again behind locked doors.

A different nurse greets me on the other side and this one is friendlier. She's a blonde who looks like a grown-up Marcia Brady with adult acne.

"Hi," she says, real cheery. "Your brother is with the doctor right now. You can wait in the group room for a minute if you'd like. Holler for the orderly if anyone bothers you." She indicates a sturdy man hovering around the perimeter of the room. "But they won't."

She holds her arm out, indicating a common area with a few chairs and couches, a TV as the centerpiece, and a couple of tables around the sides.

About six men are scattered around, not counting the guy in the corner, who is so immobile and pale that he's almost invisible. I don't even notice him at first; I think he's a piece of furniture. I find a chair as far from anyone as possible and sit down, crossing my legs and waiting with my hands in my lap. I look at the TV and try not to look back at the patients staring at me. I stare ahead at Dr. Phil. There's a married couple on the show. They're unhappy. Something about sex. The man thinks that paying his wife for sex seems like a good incentive. Dr. Phil will fix it in the allotted time, I'm sure. He'll fix it or it wouldn't be a show.

I can't help it; I look around and wonder about people's odds.

What are the odds for the guy who looks maybe Jewish, yeah, whatever, I know, but some people do look Jewish, and kind of handsome and who's wearing a tracksuit and has an older lady visiting with him who looks like she's recently been attacked by a vampire? He looks kind of like an accountant or something except the pockets of his jacket are overflowing with crap: pieces of wadded-up paper and eyeglasses and bandannas and cigarettes.

Watching TV with me is an older black man with nearly white hair. He wears a neat flannel shirt buttoned up to the top, a pair of khaki pants worn shiny at the knees, and those old-man, brown leather shuffle slippers. He's not in hospital jammies or anything and he looks normal, except he leans forward in his seat so far that I am sure he is going to get up any second, but he doesn't. The man hovers on the edge of movement, but doesn't move. He stares at the screen.

A sloppy, angry-looking, fat white guy with a few strands of greasy hair sits in a wheelchair, working with his hand on what looks like an endless puzzle. He bursts out in profanity uncontrollably every few minutes. When he shouts, "Nigger-loving fuck cock," I can't help but study the expression on the black guy's face, but there's nothing. No wince. He doesn't even notice; he's that far away. Or he's just used to it.

I stare at the faces on the screen, so self-satisfied and sincere, but I listen instead to the accountant and his mom. I don't want to make eye contact, but I steal a sideways glance at them. The puzzle assembler has a weird clucking in his throat that reminds me of Missy. Every few minutes or so he spits on the floor next to him.

I wait forever, like I could hear a clock ticking if clocks still ticked. Dr. Phil is wrapping it up, everything all better of course, by the time a young doctor with gold-rimmed glasses walks up to me. He has a big baby face, pudgy and red with all his features scrunched up in the middle. He carries some files under one arm and I can see he's already thinking about the next thing he is going to do. The embroidered name on his smock pocket is Dr. Walker. He wears the same smock I wear in beauty school. It seems unfair to him, with all that school.

I stand and shake his hand and then we sit down, each facing each other.

"Your brother Jacob is suffering a recurrence of his schizophrenic symptoms, which is disappointing but not unusual. In his case we assume that there were a number of acute stressors that precipitated this recurrence. We also suspect he stopped taking his medication a few weeks ago. Does this seem correct to you?"

I think back. When did it start getting really bad? It's hard to believe it's something as simple as a pill.

"It's hard to say. I don't know exactly when it started getting worse. It's hard to tell just what's his normal self. There's always a little bit of crazy."

"Excuse me?"

"Like, he hears voices sometimes. Even when he's well."

"Then I wouldn't say he's well. I'd say his symptoms are controlled to a degree that he's able to function in a limited way. I'm afraid that may be the best we can hope for in your brother's case. I think it's important to understand that you can't put too much pressure on him by carrying expectations that he'll live independently or hold a job that isn't extremely undemanding. I was able to locate his records. It's my understanding that he resides in a halfway house, is that right?"

"Serenity."

"That's very good. I would say we could strive to stabilize him to the point that he can gain that degree of independence again."

"How is he now?"

"Symptomatically, your brother is suffering from auditory hallucinations, inappropriate or magnified emotional responses, and paranoid delusions. Initially he was in seclusion because he was refusing meds but he's being more cooperative now and we have him on his former dose of risperidone."

"He hates them. His meds."

The accountant slaps his own thighs and jumps back from the table.

"That, unfortunately, is also quite common. It would be tremendously helpful if his community of support, most important his family, continued to encourage him to be consistent with his medication. Otherwise he has little hope of functioning in the world."

"Is it genetic?"

"How do you mean?"

"The schizophrenia."

"Ass-licker," says the puzzle guy.

"Well, there's possibly a genetic component to it. It doesn't indicate on his chart that schizophrenia was evident in either of your parents."

"I don't mean his parents. Our parents. I mean a baby. If Jake had a baby, would the baby be sick, too?"

The doctor seems a bit taken aback. As if this is not his favorite question. He says, "Some people say there is a thirteen to fifteen percent chance of the offspring developing schizophrenia, but that is by no means set in stone. Schizophrenia is a brain disease, but there's a lot about it we don't understand."

This baby has a chance at being okay. It's all any of us has, really.

"I've started him on a course of his normal medication in conjunction with something to calm him down and something to help him sleep and we have him on constant watch for the next two days. At that point, and then again at two weeks, we reevaluate. It's hard for supportive families to hear this, but what matters is his response to the medication. Period. If he was one of the percentage of people who were going to recover completely from this disease, statistically, he would have done so already."

Something smells too sweet, like rot, and I try not to breathe through my nose.

With this the doctor gets up. He's been conscientious and patient and now he's moving on. "I'll let you see your brother briefly now. Please keep your visit short. It'll be better if he doesn't get overexcited."

"Thank you, Doctor," I say to his square, white back as he strides off.

I turn in my chair, watch the entrance of the hallway where the doctor appeared, and wait for Jake. I feel like I'm going to puke again but it's not uncontrollable this time, just vague and hovering.

I know it's contrary to what the doctor says, but I can't

stop thinking that if I can just reach the Jake that I know is always there, always whole, always sane—if I can speak to that part of him I can tell him to come back.

Jake rounds the corner and he looks wrong. He's not wearing any hat, which he normally always does, and his hair sticks up in little tufts. He wears a T-shirt and thin hospital pajama pants and he looks spotless white clean, like I've never seen him. There are usually smears of grease and paint and grass stains, the colors of his messy life, all over him.

He stands with bare feet and looks at me from across the room as if he isn't sure who I am. I get up and decisively go to hug him. He kind of hugs back, but the hug is limp and uncoordinated. The electricity I feel off his skin is strange and staticky, like it's discharging some internal lightning. I take him by the arm just above his wrist and lead him to the sage green sofa.

We sit facing each other silently for a moment and although his arms hang oddly at his sides as if he feels dead in the body, I see immediately that he is alive, on fire, in the eyes. A torrent of rage swirls behind them. He looks like he's listening to something but it isn't the puzzle guy and it isn't the TV; it's something else. He's looking at me but looking past me. He's listening to something I can't hear. I take both of his hands between both of mine, how he always does with me. I'm hoping for the magic words.

"Are you okay in here?"

"This is a church. This is my house."

"Are you okay?"

"You come so far and this is what you ask? Okay means nothing. I am the reincarnation of the Son and I see what the others can't see or they wouldn't have let you pass. I see that you have the eye. My wife and the living embodiment of the mother-father continuum. It's the woman that is the body. The man, the man, the man is never the shifting sands of the time woman body. The man is the spear, is the rock."

Jake looks me right between the eyes.

"The eye of the angel. It glows, but it's crossed. Uncross it and it will glow with the light of a thousand suns from the center of your forehead. You are most welcome here."

His posture is emphatic, his body totally still except for the twitch by his left eye that is more pronounced than usual. I try to remember if when I met him it was this bad. At the treatment center he told me he was Jesus and said that I was his wife. His mother and his wife. I thought it was the drugs. All those intravenous psychedelics he did. Now I see that I didn't understand at all. I feel like the world's biggest fool.

"Jake, I love you." Those worn words, an embarrassment. They're the best I can come up with. Somewhere in me they're true. And somewhere else they're not true at all.

"I am the reincarnation of Jesus Christ of Nazareth. I am reborn forty times. Forty camels and forty cars and forty machines. I am the first living soul. I am born again and working toward your second redemption. This is the house of God but they don't know it. This my house; I am here," he says, looking around to make sure no one is listening. He speaks in a whisper, leaning in so close to me that I can smell his breath like chemicals, like poisons, rising out of him.

"They are gods, too, but they are empty gods. They are empty pretenders attempting to control me through electronic and chemical means. This morning already they implanted seventeen thoughts into my brain. This is an institution known for its brainwashing, but I have no wish to be a zombie. Even if it means admission into the zombie life with its many rewards. Still, they are empty rewards granted by empty gods. I have no interest, do you understand? I will not be made their zombie slave. I will die first and all the world, including the empty god and their machines, will die with me. They will not believe that I only keep them alive by not looking behind me and to the left, where death sits."

He begins to get angry and little flicks of spit spray onto my face.

"Can you try to come back?" I stare hard into his eyes, trying to will him into a second of clarity. I press my hands into his and I beg him. I get it now. I get it. But even so, there's the possibility of a miracle, right? Althea says that enlightenment can happen in a single moment.

I was never one for telling him I loved him. He would say it and I would say things like, "That's sweet." I said, "I love hanging out with you." I said, "You're funny." But I never said, "I love you," because I thought it was bad luck. A bad omen. That's how much I understand about omens.

"I know you are not a clone against me. I know that you are my wife but you also have seven other names of which

I only know three and some of them are empty. And I look at you and see that you are here under an empty and false name. You have showed me a false birth certificate and I have been true with you because mine says Jesus Christ and I am compelled to tell truth and live truth from now until I judge. And I tell you that you are a house. Every man is a house. Some move clockwise and some move counterclockwise and some are ranches and some are crumbling and some are palaces on fire and some are bare to the pegs."

The puzzle guy interjects, "Fucking cocksucker."

"Jake, you have to take your meds and try. You have to get better and come home, okay?"

Jake rears up out of his physical frozenness. "Do not ride the horse of the empty gods and come to me with their instructional manuals. I have respect for the empty gods in spite of their attempts to brainwash me and I have respect for the devil himself in his place but not for you. Not for you. I pity you because you were misguided by the deeds of a false father who was not the fault of your twenty and six rebirths but who did hurt you nonetheless and I have nothing if I have not compassion."

He grabs me so hard by the neck that I know it will bruise and he starts shrieking, his voice crackling with crazy. "You now look to a false god and for that you are at fault. Pull your veil. Uncross your fire eye, mother of God."

The nurse is on his way running across the room but not fast enough. Jake winds up with his right arm and with the knobby backside of his hand he belts me so hard across the face that he knocks me off the sofa to my knees. The impact disorients me and the thud of it echoes through my bones. I kneel there with my hand to my face and my eyes closed. I don't watch them restrain him and drag him back down the hallway where he came from. I open my eyes again when his shouting grows dim.

I look around after a moment and, except for the statue in the wheelchair, all the other patients are staring at me with their mouths slack. The puzzle guy laughs. The accountant extracts a pair of glasses from his pocket and a bunch of change clinks dully to the linoleum, as well as a few Q-tips and some wads of paper. The rest of them look at me and I look back.

Marcia Brady squats down next to me and puts her hand on my shoulder. She moves my hand away from my face and looks at where he slapped me.

"Looks like he gave you a good whack. Probably have a bruise tomorrow but I think you'll be all right," she says, helping me to my feet. "He's a wild one. Needs a while to settle down. Try coming back in a week or so when his medication has a chance to balance him out a bit."

I walk past the old black man and then I stop and go back. I stand in front of his view of the TV and after a minute he looks up at me with a tilt of his eyes so slight it is almost imperceptible.

"Here," I say. I take Milla's Kitty Hawk out of my purse and remove her little wings, which are torn and crumpled by now anyway. I guide his dry hand and wrap it around the plastic doll, holding it there until he takes the cue and grips it himself.

They buzz me out the first door and I am stuck in the dingy, off-white box between the doors for a heartbeat before the second one buzzes and I move through it and into the hallway, where I am free to go.

Rhythmic throbbing in my head from where Jake slapped me replaces all thought. I take a step with every two throbs. Every step gets me closer to the car. There is nothing more to it than that. I swallowed a tennis ball and it is stuck in my throat. Something tugs at my stomach from behind.

When I reach the car, I change into my school uniform. The clock reads 11:11. Time still to make it back to school so that I can clock in after lunch.

Jesus is glaring off my windshield. Jesus is in the crumbs on my seat. Jesus is in the edges of my teeth.

Nineteen

I584 hours down. 16 hours left to go.

It's been a week and my bruise has faded to a purple-edged army green.

I sit rolling wet set number one hundred and ninety-seven of the two hundred that are required. Three more wet sets left to go. Two more heads of finger waves. One set of acrylic tips. I'm nearly there. Eyes on the prize, Bebe.

A tiara sparkling in the flicker of the fluorescents perches on the edge of my station. I plan to wear it to graduation tomorrow. Javier and Violet each have slightly different ones. Javi bought them for us downtown. Mine has a heart at its peak, with a giant rhinestone shaped like a teardrop hanging at the center of it.

"Girl, you haven't cracked so much as a smile in an entire week. This is *no bueno* for the *bambina*. You can't give her only sad food to eat. So what her papa's loco? So raise her with your nice lezzy friends. Little Bebe Jr. can have three mommies. Come on, now."

"When did you turn into my Mexican grandmother?"

"I am Guatemalan, honey, not Mexican. The rest of this continent isn't just all one country."

"Thank you for the geography lesson."

But he's right. This flat fog is no good for the baby or for me or for anyone but I can't shake it. Someone has kicked out the prop that was holding me up and now I can't straighten my spine. I'm sure it has something to do with the fact I stopped my medication and something to do with this incessant nausea and more to do with my life. There's a blanket over my head all the time, one of those army blankets. I can smell it like moldy wool. Everything looks distorted like clouds blowing through my eyes. And my hands. My wrecked hands weigh a hundred pounds each, my scars itchy and stiff. I'm catatonic and slack jawed and lost. I'm nearly at this graduation I worked all year for and I should be feeling celebratory. And here I am with shit all complicated as usual.

I thought about getting rid of it the day after Jake belted me. I called and made the appointment for the consultation, but when the time came I pulled right up next to a parking spot right in front of the clinic, and I couldn't back into it. It wasn't even a decision. I kept the car in drive and pushed my foot down on the accelerator and moved forward. I even went around the block again, but I didn't try it a third time. I'm not sure if it was some weird guilt that stopped me or if it was the fact that I've had it with losing everything I've ever had.

I roll Kitty's wet, limp hair methodically but sloppily. It'll be a shitty hairdo, but they'll give me the point. I only need three more points. One roller behind the other. One foot in front of the other. I want a cigarette. I want a vodka martini.

Jesus is in this pin curl. Jesus is sparkling out of Vera's navel ring. Jesus is in my latte.

I don't know why I play this Jesus game. It meant something maybe a long time ago. I can't remember.

Javier styles his doll head with a look of intense concentration on his face that's not brow-furrowed and strained but rather is remarkably calm and almost beatific. He's been working on this hairdo since yesterday. As for Kitty, her hair is now an even brighter shade of candy-apple red than usual. He did the same color on my head. It was meant to cheer me up.

I haven't tried to get in touch with Jake. I think I won't for a while. Some things are hard to go back to.

Javier takes the tiara off the end of his station and places it as a final touch on Kitty's head, then turns her in my direction and presents her to me with a *Price Is Right* gesture. "This is my vision for you, darling. This is how I see you tomorrow. We'll spend our final hours here making each other fabulous for our momentous occasion. Paul is home baking his famous cupcakes right now. And my sister is bringing a blender for the margaritas, though yours will have to be a virgin, I'm afraid."

The hair is beautiful. With the tiara on, I'll look like a Miss America 1962, except less slim, less graceful, less pretty.

Violet is working on her look for tomorrow, which is sadly a bit off the mark. Her doll head has festive green streaks, but the updo looks like something a girl from back in Toledo would wear to the prom: a big bubble with sausage curls hanging from it like streamers.

I wander back to my locker to pull out some extra rollers and the phone buzzes in my pocket.

DON'T ANSWER.

But I do. I do answer.

"Baby! You picked up."

I get a feeling of crazy relief hearing his voice, as if I found something I lost. But I don't let on.

"Apparently."

"I miss you, Baby. We have so much to talk about."

"Like?"

Billy gives me some whole line of shit about apologies to be made and explanations and responsibility and not having any future until we straighten out our past. And I don't know why I agree to go to dinner with him other than the fact that I want to keep hearing his voice.

How we got to L.A. was the bus stopped here and Billy got off and without him there was nowhere left to go.

After a few weeks sleeping head to head on their manager's sectional, the manager got sick of us and helped to find us a little place—a dark studio with its own entrance around the back of his neighbor's house right in the center of Hollywood. At that time the band was still hoping that Billy would pull it together and we would be back on the road. Aaron would have a gig again and I could quit work at the Jet Strip and we'd be moving fast to somewhere new.

Our little room was gray and tiny. Gray walls, gray carpets, gray Venetian blinds. It was so small that you could almost lie in bed and grab a beer from the minifridge without getting up. There wasn't much room for our stuff so we stacked our clothes in crates. There was a minuscule sink and a toy stove and sometimes I even cooked. Mostly frozen stuff like breaded frozen chicken cutlets, Tater Tots, and string beans, but Aaron never complained even though I know he didn't come from eating like that. His father had been a different kind of jazz musician than mine, the kind that teaches at Berklee and gets interviewed on NPR. Still, he ate the chicken I made and was careful about not making me ashamed and that seemed like reason enough to wait quietly for things to get better. We ate on the bed or on the floor and set out places like it was a picnic.

I wasn't unhappy in that waiting place, waiting for things to change. I danced four nights a week at the club and he practiced or composed or whatever during the day while I made myself invisible. I shrank into something tiny and translucent on the bed, reading and watching his back as he hunched over and played, sitting in one of those fifties kitchen chairs with chrome legs and a padded vinyl seat. It was the only other furniture in the room. He blew a few notes or strummed the guitar, then sighed and jotted things down in a notebook that rested on top of the minifridge. I could have just faded into the comforter and spent forever invisible in that room with him. If I had ever wanted more I'd forgotten about it.

We went out once in a while to shop or go to the movies. We went to parties at artists' lofts or downtown clubs. About once a week we started smoking crystal with this couple we met at one of the parties, who lived out in Thousand Oaks. We would drive home through the hills and park at the overlook along Mulholland at five in the morning, where we'd look out at the flickering lights studded across the broad plateau of land that rose and fell, rose and fell, like it was breathing. I remember thinking that we were a part of each other and part of the car and the road and part of the whole beautiful ugly city stretched out before us. Every light was like a cell in a big organism that was us, and we were it. And I understood that I was a part of something bigger than us and bigger than Zion or anyplace like it and maybe as big as music or something equally boundless.

But most nights that I didn't work we stayed home and Aaron got progressively more despondent about the band. We took more pills, drank more, smoked more dope to keep it all fuzzy and warm, but really I knew, I saw, he was sliding away from me. He lay on the bed, arms behind his head, flat gaze at the TV set. I curled sideways into him, resting my head in the curve of his neck and my hand on his belt buckle. I remember he laid his palm on my head for a heartbeat. I remember he turned his lips to my hair.

What we were waiting for was for Billy to get right, to get off the junk, to go straight. That or for Aaron to score another gig, but Aaron was so busted up about Billy letting him down that he wasn't going to any other auditions, so effectively what we were waiting for was for Billy and Billy alone to save us. Billy lived in a guesthouse as dark as ours on a heavily Russian street in West Hollywood. When we went to see him, thick ladies would stare us down as we crossed paths with them on the sidewalk. The air wasn't friendly.

Billy called with ideas. Come over right away and listen. He never went out. Half the time when we got there he'd forgotten why he called. He always invited me along as if it was an afterthought, but I knew it wasn't. I knew I was as much a part of the equation as Aaron was. For a while, when the phone rang and it was Billy, I thought it might be the news that they were going into the studio or that he was booking another tour. But that was never it. It was always some idea he had that he couldn't tell us until we came over. Or it was an invite to a swanky party, but we had to come over to his house first to get him. There was never any party but we went anyway because it was an unwritten rule of the universe that you showed up when Billy called.

The last time I saw Billy was at the funeral, but the second-to-last time was when we got the guitar. The guitar I still have now. We knocked on Billy's door and he answered in loose jeans and a green sweater with a hole worn in the chest that you could see a small circle of white skin through. His wild curls were matted nearly flat on one side. He let us in without a hello even, looking confused like he forgot he had even invited us over.

I know that Francesca stopped over and cleaned up for him once in a while, so it wasn't totally filthy, but it stank. The apartment smelled like a thousand dead cigarettes and some burning plastic mystery poison. It was a one-bedroom with a barely used kitchen off to the side that had an empty fridge with some cans of SpaghettiOs and Coke and a stick of butter from last year.

The rug was gorgeous, with a blue-green underwater different-color sheen depending on which side you looked at it from. The furniture was modern and looked like sculpture, copies of famous designers I'd never heard of. Aaron told me but I forget the names now. The futon on the floor in the bedroom was the only afterthought, but Billy said it was because he was into Zen simplicity. The painting on the wall was one block of a slowly shifting shade of gray, shot through with a yellow horizon line. Relics from a better time. Like I said. Billy was famous, or whatever that means if you're a jazz musician, but still. He was.

We sat on the couch without an invitation. He ambled over to the suitcase Fender Rhodes organ in the corner that he bought right out of a church in Tennessee one year when he rolled through there on tour. I watched as he played a scrap of something I didn't understand, humming over the top and shouting explanations of certain bars to Aaron—what would go where in the arrangement. His fingers were white and long and looked clean and soft, untouched by elements or dishwater or time, though Billy was at least forty. The music was a mess. Not that I really knew, but I suspected he might have been making it up as he went.

I looked up at the ceiling. Directly above me was a spider spinning a web. The spider hovered for a minute. If the spider went left, I thought, they would tour again soon and everything would be okay. The spider went right. I wished even then that I could stop looking for signs.

"I dig it, man," Aaron said when he was done. "When can the other guys hear it? When can we play it?"

"Soon, man, soon. I'm not ready. When I'm ready we play it. Now, run out and get us a bottle to celebrate, because I'm out. Leave your lady here to help me cook."

He was punishing Aaron for bullshitting him. He knew it wasn't any good. And there wasn't anything to celebrate. But another unwritten rule of the universe was that you gave Billy what he asked for. Aaron left grudgingly.

When he was gone, Billy moved over to the couch and opened a funny little swing-out drawer in the cherrywood end table and pulled out some blackened foil with a half-smoked glob of tar heroin sitting at the end of a charred trail in the center of it. I'm pretty sure he was shooting the dope when no one else was around. But socially he smoked it.

"Fucking California," he said, meaning the dope. It was better in New York.

He lit a lighter underneath it and took a long hit off it before offering it to me. Aaron and I were by no means full-blown junkies like Billy, but we were chipping pretty regular by then and we were well on our way. It was Billy who had turned us on in the first place. I took the straw, soggy wet with his spit, and pulled a hit of smoke through it, leaning back against the couch and holding it in my lungs for as long as I could. And there it was. The okay. I imagined the fixing, the healing, the profound experience of relief traveling through the walls of the capillaries in my lungs and being carried by my blood vessels to the very extremities of my body. Like the films they show you in health class that explain the respiratory system and the circulatory system. Breathe in oxygen, breathe out carbon dioxide. Except it was heroin. Breathe in heroin. I wouldn't ever breathe it out if I didn't have to. I would stay there, breath held, time stopped, in my bubble of okay.

"I need a lady," said Billy, dragging his gaze off the ceiling and onto me.

I breathed out, keeping my eyes trained on the light fixture. "You need to go out more to get a lady."

He sighed, real dramatic, and we sat there for a while, him looking at me and me pretending like I didn't notice. I loved Aaron desperate crazy but I still wanted to kiss Billy right then. I think it was because Billy had a way of making me feel needed, as opposed to my suspicion that I was eventually going to be expendable as far as Aaron was concerned. Of course, Billy didn't really need me, either. But it didn't cost him anything to pretend.

"You play anything?" he asked. I'm pretty sure he knew I didn't.

"No. My dad was a horn player. But I don't play. I wish."

"Right. Everyone says that. I wish I could play. What would you play?"

"I don't know. Maybe guitar. Nothing fancy. But just to be able to play a song."

"Pick it up," he said, pointing to the vintage Martin sitting on the unmade futon in the other room.

"No. I don't even want to touch that thing. I'll drop it or something."

"You'd only drop it on the bed. Come on. Pick it up."

I felt like I was doing something wrong when I sat down on the futon and put the guitar in my lap with my hand loosely around the neck like I was waiting for a request. I was flushed in the face and foggy from the drugs. Something about Billy made me red in the face and chest.

"Looks good on you," he said. Then he walked over and sat down behind me.

He put his left hand over mine and moved each of my fingers to an uncomfortable spot.

"Strum it."

I tentatively ran my thumb across the strings. It sounded awful.

"Press harder and try again."

I did. And there was a chord. The most perfect thing, a chord.

We sat there playing like that for a minute. Then he formed the chord shapes with his left hand and I strummed the strings with my right. He pressed his chest against my back and rested his face against my hair. It was so strange to lean into him. I never even touched his hand usually. We weren't cozy; he was more like that with Aaron. He smelled like little boy sweat, like he'd been running around outside in the cold, sweating under his big coat. But I knew he hadn't been outside in days.

He played "Dead Flowers" and he sang light into my ear and it was nothing really. Like standing with my back to the band during sound check and feeling the music close to me, but not close enough. I knew when we put the guitar down it would be like it had never happened. He was just making me uncomfortable because he could. And because Aaron and I were caught in his web. His grip grew tighter as his world got smaller. Billy had to burn down everything around him and rise from the ashes again and again. That's what kept things interesting for him. Stick around long enough, you knew you would wind up a casualty, too. But you stuck around anyway.

When the song ended he left me sitting on the bed with the guitar.

"Do you like yourself?" he asked.

"Ask another question."

Aaron came in then. Stood in the door with the paper bag in his arm. He had picked up some cereal and milk along with the scotch.

"Any luck with the SpaghettiOs?" he asked.

He didn't mind, really. It was only Billy. It was only a few chords. It was only me, after all, and I wasn't going anywhere.

There were no SpaghettiOs made, so I poured three bowls of Cheerios while he broke ice from the plastic molds in the freezer and poured two fingers of scotch into each of the heavy crystal glasses. Billy was married once. He still had the crystal.

He handed me the guitar as I walked out the door.

"To borrow. To learn on."

Only when Billy gave me the guitar did Aaron start to bristle. Once we were in the car, he said, "What the hell were you two talking about? Do you have any idea how much that guitar is worth?"

I still have the guitar. I still haven't learned a thing.

Part of me never wants to see Billy again and part of me knows that I see him every day in my head anyway. Every day I think of Aaron and I find that Billy is there, too, our strange little triangle. I pretend I'm fighting to live in the present but really I'm having an affair with the past every secret moment. Talking to Billy feels like the most delicious admission of guilt. I've been pretending to be with a crazy man when really I've been with you all along.

We agree to meet at eight at a local Indian restaurant. It's the night before graduation.

1592 hours down. 8 hours left to go.

Twenty

I shower back at the house and borrow a black dress from Chandra that is too small for my boobs, too fancy for Indian food, and too flimsy for the cold weather. I pull on a tight pair of fishnets. In dim light, when I wear fishnets, you can't see the scars on my legs unless you look close.

The bodice of the dress boosts my now quite spectacular tits into a perfectly sculptured rolling porno landscape. I am pitched sideways with a strange sadness and a new stirring of what I suspect is anger. Anger at this alien being in my body and anger at myself for the thousand obvious reasons. Everything looks blown clear by a cold wind. I am that kind of altered. As I dress I feel wildly reckless. Thoughts of Jake and the echo of his slap roll through me in unguarded moments. Fuck him, I think, looking in the mirror and teasing my hair into a sixties-style half updo resembling Javier's Sharon Tate doll. And fuck me. Fuck me while you're at it.

I apply about four gallons of liquid eyeliner and a bucket

of shiny pink lip gloss, while kneeling on the floor in front of the full-length mirror we have wedged up against the side of the dresser.

Violet lies on the bed behind me reading *Lithium for Medea.* She looks up when I stand and straighten myself out. She has already expressed her disapproval of my seeing Billy, but she's through with scolding me, I guess.

"Wow, Bebes. You look really pretty."

She's right. I do look pretty. I don't know what I'm expecting out of tonight—a confrontation, an apology maybe. Or maybe just to see the face of someone who knew Aaron like I did. But I do know one thing. I want to remember what it was like to be pretty.

Billy is seated at an outside table underneath the heating lamps. The gated patio is covered with low-slung vines and glowing lanterns, like a tiny paradise off a seedy stretch of Sunset and Normandie. I see him and my heel immediately catches on an irregularity in the pavement. I stumble and then try to smooth out my step, to smooth out my skirt. His hair is the same. He has the same profile. He sees me and stands.

For a moment I feel an intense relief flood me, as if I've suddenly been given back everything I lost. Then just as quickly I remember, no. No. Billy wasn't what was lost. But he was so close by, you could almost confuse the two in the low light, in the late, late winter.

"Baby."

"You can call me Bebe now."

"Didn't I?"

Billy kisses me on the cheek and holds me against him for a beat longer than is comfortable.

"You look beautiful."

He pulls out my chair for me.

"Yeah, well, you look exactly the same."

"But I'm not the same," he says, resuming his seat.

"So I read."

"Press is press. You know that. It's not the whole story. You should learn the whole story. That's why I called. But first, I'm starving."

As he says it, a shy-looking waitress appears and puts a Kingfisher beer down in front of him. There's a glimmer of impish mischief in his expression when he turns toward her and then a shadow of that drug addict sad damage when he turns the other way. His face has always been alive like that. He's one of those people who look like a totally different person in every photograph.

"Would you like a drink?" he asks. The waitress looks at me with her pen poised above her notebook. The colored lights strung across the patio give Billy's wild, white boy afro a red halo around the edges. I look at the beer.

"No, thank you, water is fine."

"Come back in a few minutes," says Billy.

"You said you were sober."

"I am sober. Six months now. This is just a beer."

"You can't be sober and have a beer."

"Yes, I can. I'm sober from all illegal narcotics. My problem is with drugs. Beer isn't my problem, so I can have all the beer I want."

"Okay, Billy. I'm gonna go now," I say.

"Wait, Bebe. Don't go. Please. I need to talk to you. You're not the only one who loved him, you know. If it makes you uncomfortable, I won't drink. Okay? Just sit down."

I surrender. I sit. I don't want to leave anyway.

"Good. Let's order," he says. "Shall we?"

Billy shifts gears and explains to me the difference between northern Indian food and southern Indian food. He tells me that he once went to India with an ex who was into Sai Baba.

"Long before I met you. When there were different times for all of us," he says.

Billy is a jazzman at heart but how he made himself a star is by collaborating with rock musicians and also by writing a song that was covered by a pop star in the early nineties. He gets me laughing with stories about Bono and some rap producer who doesn't have a stick of furniture in his house and a guitarist who eats nothing but enchiladas with ketchup. We're most of the way through dinner before I realize that he hasn't told me why he called and also that he's nearly made it through three beers.

"It's getting late," I say. "I have an important day tomorrow. I'm graduating."

"From cosmetology school?" He doesn't bother to hide the derision in his voice.

"It's a good gig. It's my ticket out of town."

"You and your tickets out of town," he says. "We haven't even talked yet. Okay, I'll tell you what. I have something I want to show you. I live right across the street here. Come over for a quick minute and then I'll let you go and I'll never bother you again. That or you can come to my show at the end of the week. Your choice."

I agree to go with him, not because I believe anymore that he has something to show me or even something to tell me, but because I can't bring myself to say good-bye.

He offers his arm as we cross the street. I take it just above the elbow, but don't lean on him. Billy is only a couple of inches shorter than me in my heels, which still makes him about six feet tall. Usually I tower over men when I wear heels.

He lives in an old, five-story brick building, which has somehow weathered the many earthquakes without crumbling.

"When did you move?" I ask.

"I moved when I quit dope. Got to change up the feng shui when you do that kind of thing, you know?"

We walk up three flights to a clean, one-bedroom apartment with a wall of exposed brick. Brick walls always remind me of Toledo. Strewn around are a few pieces of midcentury furniture and some expensive vintage music equipment. I don't see the old organ anywhere.

I follow him to the kitchen, where he immediately opens the fridge and grabs another beer. An urge to drink washes over me, as powerful as any I've felt since I quit. Some sharp-fingered demon hand reaches through my back just underneath my shoulder blades, grabs my heart, and squeezes. The only thing that will relieve the terrible pressure is a drink. I can smell the yeasty sweetness from across the table like it is the most natural thing in the world. Part of your sweat and your blood. Don't you need it like water to survive?

If I drank a beer it would be the final stone out from under my tenuous foothold and I would go sliding down the mountain. It would be the end of trying to hang on. My muscles ache from clinging to the last stone all day long every day. I'm sick of gripping so hard. I'd almost rather fall.

My head, my body, my soul demands a beer. And I'm not being dramatic here. Within the course of a minute, my logical faculties have reasoned it out. My deep nihilism has put in its vote. My exhaustion has echoed a resounding yes. I don't want to sit here sober and always apart from it all and aware of every little thing. How my nose is stuffed up and how the world is at war and how Billy laughs with a bitter edge and how the polar ice caps are melting and how it is hard to sit like a lady in my too-slutty dress and how Jake is locked in the VA hospital and how Aaron is nowhere at all and he never will be. Oh, yeah. And how I'm pregnant. And that, too.

I decide to ask for a beer. Better yet, to reach out and just grab Billy's and take a sip. It'll be cute. No one will care because no one will know. One beer. One beer won't hurt a baby. Maybe enough beers and I'll find the courage not to have this baby after all. Billy will grab another beer. I'll finish his, and then drink another and then another until I pass out and wake up here as if it's happened a million times before. I'll quietly take care of my little problem and then I'll slip seamlessly into his life. Be the drunk hairstylist girlfriend of a drunk legend. I'll move straight from Serenity House into this pad with the brick wall and the fancy guitars in the corner. I like his face, I think. I always liked his face.

Drink now, I tell myself. Just fuck it. But my body doesn't move. I will my arm toward the half-drunk bottle in his hand. Now. Now before it's all gone. But some neural connection is severed and my hand stays by my side. It even moves for a second to readjust my skirt, but it doesn't reach for a beer. Outside of my skin and in the air of the room, things are moving like they have been all night but on the inside, the soft dark of my brain goes still. And I can only think some supernatural force holds me back that's more powerful than all the will in me pushing me forward. At a different time I might have called it Jesus, believed that Jesus is here holding me.

Jesus is in the slick of my lip gloss. Jesus is in the bones of my wrist. Jesus is in the lines of my forehead.

Then my outsides and my insides sync up again and the sound clicks on and I'm back in the mix, but I don't reach for a drink. I want one but I'm not going to have one. The moment of reaching has passed.

"The reason I called you was that I wanted to play this

new song for you. I wrote it just after he died but I only finished it a few weeks ago."

The scenario is so familiar. He picks up an acoustic guitar from where it leans against the wall. I sit with my back against the opposite end of the couch and slip my shoes off, putting my feet on the cushion next to him.

He lays out some salty, smoky, whiskey soul magic, words slurred but chords impeccably precise. This drunken asshole. He has the songs in him that I've longed for all my life. That I haven't been close to touching since Aaron died. Aaron could play anything—trumpet, guitar, piano, percussion. When Aaron played, I used to wish I were him instead of me.

But I don't wish I were Billy right now. I can see the tragedy flames licking at his hems. I've learned to spot them by now. You might even call me an expert. And I can see clearly that Billy may have gotten away with murder for this long but he won't survive much longer. He'll be lucky if he lasts the year. There's already a road map of waste all over him.

He stops the song abruptly before it's over and he runs his hands over my shins. I pull my legs into my chest as if he burned me.

"Poor legs," he says. He looks like he's about to start crying. "Poor legs."

He leans in to kiss my legs and I hop off the couch.

"Stop it."

"You remember him all wrong. You always had it all

wrong about him. Guess what? It's not my fault. It's not yours, either."

He puts the guitar aside, stands, and reaches for my face. I don't say no when he kisses me. I never have been able to stick by a no with him. No one really can, so I don't feel too bad about it. He must have brushed his teeth a beer ago because spearmint chalkiness takes the edge off the alcohol taste of his mouth. But I can still taste the beer. I breathe it in and try to imagine I am growing drunk on his fumes. I could catch a buzz rubbing on his skin.

He's starting to sweat the beer out his pores and it smells sour but not yet sick. I know how it'll smell later. I know how it'll smell in the morning because it's one of the things I remember about my pop from just before he died. I remember how their bedroom used to smell in the morning after his night sweats. I feel like I'm cheating. I'm not sure on who.

"I can't do this. I have to go."

"I understand." He pulls away and slips his hands into his pockets, quickly contrite. "I'm sorry. This isn't why I called you. Come have a quick smoke with me on the roof before you leave."

I love rooftops. I love a view from anywhere. Any vantage point from which you can see further than the immediate ground in front of you.

I climb the three flights wearing the beat-up overcoat Billy has given me from the back of his door, the kind of coat you could wear in Ohio. Too many hours awake and I really want a cigarette and I can feel my life straight through to my bones. But even so, when the dark sky opens up over us, from just five floors up I could almost love L.A. My heart spills over the edge of the rooftop and streams out through the grid of the city and I feel how many big dreams are floating around out there. This town where the dreams are long, broad strokes and the execution is delegated in impossible details to a million grunts. The weight of the wealth in one small corner of L.A. should tip the scale so badly that the whole thing turns over and slides off into the Pacific. But still, from here I could almost love it. In front of me, the lit-up switchboard fades until it dissolves in the dense haze.

Billy walks unsteadily around to the side of the building that pretty much just faces the brick wall of the building next to it. On that wall is a fifteen-foot-long painting in shades of gray, as if it was a black-and-white photograph. A woman with long black hair and giant dark eyes floats with wings and a halo in front of a marshmallow cloud. She has no feet, only a long, white, flowing dress.

"Julio did that. He lives in the pad downstairs from mine. His lady died of an overdose last year and he painted that for her."

"It's cool," I say. "We should all have someone to paint us like that."

"When we die?"

"Whenever."

Billy reaches for me again and this time I see it coming and try to dodge him. I've imagined a thousand times Billy showing up at my door and putting his arms around me. And in my mind it felt like being rescued from how alone I was. It felt like such a relief. But on this rooftop with his beer breath and his foggy eyes it's not like coming home at all. Unless home is somewhere confused and pathetic. He grabs my arm as if to stop me from pulling away, then reconsiders and drops it.

"I was just a junkie," he says evenly.

"What?"

"You can be angry at me forever if you want but I was just a junkie. I wasn't your boyfriend. I wasn't the one who pimped you out to an airport strip club and then sat around getting high all day and hating you for it and fucking every other idiot he could get his hands on. He played a mean trick on you when he died, Baby. If he had lived you would have figured out quick that he wasn't perfect. He wasn't a saint. He wasn't even very nice to you, frankly."

"Is that what you wanted to tell me?"

"Yes."

"Great. You said I could never see you again or come to your show Friday, right? I choose never."

"I'm trying to save you from staying married to him. You loved him. He treated you lousy. He's dead. That's all. It doesn't help to be delusional about it."

I turn to leave. I look up one last time. Dark sky swirling with darker clouds lit with golden shorelines. I guess it is maybe a three-quarter moon tonight. Not as bright as a full moon.

He's wrong. The last stone gives way from under my

heel and I start to fall. It did help to be delusional about it. It helped me not to feel ashamed on top of everything. Don't go, I think. But it's me who's leaving. I wish I could rewind to the part where Billy was playing the song.

I drop his overcoat on the tar ground before I walk into the stairwell, down the five flights, and out to the street. I don't bother running. They never follow.

Twenty-one

I look at the dashboard clock and note that it's two A.M. I'm out way past curfew. I'm high from the rooftop adrenaline, rushing too fast, my brain clicking forward. If I don't get away with this curfew violation, if I can't lie my way out of it, if someone sees me come in this late, Susan might really terminate my contract. How could I be so stupid? What did I think I wanted anyway, seeing Billy again? What was I doing? I imagine I can still smell beer in my hair. And there it is again. My intestines seize and I want a drink with a desire akin to wanting a chair to sit in after a twelve-thousand-mile walk.

So how this works is, there are things you're supposed to do when you want a drink this bad. I have a list of people I'm meant to call if something like this happens. I'm supposed to breathe. And foremost, I'm supposed to pray. Now, I'm not opposed to praying. I do it when I'm meant to do it. You know, God grant me the serenity blah blah. I don't think there's anyone on the other end of the line but I figure maybe I'm the one on the other end of the line. That I'm the prayer and the prayee. And I need to hear that stuff. I need to hear it way more than the bullshit I make up on my own. So pray. Pray, you idiot. But I don't pray and I can only explain why by saying that for some reason I'd rather chew tacks. I'd rather gnaw off my own toe. I'm sick of the words and I'm sick of making shit up about God so I can say them and not feel like a total hypocrite. And I hate God for making it so hard. And I miss God. I miss him every day.

I drive and drive with nowhere to land. There is nowhere to go but Serenity, and I'm not prepared for that just yet. Now or an hour from now makes no difference. I'll get away with missing curfew or I won't.

I drive and drive and wonder where the people in the other cars are going. So many people out driving in the middle of the night. I drive and drive in circles on the looping ribbons of the freeways, remembering choices I made—a whole string of them that felt barely even like choices. Ending with this moment and this choice. It's real simple. You drink or you don't. Ending here and starting where? Starting with the drink my father gave me when I was five, somewhere at Grandpa Ralph's house with that stuffed wahoo fish on the wall. Starting when my pop married my mother. Starting when she didn't take me to the funeral. Starting with I miss my pop every day still. Every day.

No. My life as it is now started with the choice I made to leave Toledo with Aaron. I was born again when Pastor Dan lifted me out of that water and I was born yet again when Aaron walked through the door of Rusty's. And it shouldn't happen that way. It's not supposed to. Once is supposed to be enough. But I know that I was born the day I met him. I was convinced it was my destiny to follow him. God had sent me a ticket out of Toledo. Hit the road with a traveling jazzman and head west toward the coast. I wasn't even scared. I believed in signs, in road markers from the Holy Ghost. I was sure it was only the first of many.

I drive east down Sunset from where it turns Mexican to where it turns Chinese, then snake onto the side streets where it turns downtown—tall canyons of buildings and seedy streets lined with residential hotels and gated storefronts. And I pass by a legion of the forgotten. A night army of shuffling souls clad in rags. I know a corner near here with a doughnut shop that you can park at and some kid will pop up at your window with a mouthful of heroin balloons. You don't even have to get out of your car. Everybody is in such a rush, but come back ten years later and nothing has changed. They were in a big hurry to leave and come right back. Though I'm a block away, I still feel the black hole of it behind me. Pulling at me.

The last stop on the tour was L.A. We rolled through the country in a state of suspended grace with no real destination but California. We wouldn't stop in L.A., Aaron said. Never L.A. We'd get right on the train headed for San Francisco. San Francisco with fog-shrouded hills and music echoing through the streets.

I'm not making it up when I say I was happy right then. I wouldn't have traded my now for any kind of future. It was my only time. Sharing the motel rooms and lying around after shows on synthetic bedspreads, passing around the bottle and smoking rolled cigarettes while we talked aimlessly about music or home or our families or our fantasies or whatever. I washed our shirts and underwear out in the sink and hung them on shower rods and across the tops of the doors to dry. The whole band called me Baby instead of Bebe. It was a jazz thing. I was a part of something.

I drive past downtown to where the warehouses and the artful graffiti make me think of Jake, then over the bridges that cross the railroad tracks that make me think of leaving or make me think of Europe or somewhere I imagine there are pretty bridges.

Driving with Billy and the band, moments for Aaron and me alone were rare and precious. My thighs sliding under his long fingers. The creases where the pink of his palms bled into the caramel brown spanning the tops of his hands. I watched him touch me. Him next to me. How pale I looked.

We lay across the seats of the bus and smoked pot and he told me about how we were going to make a family of gypsies. How we were going to be famous and it was going to be life on the road but not in a crap bus like that one. In a beautiful bus that was just like the nicest hotel room you could ever imagine, but on wheels. He would play and I would sing and our little babies would be a caravan of prodigies. And when we went home, we'd go home to California in the sun, where our den walls would be plastered with gold records.

Half-dark bus lit milky blue with streetlights rolling by us, on a highway somewhere near Pittsburgh. Eagles on the radio singing *I'm already gone*. Wake up in the Indiana morning. Wichita. Omaha. Cedar Rapids, Iowa. Cow towns. Deep blue sky and road signs. Hangnails and dirty hair and Dorito dinners and walls of exhaustion.

When we drove through the night I slept holding tight to Aaron and tight to what was left of me, but I felt something new growing. A new possibility—hazy, so I couldn't quite picture it. Who I truly was inside, or at least who I was going to be. I believed that I would land in California and it would feel like home. I miss my Aaron so much that it hurts like I swallowed glass. All the time still.

I drive into East L.A.—the Mexican groceries and upholstery shops and churches and schools and the rows of small houses with illegal additions that back right up to the houses next door. Asphalt lit yellow by the streetlights. No one around anywhere, just cars. Red Dodge minivan, green grandma Chrysler, white piece-of-shit Toyota truck stacked with cardboard.

Some days during sound check I would walk around the front of the stage with my back to it, pretending like I was going somewhere. I moved as slow as possible and tried to feel it. How it is to have that wall of music behind you, traveling through you. You can get drunk on it, like how you can get drunk on a choir. I tried to imagine what Aaron felt or what my pop had felt up there, weaving in and out of the blanket of sound with their own. I could catch a handful of it, but it slipped through my fingers like water. Then I would turn and watch like every other dumb audience member and know that was all I'd ever be. At best I might be a muse and hope that it was enough.

I drive with the White Stripes blasting from my shitty, distorted radio. Her driving kick drum and the desperate warble of his voice. *A seven nation army couldn't hold me back.*

I was a stupid Toledo girl. I had no idea about the dope until it was there in front of me. I thought Billy was just drunk, crazy, depressed.

As a rule, Billy was the only one who got his own motel room. One night Aaron was in Billy's room talking band business, but he took way too long. I felt jealous and went to knock on the door in case it wasn't business and they were partying without me.

Billy said, "Who is it?"

"It's Bebe."

"Come on in, Baby."

I opened the door just wide enough to peek my head in.

Billy lay on top of the flowered bedspread on one of the double beds, real happy and sleepy with a devious half smile. Aaron was half sitting up on the other bed.

I want to call Mom but it's too late. I want to call her and not tell her anything's wrong but just hear her voice be happy that I called. I don't tell my mom the real things because they just hover in the two thousand miles of air between us and dissolve. They never reach her. But I think about how she used to sing me the song about the taxis, how she'd lie there with me until I was asleep every night. I don't remember a night without her when I was little. At least not after my pop died. She'd lie next to me and sometimes I'd feel her shake like she was crying without any noise. And that memory wars with the memory of the phone call I made to her when Aaron died. I wanted her to cry for me. Not just shake silently. I wanted her to cry. Because she lost my pop so young I wanted her to have some wisdom for me. A magic trick for how you live anyway. What she had was nothing.

"Oh, honey. Sometimes things are so terrible in life, but they get better. Sometimes they get terrible again but then they get better again. What doesn't kill us makes us stronger. I always say, when life hands you lemons . . . ," she'd said.

"Lemons?"

She didn't come to the funeral. No money for a plane ticket. No time off from work. I don't miss her. Hardly ever.

Billy wasn't wearing his usual sunglasses and his eyes were glassy and glittery. He patted the bed next to him, but I went and sat where Aaron was, instead. Billy looked so thin without his coat on, in just his T-shirt and his suit pants. His pants were hiked up by how he was lying, exposing his bony ankles and white feet lined with thick blue veins. I felt a pang of affection for him. How could you not half fall in love with Billy? He was so arrogant, so charmed, so lost. We followed him wherever he went. I missed him only sometimes before tonight. I don't think I will again.

I drive past Payless ShoeSource, DaVita Dialysis, 99¢ Only, Lavanderia, Chinese Food Bowl, Pizza We Deliver, Kragen Auto Parts. Something about the driving has sort of settled me, at least enough that I don't even want a drink anymore. I just want a fucking doughnut but there are none to be found. I just want to find the fucking freeway entrance, but I can't find that, either.

Aaron called Billy's hair a Jew-fro. Billy wore it long and wild like Noel Redding, the bass player for Jimi Hendrix. Aaron told me that Noel Redding hadn't even been a bass player, he was a guitar player, but he got the job because of his hair.

I drive over an overpass, a flimsy railing between the Honda and the air, a long-enough drop between the upper deck and the cars crossing beneath. One move—brain impulse to muscle twitch. One fat, courageous, impulsive move and I would cross that invisible, ever-present line. Sometimes I see the line out of the corner of my eye like a shadow, the line you could cross between Here and Not Here, Alive or Dead. But when I turn to look at it straight on, it disappears. If I turned not just my head to see it, but the steering wheel, too, I know I'd see that line clear as day. I'd see it clear when I crossed it.

A few small lines of coke were laid out on the fake maple nightstand next to the base of the fake brass lamp. Billy saw me spot it.

"Help yourself," he said, gesturing toward the drugs.

"Thanks," I said and leaned toward it, holding my hair back. But as I bent over, Aaron put his palm flat to my chest and stopped me.

"Careful," he said. "It's not coke. Do just a little, okay?"

"Okay," I said. And I did. Just a little that night.

I turn and head back because you can drive and drive but where is there to go really? I'm empty hungry, my whole body a ravenous void to feed. My mind is like a carnival ride gone wild off the rails. I still want liquor and pills. I want a warehouse stacked with heroin. I want an ocean liner full of cocaine. But there's the baby, and even if there wasn't the baby there are the shadows. I'm also fucking starving, so I turn toward where I know there's a Ralph's.

The air through the open window rushing wet on my face smells like rain from earlier in the evening, though I don't remember it raining. The pavement hisses as I drive and drive on the freeway with the late-night radio blaring.

The grocery store parking lot is nice late at night: dark gray and quiet, embossed with an Aztec hieroglyph of yellow lines. The only soul in sight is a nodding bum in a Santa cap. When I get closer, I see the bum is a handsome guy with a matted blond beard who was probably an actor five or ten or fifteen years ago when he came to L.A., like I came here, like everyone comes here. We must have the best-looking homeless population in the world. I'm glad he nods off as I pass by him, because he doesn't ask me for change.

Jesus is a Krispy Kreme Kit Kat caramel candy sugar coma. Jesus is a salt and vinegar potato chip ranch dressing heart attack.

I want anything to make me forget. I try to walk purposefully, but not too desperately, through the aisles. I maneuver around a couple of dazed-looking club kids. A pixie girl wearing a silver minidress and glittering silver makeup stares wide-eyed at the cereal. She's so delicate, so dainty, so pretty. She reminds me of how I left Milla's little Kitty behind. The girl's gay boyfriend stands behind her wearing rainbow platforms, turquoise hip-huggers, and a Starsky and Hutch orange leather jacket. They each have a gallon of Gatorade tucked in one arm and the boy carries a box of Lucky Charms. One sad old lady wearing weird eye makeup pushes a cart with some fish sticks in it. The floors glow green from the fluorescents.

I go back to the dairy case to look for the rice pudding, planning to open one and eat it right here in the store. I do this sometimes. But when I get there, I realize I don't have a spoon. How this works is you have to get the spoon first from up at the front.

The whipped cream cans are lined up like little soldiers. I grab a cold cylinder and aim to shoot the whipped cream straight into my mouth.

I don't know what happens, where the lapse is between thought and action, but I don't tilt the can the right way. The choice isn't a choice; it's pure momentum. I hold the can upright, push out all my breath, insert the plastic nozzle in my mouth, and suck the first spray of sweet sour limp liquid and then the slightly chemical-tasting nothing cold air. Suck and suck and let the poison fill me up and then hold it in my lungs until they ache. Perhaps the lamest relapse in all of addict history—sucking whipped cream cans at a Ralph's.

I am already reaching for another one as the sparkles close in. I can't feel my mouth and then I can't feel my body. I sink to the cold floor in front of the dairy case and, when I begin to come around, I see a red-aproned fat white man hurrying toward me. I gauge that I have time, grab for one more can, and suck the nitrous out of it as fast as I can.

Far away in my body, someone's hands drag me by under my arms. By the time we reach the door, I've regained consciousness. I scramble to my feet as he attempts to haul me out. He keeps stopping to huff and puff dramatically.

As I stand up, I hear him say, "Sorry, Manny. I'm going as fast as I can. She's a big un."

"Wait, please. I'm sorry," I say, straightening my dress, which is hiked up around my waist. I try to sound reasonable. "I have to pay for my merchandise. I just need to grab a couple more things first. Please."

I'm gone. Somewhere in that nondecision decision, I gave up. All this trying so hard to change and love and live. I wasn't trying hard enough and now I'm done trying at all. Fuck it. My eye is already on the liquor aisle.

Three red aprons line up, making a wall in front of me that blocks the door. An angry Asian guy points into the night, into the early parking lot morning.

"Please leave these premises immediately, ma'am."

"Please. Let me back in. I won't do it again. It was just a teeny mistake." I make the baby girl face with the pouty lips and the blink blink eyes. They are unamused. What are they so serious about? What the hell do they care if I suck some chemicals in their aisles?

It dawns on me that I can't buy liquor after two in the morning anyway. I wish I'd stolen a bottle of vodka. I wish I had shoved some food in my jacket first before I got myself thrown out of the store.

"Okay, okay," I say, totally logical. "Listen. I'll blow all three of you for a bottle of Absolut and a package of Snowballs right now. I'm serious."

This seems like a reasonable idea.

"I have your bottle of vodka right here," the Santa bum pipes in, grabbing his crotch. He still squats against one of the columns in the grocery store entrance.

The clerks stand there, shoulder to shoulder, serious and pimply and pale green. Two of them look at each other, as if considering the offer, but the angry Asian guy stares them into submission. He's the rule guy. He's the boss here. Apparently it's more important to him to be the boss than to get a blow job.

What the fuck is wrong with these people? What the fuck is wrong with me? Am I so ugly? Have I lost all my powers of persuasion? I can't even get a fifteen-dollar bottle of liquor out of a couple of night-shift grocery clerks? Even with offers of oral sex? I've fallen so far so fast. It hasn't felt fast. It's felt like forever.

"Oh, come on," I say. They stare at me wordless.

"Homos!" I shout at them as I turn and walk ungracefully toward the Honda. I'm less walking and more falling toward the car. There's no liquor to be had. I think of who I can call with drugs or booze, but I don't have anyone's number.

The cool thing about being pregnant is how I stopped feeling alone. Like there's this other glowing presence with me all the time. But I just killed it. Not the baby. The baby's still there I think. I killed the feeling and I'm back alone again. I have to get rid of this baby, this probably crazy monster fetus. I've got to do it tomorrow. And with that thought the night crumbles in front of me. I'm going to get high. Whatever I have to do I'm going to get high and I'm going to stay that way as long as I can.

Jesus is nowhere. Jesus is nowhere and nowhere and nowhere.

Frantic inspiration strikes me. I dig through the mountains of crap in the trunk of my car and pull out the plastic gas can, red and yellow like a child's fire truck toy. I have the gas can and the tube stashed in case I get down to my last dollar, run out of gas, and need to pillage from a good samaritan. This embarrassing scenario has happened before, is why they're in here. Is how I know how to siphon gas in the first place.

I fall to my knees on the pavement next to the car, unscrewing the gas cap with a pop hiss. I thread the clear tube like an IV into the metal pipe. I set the can in front of me and put the other end of the tube between my lips, sucking out the air until a mouthful of burning acid piss poison floods my mouth. Then I fill the can with a small amount of gas and pull the tube out. The relief starts even before you get high. It starts the minute you can see the finish line. Eyes on the prize.

Kneeling on the blacktop in front of the gas can, I unzip the back of my dress and shimmy the top half of it off my shoulders. I unsnap the leopard print push-up bra, hold it against the nozzle of the gas can, and saturate the padding. I open the door and crawl into the driver's seat without even standing up. I wrap the gasoline-soaked C-cup around my nose and mouth and I breathe and breathe and breathe until my head caves in and there is nothing but floaty blackness and my arms drop like weights to my sides and everything is so heavy until it is so light and there is only the twinkling dark and nothing no feeling just nothing.

The solidity creeps back in beginning with my extremities and a current of nausea surges through me. I open the car door and vomit onto the asphalt. As I hang there, trembling, waiting for the next wretch, about a foot to the right of the curry whipped cream splatter I see a broken beer bottle, tossed out a window by some asshole who wanted to tell God he didn't give a shit about anything. Most of the bottle is shattered, but the bottom stayed intact, with one tooth of a shard sticking up. I lean just a little farther from my perch, carefully grasp the piece of green glass, and place it, still wet, onto the dashboard in front of me. A delicate hem of light highlights the perfect edge of the shard.

I can't imagine living after this moment. I close my eyes and lean back and imagine that the suicide ghost surfer who owned the car before me is a warm boy with a shoulder I can lean my head on. I pretend he's with me and he is. He's white pale and the blood has pooled at his feet. I know it sounds ghastly but it isn't. It's like having a friend. He sat in this same seat, cut his wrists, and bled to death as he stared out at the ocean, the dark shapes of the other surfers drifting over the waves. He had once felt flickers of the joy that the morning ocean held for the others. He had once believed that their purpose could be his. But always he wound up back to blinking the water from his eyes and thinking, born again and again and this is all there is? It's not enough.

Would it be undignified to join him right now, like this, in a Ralph's parking lot with vomit crust on my dress and the car smelling of gasoline? I only need to not feel so sick first. I only need to find the strength to sink the glass into my skin. It's the thought, the always thought, the one I don't talk about too much because people get all worked up about it. The one where I drive wild up in the canyons until I find the perfect cliff to launch off. The one where I push the plunger down and the next moment doesn't exist.

Maybe I'll find them waiting for me, Aaron and my dad and the surfer. Not that they'll be sitting on a cloud with wings growing out of their backs, but I think that I'll find them. I'll find my Aaron again in a realm of boundless forgiveness. We'll be together and be more than the sum of our choices.

Here it is, the perfect piece of glass. Waiting for me like God planted it there. Like God is saying go ahead and let yourself off the hook already, you're so far beyond saving.

I mean to do it after I rest my eyes for a minute, but instead I surrender to sleep. When I wake, the windshield has shattered into a spiderweb of cracks and I think how it almost looks pretty. When did I crash? When did the sun rise? The daylight is so bright, this relentless white flame, that I try to put my hands over my eyes but my arms are so weak I can't move them. I wonder if I did it and I can't remember.

I can barely turn my head to see the surfer sitting next to me. He looks just like I imagined, with a tangle of sun-bleached hair and eyes like they sucked up the sea itself. He smiles at me. He's fine now. There's no more blood on the floor and his arms are sealed up with perfect skin like he never took a razor to them. What about my hands, I wonder? Are they healed? I think that if I look down and see my hands are healed then I'm probably dead. I don't look.

The surfer has a look on his face like he's perfectly balanced on his board and riding the highest and wildest wave. He's tan and shining and he's winning, he's flying. And I know—this is who he is. This is who he was really. I wish he could have seen himself this way. It's a gift of mine. I can see people how they are in their dreams. Like how Javi can give people the haircut they have in their dreams. And if you can do that, I guess it becomes like your job or obligation or something. Or even your purpose. It can become your purpose to see the people no one else sees and to see them truly pretty. I have my beauty school graduation today and for today my wrists will stay.

I say to the surfer, "Please go on ahead without me. I'll catch up. I'll catch up with you."

I wake for real and open my eyes. I'm sitting in the driver's seat shaking with sobs, my face wet with tears. I must have been crying in my sleep. The windshield is whole and so am I.

And what I say to nothing, to the milky light of the approaching dawn is, "Please go on ahead. I'll catch up. I'll catch up with you."

And I mean it. I'm ready for Aaron to go on ahead of me. I can't hold this guilt anymore. And I don't seem to be dying.

The car smells like a gas station. My mouth is cracked and dry. Drool coats the side of my face and the top of my dress hangs off me, barely covering my boobs. There's a toxic taste in my mouth so strong it creeps up the back of my throat and into my nose. The taste makes me gag, but I breathe through it and through the throbbing of my poor head. I put the car in drive and head it toward Serenity. Because this morning is as good as any to be born again. And you might call me an expert.

Twenty-two

When I walk in the door, I immediately know that I'm fucked. The living room is washed in pale light and Susan Schmidt, looking hastily dressed and wearing no makeup for the first time I have ever seen, sits there with three of my sleepy housemates. They talk in low, concerned voices. My stomach lurches as I enter in last night's crumpled dress with my shoes in my hand. But this is how it goes. You do shit and sometimes you get away with it and sometimes you don't. Some people get away with everything. I don't get away with much.

All four of them look up at me, real grave. Althea looks down and Missy looks at Althea and Violet looks at me with helplessness in her eyes and I know that at least she has been defending me.

"Hello, Beth," says Susan, all grim and self-important. "Would you please take a seat?"

I throw myself down into the ratty recliner and cross

my legs. I fling my arms wide over the armrests. If this is it then this is it. I'm not dead and the full possibility of that fact alone moves through me like a speedball, nauseating and thrilling. I'll miss this place. This has been my home. But I'm not about to grovel to someone who knows me so little that she insists on calling me Beth.

"You know I like you, Beth, but you have committed some very serious infractions here. Do you have an explanation for why you stayed out all night, violating your curfew and making your friends sick with worry? I've already called the police and reported you as a missing person."

"Not far off the mark, I guess. But I hope to find myself soon."

Susan Schmidt rears up in her seat like an angry cobra. She has been dragged, at dawn, out of her cozy bed in her swanky home bought with her family money and now I, a soon-to-be homeless, half-crazy, knocked-up, gas-huffing skank, am being cryptic with her. It offends her sense of hierarchy.

"In light of the position you're in, it may be wise to drop the defensive cleverness and try to have an authentic conversation."

This conversation, authentic or not, is totally pointless. I know well that there is no saving myself at Serenity and I am not about to hash this all out on the coffee table with Susan Schmidt. Plus, she's right. I pushed the boundaries a little too far and broke them. It appears as if it's time to leave.

I look at Violet. Fat, silent tears snake down her cheeks.

She wipes her red nose with her leopard print sleeve. It was Missy, I bet, who called Susan. She's frozen and looking down at the carpet with those haunted bug eyes of hers. For a full-blown paranoid schizo, she sure is a company man. I bet she thought she was doing the right thing, though. I can't really blame her.

"Well, kids," I say. "It's been fun."

"Why are you so defiant?" Susan asks.

"Bebes, please. Please," says Violet. "We have to talk about this. You can't leave. Where are you going to go?"

I stand, pivot, and head upstairs to pack my stuff. There isn't much of it and it's fit in the Honda before.

"Wait, Beth," Susan calls after me, scurrying to the foot of the stairs. "I think you owe it to yourself and to your housemates to process this situation with honesty and closure. We have to make a plan for you. We're concerned about your well-being. We don't want you just to run out onto the street."

Susan's entreaties echo through the hallways but don't follow me upstairs. When I get to my room, everything looks neater than I left it, which is a sure sign they've gone through my shit.

I look around the room at Violet's goth goodies, at the dust along the top of the moldings, at the place where the window doesn't close exactly right, at the precious guitar leaning against the side of the dresser. I've lain in my bed here many hours just looking around, unable to get up and actually do anything. I know every crack in this ceiling.

My bravado drains into the floor and my stomach cramps. I wasn't expecting to leave so soon and with nowhere else to go.

I take my shirts out of the closet and fold them neatly into my duffel bag, thinking about a lunch I had with Jake. Two months ago, Jake and I were languishing in the same apathy: trying to not drink and to figure out a way that living in this world might suck a little less. Maybe wild success, maybe a good fuck, maybe saintly spiritual devotion, maybe a package of onion rings, maybe a trip to the Grand Canyon in a trailer or to Peru in a goat caravan or something. Sitting over black and white shakes at the 101 Cafe, we mused about it. The next junked car he had his eye on fixing up. His next doomed straight job. My soon-to-be career at a fancy Beverly Hills salon.

Afterward we went to Griffith Park and hiked up one of the trails to an overlook called Dante's Peak. We both thought that was really funny. When we turned back, there was this particularly steep stretch that he ran down with his feet barely touching the ground and his arms out to the sides and I swear he was almost flying. That's what this leaving is. It seems like a steep downhill, but maybe I'm just about ready to take off. That's the thought that keeps me packing.

Violet wakes Buck, and Buck helps me carry my bags down the stairs. The three of us walk out into a bright, cool spring morning. My graduation day. As I walk out the door of the sober living, a curtain closes behind me. I am moving, but I don't know in which direction. Susan hovers in the doorway as I hug my friends good-bye. The sincerely concerned look on her face surprises me. Have I been right about anything?

"Where're you going? You want I should come with you?" asks Buck, but she's still in her robe.

"I'm going to school early today. Because my hair is fucked."

Jesus is in the soles of my feet. Jesus is in the tires of my car. Jesus is in the wind at my back.

From the look on Vi's face, I think I probably said that last part out loud.

Twenty-three

I592 hours down. 8 hours left to go.

I have the timing of a trapeze artist. I hover in midair right now, but I can see the bar of the next trapeze swinging toward me. I have to grab hold and hang on with all I've got until I get dropped off somewhere new.

With a half hour to go until school opens, I sit here in my car and struggle to keep my eyes open. A half hour to stay awake and then eight hours to get through and I'll have completed the sixteen hundred hours required to be a licensed cosmetologist in the State of California. Then I only have to pass my State Board and I'll have my license. That's what I'm thinking. That's all I'm thinking. I picture myself stylish, you know, a little eccentric—a nose ring, a hot pair of boots—greeting my next rich client with a double cheek kiss. The clients will think I'm so unusual and chic. My hands will be a subject for gossip, but what better place for gossip than a hair salon?

Did you hear she crawled out of the car across a road full of broken glass?

Tragic. Fascinating.

The other hairstylists will be like a little family. Maybe Javi will even be there. We'll drink margaritas together after the salon closes on Friday night. I'll have a fabulous little apartment with a vintage yellow kitchen all lit with sunshine. Is there a baby in the picture? I don't have an answer to that one.

I feel like I'm on heroin, but I'm not. My eyes keep closing against my will and I have to open the car door to puke twice. At least the puking wakes me back up. Close my eyes and I see a wall of sickening orange—the daylight behind my eyelids.

And bubbling beneath the sunlit kitchen is, What have I done? What have I done? Sometimes the damage of a moment's mistake is immediately obvious but sometimes it takes much longer. Huffing gas is no good at all. Definitely not good for unborn children.

Still fifteen minutes early, I get out of the car and walk through the deserted early morning streets toward the school. I wear my school uniform but carry the mint green 1950s cocktail dress that Javi and I bought at Jet Rag over my shoulder, the skirt of it blowing behind me like a banner. Through the arched picture windows, I see Miss Mary-Jo, Miss Hernandez, and a few of the students setting up inside. When I open the door, the overpowering smell of cheap shampoo and setting gel sends me running to the bathroom to barf yet again, nothing left in my stomach this time but bile.

When I emerge, pale and shaking, Miss Mary-Jo bounds toward me, her mushroom hair bouncing with each step. She stretches her short arms wide and I brace myself for the hug. I bend down so she can reach me. She gives me a smacky wet kiss on the cheek.

"You are too much the partying last night," she says, wagging her finger at me playfully. "You look like a dragging cat."

She leans in and whispers, "If you were to go upstairs and lie down on the carpet behind the upstairs lockers, I surely would not be seeing you there, and I am the teacher of upstairs today." She gives me a wink with one heavily mascaraed eye. There are angels everywhere.

I do exactly as she suggests. I go upstairs behind the back lockers and fall to my knees on the thin stretch of crappy carpet. I wedge myself against the wall, my textbook under my head and my smock over me like a blanket, and fall into merciful blackness. Far away in the awake world, I hear the students start to arrive: giggling, shuffling, equipment tumbling out of lockers, the slam of metal on metal. I hear it behind my sleep and through it but it doesn't wake me up. I'm as comfortable on this floor as I have ever been. I think maybe I'll never get up again. And with that thought comes the tears.

Vera and Lila hear me and peek their concerned faces around the side of the locker. I look up at them.

"You are sick, honey?"

"I'm okay. Thanks. I'll be okay," I say, unable to even try to be convincing. I wipe a stream of snot from my upper lip.

"We go to get your friend for you."

And in what seems like an instant, Javier appears, his hair an incredible new shade of sea-foam green.

"Oh, good," he says when he sees me there unshowered with my hair unbrushed, my face slick with snot and tears. I repeatedly clutch and release a corner of the smock, which lies in a wrinkled ball beside me. "Now I have something to do with these next eight hours." He thrusts one hip forward and plants a decisive hand on it. "It's going to take at least that long to get you looking pretty."

"I did a bad thing, Javi."

"Stand up, Frances Farmer," he says, somehow managing to have disgust and love in his voice at the same time. He reaches his hand out to me and pulls me up. The head rush almost knocks me back down but I steady myself. "You can tell me all about it while we fix your hair."

That's what I need. A new hairdo. Have I mentioned that a new hairdo can change the course of your whole day? It can change the course of your whole life if you let it. That's why I came to beauty school in the first place. If I told you anything else, I was lying.

The teachers are festive and lax today. Even Mrs. Montano has stayed holed up in her office and hasn't attempted to quell the rising excitement. The graduating Armenian girls have cooked an incredible banquet and arranged it in a beautiful spread on tables they pushed together in the lunchroom. They chat while hanging streamers and those accordion-style paper bells. The school looks ready for a bridal shower or a prom. Some of the students' husbands and boyfriends start to arrive, towing little girls in organza dresses and patent leather shoes and little boys in tiny suits with their hair slicked down. The men carry lavish bouquets of flowers and set them on their wives' stations, recently cleared of equipment for the last time.

At the end of the day, after Javi has styled my hair to perfection, Javi, Vi, and I decide to change into our party clothes. Candy follows us back to the locker bays. She has been tailing me around all day trying to get the dirt.

"Bebe, oh, my God. Did you get kicked out for sex? Come on. Tell me about it. Please. I'd tell you."

"No. Sadly. Not sex."

"Was it drugs? You can tell me. Do you have some? Can I buy some?"

Javier styled Candy's hair into the most incredible white girl afro-puffs I've ever seen, complete with red and orange and pink extensions. The height of it (and probably how tight he pulled it) does wonders for her double chin. She's on my nerves less than usual today. I even feel kind of sad that I won't see her again. The sad isn't about her specifically, but about Serenity. Where will I go now?

I change in the cramped bathroom, trying my best to clean the smell off me from last night before putting on my party dress. I spritz on a little vanilla oil and pull the dress up, the slight curve of my belly etching a wrinkle into the taffeta. I fasten the zipper, the stiff bodice encasing me like comforting armor. I look down and realize the thing I've forgotten. The thing I never forget—my fishnets. Emerging from under the bell of the dress, my legs look like the logs of ground turkey meat you see in the butcher's display case. The thick keloid scars snake from my feet to the tops of my knees, the memory of the crash engraved into my every day. I don't want to take off my pretty, pretty dress and put my polyester pants back on. Instead, I step my bare feet into my shoes, slip the straps around my heels, and don't look down again. I look straight ahead to where I'm going and resolve that if people stare I'll look them dead in the eye. I'll look right through them.

I join Javi and Violet where they are primping in front of their stations.

"The dress, darling. It's perfection. You're Grace Kelly meets the B-52s. You do honor to the hair," says Javi.

My hair is magnificent. The candy-apple red, foot-high confection took him a full three hours.

Javi is dapper in his shiny boots, black bell-bottomed pants, and a Pucci pattern blouse that perfectly matches his new hair. Violet wears a veil and a hat fashioned from an enormous black silk rose. She made her own outfit and it's a floor-length, Victorian-inspired, deconstructed dress complete with corset and bell sleeves and chicly shredded edges. She's much better with clothes than with hair.

I take my place next to them, all of us fixing our makeup in the mirror. I dip into Javi's iridescent white eye shadow, Violet does her lips burgundy blood red, and for Javi it's about the lip gloss and just a touch of glitter on the eyelids.

We declare each other flawless. Javi and I turn toward the mirror and don our tiaras, the crowning touch.

Twenty minutes later, Javier's sister is blending margaritas by the shampoo bowls. Mrs. Montano has already broken into Paul's cupcakes and she carries a double chocolate in one hand and a margarita, no salt, in the other.

Me, I'm not drinking. Because yesterday was yesterday and today I am probably still pregnant, though I can't be sure. Some days seem like the end of your life but then they aren't and you still have to figure out how to wake up again.

Buck shows up and she's made an impressive effort to look like Nick Cave instead of Johnny Van Zant, which makes me think she really loves Violet. Violet glides around in that somber Victorian mourning getup but she can't help it; she looks happy.

Buck barely says hello before she starts talking San Francisco. She's on fire with a plan for our future; she's been at home plotting all day.

"Here's the evil plan," says Buck as Violet reaches over

with her pinkie to wipe a spot of frosting from her upper lip. "You stay on Javi and Paul's couch for a couple of weeks. We wait for you to pass the State Board and then we hit the road. The three of us and baby makes four."

"I can't go with you. I can't just leave Jake. How can I?"

"So what? You can't. So neither can I. So come anyway. What the fuck? What else are you doing? You want to stay here and wait for your crazy-ass boyfriend so that the two of you can find a freeway underpass where you can hang out and sniff glue for a while? He doesn't want a real life. You do. Or if you don't you should."

"I don't want to talk about this now. I want to dance."

Lila brought a boom box and her *Hits of the Seventies* cassette tape. The Armenian girls love it and Miss Hernandez loves it and a quake can even be detected in Mrs. Montano's wide rear when "Celebration" comes on. The cultural walls and teacher-student hierarchies dissolve and we all start dancing with each other in the aisles. The students who are graduating are all flushed and dressed up. The students who are still working on their hours wear their uniforms and look jealous, but are having fun anyway. It's a long time, 1600 hours. Let me tell you. It's a long year of your life.

"Dancing Queen" comes on and I find an open spot in the aisle where I sing and spin in my own world with my arms up in the air. *Having the time of your life.* I stop in midspin facing the back door. Through the milling, laughing crowd in the shampoo room I see a figure looming in the doorway, backlit with the yellow late afternoon sun. Eddies of dust catch the light from the open door as they swirl through the air.

Jake. How did he get out? How did he get his clothes back? He wears paint-splattered army fatigue pants and a filthy thermal shirt with the cuffs cut off at the wrists so that the sleeves are frayed around his broad forearms. He has his usual combat boots on and a torn T-shirt tied around his head like a gangster or a pirate. The crowd instinctively parts, forming an aisle in front of him. His arms hang down at his sides and he looks straight ahead, which is to say straight at me. In his right hand is a dense, magnetic presence: the L shape of a gun. The same gun I shot off his cousin's back porch in Joshua Tree. Violet approaches with a couple of sodas and she sees him at the same time I do. I hear her suck in a lungful of breath.

"Call Susan," I say.

"Susan?"

"Just call her."

I don't know why my mind turns to Susan but I feel somehow that she'll know what to do. I think that maybe I haven't been fair to Susan. That maybe I haven't been seeing people right.

Vi fades backward into the front room. I glance around quickly. I don't think anyone else has spotted the gun. They ignore the weirdo in the doorway and go on with their party. Javier's sister keeps up the constant white noise of the blender.

Jake hovers with a menacing, caged energy. I walk slowly toward him and I am floating, drifting. He scopes out the landscape, looking for enemies hidden in the bushes, under the shampoo sinks, in the chipped pink Formica cupboards, behind the door of the supply closet.

As I approach, he lifts the gun low at his hip like a cowboy, pointing straight at the center of me. I keep moving forward.

Jake grows more rigid with tension the closer I get. I walk until I can feel the gun pressing into the bodice of my dress right at my solar plexus.

"Jake."

"I'm not Jake. That is my false name," he says in a whisper through clenched teeth. "That's only on one of my birth certificates. I have four. This is my right to be known by my real name. They steal it, the baby killers. The rapists. Who are you? Have they hollowed you out yet? This is what I have come to find out."

Abba has changed to the Bee Gees' infectious falsetto.

"They haven't got to me yet, Jake."

"I'm not Jake," he says, eyes straining, fat beads of sweat forming on his unshaven upper lip and across his forehead. "I am the Christ. I am Jesus of Nazareth. And if you are not yet a zombie I'm here to save you. You have been waiting so long to be saved. I have heard you in my sleep. There is no more time. They are here, the zombies, I can smell them rotting. Zombies with only one eye and with twelve names and as each man is a house so each man will fall. But here I am for you. Cover your face now. Do you smell it? Horrible, horrible. The smell."

Jake flares his nostrils and sniffs at the air like there is a fire. Then he drops the gun to his side, grabs me by the arm, and pulls me toward the supply closet. He quickly opens the door, glances behind him, shoves me in front of him, and closes the door behind us.

"We can wait here until nightfall. It is a myth about zombies and night. Zombies do not need the death of the sunlight. Only the death of the sunlight of the soul. The zombies of this age are day dwellers. That way they can see better who has lost faith. I can protect us here. If I don't sleep, I can protect us."

He locks the door and faces it, sitting down with his back against the unopened boxes of hair product that are stacked against the wall. He holds his gun between his legs, pointed at the door.

The supply closet is barely big enough for two. The perimeter of the floor is lined with boxes and the walls are shelved to the ceiling with rows of hair color and developer and perm solution and facial products and gloves and applicator bottles and industrial-sized refills of shampoo and conditioner. It smells like perfume and latex and bleach. My own hair reeks of the whole bottle of hair spray that Javier used to cement it into its sculptural beauty.

I stand there for a minute, stiff in my dress like an overgrown doll in the corner of a dark closet, the light and sounds of the party bleeding in around the edges of the door.

He listens theatrically, like a dog with his head cocked.

"Can I turn the light on?" I ask.

He seems startled by the question, as if he forgot I was there. "Yes," he says, not looking at me, keeping his watchful gaze on the door with its off-white paint chipping and yellowing with age. I turn on the light and the bare bulb above throws harsh shadows.

I slip my shoes off and sit down cross-legged next to him on the cool, speckled linoleum, my dress puffing out around me like a muffin top.

"Do we really need the gun? What about love thy enemy?"

"I love them. I love them so much. I just can't stand the smell of them. Every age has a Christ. I'm the Christ for this age and therefore I carry a gun. I am here to protect you."

"From who?"

"From Caesar. He is a bloodthirsty madman. He believes he is God. He is not even an emptied-out god. History will try him and reveal this. We must be careful of our prophets, He said. We must be careful of our prophets but we must have faith in our angels."

Jake gestures in the air with his gun for emphasis. He smells like chemicals and b.o. How could I have been so wrong about everything?

"They shot me up with mind control drugs and they tried to convince me I was someone I was not. But halfway through, I remembered my true identity. I remembered that I am Jesus and that is my birthright. They tried to tell me there are no zombies but at the same time their flesh was rotting off their faces in front of me. I told them I could save them but they didn't want to be saved. They will destroy me rather than be saved, but I will not let them. I had to escape from there to do God's work. I know your wish. I've always known your wish. I could grant it."

The wish thing makes it sound like a bit of Santa Claus got mixed in with his Jesus. Truthfully, I do. Of course I have a wish. But even Jesus was no genie.

Jake probably hasn't slept in days. Beyond the party noises and the music, I start to hear another kind of bustle outside the door—hushed and official voices. The music stops abruptly.

"You believe you are a slave and that you are being punished," he says, putting the gun down on the floor beside him and placing a hardened palm on either side of my face. His hands smell like dirt and metal. "You wish to be saved. But you already are. You already are saved."

I can't save Jake because he's already saved, too. But saved doesn't equal healed and his healing isn't mine to give. And there it all is, clear as an L.A. sky after a winter rain scrubs the smog away. Jake has got to finish this zombie battle without me. I'm going to San Francisco with Buck and Vi.

"If I have another wish, will you grant that, too?

"I wish that you'd hand me the gun. I wish you'd surround us in golden light and that you'd take my hand now and walk with me out the door."

I hear the whispered discussion, see the shadows passing by the light from under the door.

I lean in and kiss him on the forehead. The gun is heavier than I remembered it, tucked into the scarred cradle of my palm.

Twenty-four

I600 hours down. Plus five minutes, even.

I'm done. Graduated. The clock on the wall over the shampoo bowls says 5:05.

Underneath it stands a line of five cops with their guns drawn at me. Gathered in the doorway leading to the front room, I see Susan Schmidt and the social worker for the guys' side of Serenity talking to some plainclothes-looking guys. Behind them wait the paramedics.

One of the uniformed cops shouts at me, "Drop your weapon." Then, "Put your hands where we can see them." And all the rest of that shit.

I put Jake's gun on the ground and give it a little kick toward them with one bare toe.

Jake doesn't even put up a fight. Two large men carry him out through the aisle, limp-legged and sedated.

I follow them out and everyone files onto the sidewalk around me. Buck stands on one side of me and Violet stands on the other. Buck holds me gently by the elbow, as if to say fall and I'll catch you.

We watch as they load him into the back of the ambulance and drive off down the street. They don't turn on the lights. They don't turn on the sirens. They should have at least given him the lights.

I stand there watching until the red and white block of the ambulance is absorbed into the traffic on Brand Boulevard and I can't see it anymore. Everyone stands there with me and no one says anything until I turn around. I get this feeling that the baby is okay. And I'm okay. I haven't reached the edge of the continent with nowhere else to go.

Susan steps up and for some reason I don't want to punch her in the face.

"Would you like to come home now, Bebe?"

"Yes. I'd like to come home."

Wispy pink clouds stretch across the fading blue of the twilight. How many more weeks do we have to wait before the days get longer? It's spring already, isn't it? I guess not, because it's still March. But almost. It's almost spring.

Epilogue

We drive over the Golden Gate Bridge, with its red arches soaring over you making you dizzy, and up into the tortuous roads that wind through the impossible majesty of the Marin Headlands. If you know secret things then you know there's a turnoff where you can hike down a stairway cut into a red cliffside. The hike leads to a beach with black sand that looks like ground pepper and is so warm it makes your towel feel like an electric blanket. And you don't have to wear a thread of clothing if you don't want to and most people don't want to, it being San Francisco and all.

It's a glaring bright Indian summer. I stand at the edge of the ocean with only my feet in the cold, cold water, watching the rippling forever sky mirror. An ocean liner is a hazy toy floating in the distance. Gulls shift in circles overhead like flecks of white glass in a kaleidoscope. You can see a corner of the city across the bay like a fuzzy watercolor.

I imagine Jake plunging wildly through the waves, one

after the other, shaking his head like a wet dog when he emerges, drops of water flying through the air and catching the light with tiny rainbows. I talk to him regularly and he's back at Serenity. He's doing better. He's managing.

Violet lies on a blanket in a long white dress, with a parasol, of course, to shade her pale skin from the sun. Buck runs in boxers and a tank top along the shore, chasing our mutt, Moses, throwing him a slimy tennis ball. Moses was hanging out around back our Mission flat one day underneath where the stairs are and Violet invited him to stay.

Me, I'm in a bikini and I'm round as a beach ball, every part of me stretched and swollen to its limit. I wear my legs bare mostly now, when it's that kind of day. People rarely even notice.

I tilt my face to the sun and run my scarred palms over the slope of my belly, which looks exactly like the hills rising behind the cliffs all around us. People smile at my belly all along the beach. People want to touch her all day long, this baby.

I think about sharks and starfish and how there's no ocean in Toledo. No ocean at all. I wonder how people live like that, trapped by all that land. I wade farther into the water, breathing faster with the cold, and then I fall backward and float for a moment and I'm weightless. I'm light.

My Jesus refrain is different now, transformed without my even thinking about it.

The sunlight is under my eyelids. The sky is in my collarbone. The ocean is in the palm of my hand.

Also from Jillian Lauren,

the *New York Times* bestseller

ISBN 978-0-452-29631-2

www.jillianlauren.com

Available wherever books are sold.